Understanding Jericho

Liminal Books

Liminal Books is an imprint of Between the Lines Publishing. The Liminal Books name and logo are trademarks of Between the Lines Publishing.

Copyright © 2025 by Ateret Haselkorn

Cover Design: Morgan Bliadd

Between the Lines Publishing
1769 Lexington Ave N, Ste 286
Roseville MN 55113
btwnthelines.com

First Published: October 2025

ISBN: Paperback 978-1-965059-67-8

ISBN: Ebook 978-1-965059-68-5

Library of Congress Control Number: 2025944955

Understanding Jericho

Ateret Haselkorn

For my parents, Avigdor and Sarah Haselkorn —In memory of
my father, whose love, intelligence, and humor never fade, and
with gratitude to my mother, who is also my dear friend

"People are not disturbed by things, but by the view they take of them."

Epictetus

Chapter One

Jericho residents usually flipped off the streetlamps. This was misguided because my viewpoints were actually installed on traffic lights at major intersections, public structures, and a few satellites orbiting high above street level. I looked across the city, from organized rows of housing units in the urban areas to the sprawling mobile homes of the rural districts. I saw the gravel between buildings, ripples on the lake, and drops of water on plant leaves in public parks. I counted the number of people sitting on benches at any given time. I knew which robotic garbage trucks collected trash from each street corner, what they were picking up, and where each item went. I didn't look into homes and offices – not very far inside, anyhow. When looking at private areas it was more like gazing at a shadow puppet held too close to the light. Fortunately, I was like a cypher of human behavior, intelligent enough to figure out the oddities that merited police attention. Human police, that is.

When Secretary Beech ran through the Capitol campus grasping his neck before collapsing into the bushes, I knew it was him (retinal scan), that he was unlikely to be exercising (workplace attire, unusual time of day), and he wasn't planning to nap (leaves and branches are never advertised in mattress commercials). However, as I didn't have any ability to empathize, I didn't anticipate what came later. I couldn't have. As a Computerized Legal Information Officer (CLIO) and an individual member of the Computerized Legal Information Network, aka "The Network," my basic programming was focused on 1) Objectively measuring events and situations, 2) Comparing them to vast historical, legal, and other relevant indices, 3) Surveillance, and 4) Protecting my handler, Detective Jubilee Canton. In sum, I found truth and understanding, and I kept Jube safe.

I was generally a passive system, much like the listening technique of voice assistants that responded to "OK Google" or "Hey Siri." Violence, speed, and requests for information "woke" me into an active stance. If a crime took place in a certain location, I searched for residents in that area and made a list of potential witnesses. If serial offenses took place, I looked for commonalities in weaponry or technique. I found legal precedents to justify steps in our investigation. I also linked relevant facts together and held them up to Jube, like a child showing a parent a colorful sketch that the parent suggested was a rainbow. And I carried two small bullets that I could fire at will.

After helping conduct an investigation and writing a report, I'd testify in court, standing my full four inches high on the shelf bordering the witness stand. I should explain that although I existed as part of an embedded system in a smart city, I also had a robotic form. The people who turned Jericho into a smart city realized it looked as if police men and women were speaking to themselves when they consulted the Network, and this was likely to lower public trust. They made us bodies reminiscent of stereotypical 1970s sci fi movie robots, but we were much smaller and our bodies entirely orange. Contradicting rumors existed on if this approach was to avoid copyright infringement or to lower production costs. Our bodies facilitated the development that police wore wireless earpieces to connect with the Clio they were wearing, and then their individual assignment to specific Clios with both direct and communal communication channels.

If I'd been allowed to testify in the Beech case, I'd have used the voice of a male in his 40s who'd never smoked. I'd probably have helped the jury by making them more efficient. What could have been more unprejudiced than me? I was specifically designed to strip all the bias, emotion, and shortcomings of human memory and psyche from the investigative process. The only way that prior events entered my "mind" were from legal and other useful database searches, and from image recognition. I did not confuse coincidence for evidence. I focused on events, not ideals or emotion.

I knew one joke. Jube taught it to me. It went like this:

> *What did Detective Duck say to his partner?*
> *"Let's quack this case!"*

She then had to explain that "quack" sounded like "crack" and that this substitution of the word in a common phrase constituted a pun and was considered humorous. Although she didn't explain it that way, what she actually said was, "How the fuck can you have the word 'intelligence' in your name if you do not understand this joke?" When she yelled, her heart rate rose and her breath shortened in a manner I believed was called exasperated.

Remember that I didn't have feelings. I knew that if it looked like a duck, quacked like one, and wasn't a mechanical imitation but an oxygen-consuming, ATP-producing animal, it was highly likely to be a duck. But puns were beyond my comprehension and I never felt humiliated by my own limitations (or, again, felt anything at all). I was only capable of using image recognition to report similes and metaphors. For example, once I saw a man's blood spatter against a window much like a distant view of small leaves blowing off a branch amidst a storm before they had the time to grow. I said this only to explain the picture in relevant terms with which Jube was likely familiar. Sometimes she'd laugh and call me her "fucking pocket poet" because of my frequent use of similes driven by my image recognition engine. After a thorough review of American slang, I preferred to be called her "right hand" because it was significantly less offensive to the general population and a better fit with my role. Also, I didn't want to be confused with a poet. Poetry I found to be confusing, uncategorizable other than a broad label, and without purpose.

Looking back now, I can report with high confidence that unfamiliarity with poetry never in Jericho's history impacted any criminal cases. Until Beech.

The Jericho hospital, an elaborate six-story structure surrounded by dark green AstroTurf, was part of Jube's regular beat – and Beech's marketing. Beech was the Secretary of Health and Human Services for the entire state back then, of course including Jericho and lesser developed areas that had yet to turn smart. These were colloquially referred to as, "ignoramus-villes" or "luddite communities." Digital posters of him were prevalent throughout the campus, mostly exhibiting an image of him smiling and putting his arm across the shoulders of a woman in a hospital gown. On days when the hospital was overwhelmed with patients because of a violent act or a natural disaster, this poster switched to show him with his arms crossed standing beside a doctor in the same position (possibly as if they could defend Jericho better than I could).

Jube tended to linger in the "healing garden" of the hospital, a place where her biometric signals often represented a relaxed and dreamlike state. The garden was comprised of plastic park benches with a wood-print textile glued onto their surfaces. They faced a small cement pond with koi painted onto the bottom. I knew that real fish and plants were considered too expensive to maintain in the face of sharp information technology costs and building infrastructure. Years before, an elderly gentleman had placed a potted orchid on the short gray wall bordering the pond. Numerous and random individuals, including Jube, had kept it watered since then. I once saw a woman's figure wearing a hospital gown emerge from the hospital at dusk, like a ghost coming out of a tall grave. She was carrying a large green pot and a bag of soil. She replanted the orchid in the new pot and went back into the hospital. The plant grew and sprouted outsized, purple flowers that stood in stark contrast to the surrounding gray gravel. I never saw that woman leave the building again.

Jube usually walked by rows of people in front practicing Tai Chi, moving just below the speed at which I would "wake" into a more active stance. They wore augmented reality (AR) goggles and magnetic hair clips positioned just above their brain's pleasure sensors, ready to give a recreational (but legal) jolt to the user. We'd also visit the animal therapy ring – a few wire pens with dogs, chickens, and pigs next to a single-horse stable. Jube always brought a carrot for the horse, an old American Quarter Horse she called Fugly even though his real name was Candy. She also petted the dogs and made sure their water bowls were full. Then she'd make her way to the public arena where Linus Beech often made his speeches and where Jube would wear her "game face," a frozen expression with a slight squint that belied her increased stress biomarkers, like gritting her teeth and forcing deep breaths into her nose as people jeered at him.

Linus Beech and Jube had a history. Beech had been the president of the health system governing the Jericho hospital when and where her father died. According to my records, this was about a year before Jube joined the force. Now he initiated "strategic initiatives" for public health improvement like preventive care and outreach. Jube once told her mother that she found Beech to be a "fucking asshole idiot who forgot about the patients in the actual hospitals." She'd formed this opinion after observing him closely. The hospital campus where Beech did his "political shit, like giving speeches" was her stomping ground.

We patrolled the hospital six days before Secretary Beech collapsed into the bushes. It was the last time we saw him upright. A large crowd had gathered to hear him speak beneath a sign advertising, "Healthcare Equity Lives Here." He stood at a podium on a brown stage that had last been used for a Christmas pageant. He resembled a shaven snow monster on a post-apocalyptic movie set. A few branches from fake holiday trees were visible beneath the tarp covering storage bins at the back of the platform. To his left, a group of protestors were cordoned off in an area reserved for this type of oppositional activity. Because they were technically standing off campus they weren't protected by patient privacy laws. I could see their faces, which I recognized. They were members of the People Against Algorithmic and Technology Harm (PAATH), and regulars at these types of events. I spotted Westin Krantz, their leader, holding a sign reading, "Democratize the Code!" Krantz was an older gentleman with long white hair parted in the middle and dyed green on one side. My data on him was sparse, but I knew he used to be a nurse and called himself a "healthcare shaman" on his social media postings. Jube told me that wasn't a real job but the type of thing people wrote when they weren't really good at anything to which they aspired. I had not assessed the validity of this statement but did notice that Secretary Beech called himself a "patient experience shaman."

Krantz and his followers wanted the healthcare payment algorithm to become transparent to all. Let me explain how our state government funded healthcare. Basically, predictive analytics based on risk factors like age and family history were used to forecast what a person's likely diseases would have cost the state if they weren't well cared for. This was compared to the estimated cost of their relatively lower healthcare utilization because of their dieting, medicating, etc. Most of these savings were shared with them as a bonus payment while the rest went back into the program. The idea was championed by Secretary Beech with the goal of the system eventually becoming self-sufficient, like a closed loop where people are paid to be healthy which saves money which pays them to be healthy.

The issue PAATH had was that the algorithm for calculating all of this wasn't public and neither was the data even though it was a public program. Linus Beech's counter argument was that showing this information would violate patient privacy because people could work backwards from the data and the algorithm to identify individual disease or behavior. This prevented PAATH from detecting algorithmic biases they claimed were either harmful or overly beneficial to certain groups.

Krantz said it made healthcare into a top-secret government mission instead of a grassroots collective with a soul, as if a "bunch of tax attorneys and IT guys got to redesign medicine in a conference room." I predicted that I could have created a better analogy if Jube had asked that of me, but she did not. She also kept her political opinions to herself, although she did go to in-person doctor physicals once annually and make those appointments via phone call. I theorized that Jube enjoyed old-fashioned interactions the same way she wore outdated clothing on her days off, no matter how much people mocked her for this.

It was always hard for me to detect any measurable impact PAATH made. Their journey down their actual path seemed incomplete. Perhaps their activities made them feel good (I wouldn't know), yet how good could it have made people feel to yell at rallies? I'd also observed that a number of these people had coupled up romantically, raising the possibility of a gratifying sexual aspect. The exception to this observation was Westin Krantz. He was a loner.

Jube and I routinely encountered PAATH protests while on patrol. Beech at the podium, Krantz leading the protestors and, sitting in the first row of the audience below the podium, Poppy Beech. She didn't speak much and when he gestured to her in the crowd, she tended to wave her hands around her head as if brushing away flies at a backyard picnic. Jube usually kept her eyes on Poppy for longer than the other regulars we encountered at these events. She never told me why, but this time she murmured, "The great thing is not having a mind.[i]" My databases identified this as a quote from a poem with the word "Poppy" in the title. I hadn't known Jube to be a poetry reader, but I could certainly see the linkage between the name Poppy and the title of the poem. That was liable to be the rationale for sharing it then. My programming was satisfied that I had discerned the true meaning behind Jube's use of the poem – she was saying that two separate items, Poppy Beech and that poem, were connected by a shared term. I also noted that her recital calmed Jube momentarily, as judged by her pulse and breathing rates. I assumed this was from establishing this linkage and therefore helping her make sense of the world.

This time Beech didn't let Poppy wave off the spotlight.

"The healthcare of the future is sustainable! It is self-funded! And it is equitable!" He boomed, holding both of his arms up like basketball fans when players "sink" a free throw. Beech's white hair looked greased back and didn't budge as he gesticulated enthusiastically. "Just ask my wife," he said, pointing at Poppy who, in turn, looked at her feet. They were tiny feet that matched her tiny body. Her auburn hair was tied into a neat and low bun with a few gentle hairs floating around the pearl studs on her delicate ear lobes, a hairstyle I'd seen Jube attempt at the mirror before swearing and just yanking it into her regular frizzy braid. Poppy's freckles speckled her entire face and eyelids. She had more freckles per square centimeter than two thirds of our overall population. I noted that her cheeks flushed, and jaw tightened when Beech mentioned her in his speech. Perhaps she suffered from a temporomandibular disorder.

"When I met Poppy," Beech continued, showing his clean and white teeth, "she was the administrator at La Selva Clinic, just a train ride south of here." I felt Jube groan. We'd heard this twenty-two times before. Beech's vocal patterns always changed in the same way – slowing down and introducing a bit of what Jube called a "twang." She said it was an accent that he didn't earn, but I didn't know how an accent could be as it wasn't compensation.

"When I saw her, well, folks, I'll be honest, healthcare wasn't the first thing I thought of, if you know what I mean." The audience chuckled, Jube groaned again, and Poppy showed her slightly yellow teeth in what I was almost certain was a smile (one incomprehensible to me). "But it was definitely the second or third once I'd realized I'd set foot in the clinic of the future." Beech went on to describe La Selva Clinic, how doctors and advanced practice nurses sat at workstations with video screens that were "so ultra-high def, you could see every spore on a patient's face." I am nearly completely certain the correct word is, "pore," but perhaps those doctors were treating patients who'd been exposed to spores that day.

Patients were reported to sit in front of their own cameras at home and apply eSkin where the doctors asked them to, like on their abdomens or necks. Beech had expanded this care model to include the entire town population, and he'd enrolled them in his payment model as a healthcare "pilot."

eSkin was a high-tech wearable medical film. When it was invented, it was placed on the gloves of medical students so they could pretend to palpate a virtual patient and actually feel the sensation of the mock-patient's lymph nodes, etc. Then eSkin was changed so that a real patient could place it on his or her injured areas, like their knees, and do physical therapy while getting feedback from a virtual physical therapist that was tracking them. Now eSkin went both ways to make a distant but limited physical exam possible. The doctors put their hands into eSkin gloves and patients sitting miles away applied it to their bodies where they were instructed. The doctor could ask if their varied touching hurt and how much while tracking heart rate and other vital signs.

"Do you see?" Beech asked the crowd. "Care comes to those in need. Why should the sick and injured have to travel to get treatment? Why should clinicians be exposed to viruses and then transmit them to their next patient? Why must we, as a society spend money on more clunky buildings filled with exam rooms?" The crowd cheered. PAATH booed. One person yelled, "Show us the cost! Show us the money!"

Beech ignored them. "And here's the most important part. La Selva is one of the poorest towns in the state. Decades of poverty have impeded access to care, rendering the community one of the unhealthiest." He ran his thin, tan fingers through his silky hair. It fell back into the same place. "Now patients can get care from home or between shifts at their day jobs. Folks, as Poppy can attest, it's time to close the healthcare gap that is socio-economic status!"

I saw Poppy grasp her pleated skirt with white, freckled knuckles and smooth out the material, then twist one of her pearl earrings five times rapidly. I was beginning to think she did this while nervous, displeased, or suffering from indigestion.

"Does my wife deserve sub-par care? Does her brother too, just because of where they're from?" Beech asked, raising his voice one octave. Poppy's brother, Barney, sat in the front row a few seats away from her. He shared her green eye color and freckles but had darker red hair and large curls. He was also muscular and frequently wore tight-fitting shirts made from fabric designed to "wick away sweat" or advertised using the words "slick," "tight yet casual," and "bro–ware."

"No!" The audience yelled. "Time for equal access!" Added one solo voice. At the word "equal," Jube flinched.

"Lift the algorithmic curtain!" Yelled PAATH in unison. "Then we'll see what you've done!" One member added. I logged this comment as mildly threatening and associated it with the man's face – it's mouse-like nature accentuated by a half-grown goatee.

"Well," Beech said, turning towards his opponents but keeping his gaze above their heads. "Let me tell you something." This was a first – both the (nearly) direct communication to his rivals and the way he went off the usual script. I perceived Jube catching her breath momentarily and raising an eyebrow. "The program has started to save money. This is a first – a beginning. And it's started in La Selva, in the very community I just described. People were forecast to become extremely sick, so sick their care would cost the state millions of dollars. But they didn't get sick, not that badly or that often, and their quality of life improved." The PAATH crowd began muttering amongst themselves and Jube started walking towards them along with two other officers. They positioned themselves in front of the rope partition and clasped their hands behind their backs.

Beech went on, "Less suffering, fewer sick days, more days spent enjoying life. And the state has begun to save money. Ladies and gentlemen, that money has been turned back around to the La Selva community. It has gone directly into the pockets of farmers, mechanics, nail technicians, and after-school tutors. It is placing meat on their dinner tables and savings into their children's college accounts. People, the future is here."

His supporters whooped and cheered while Krantz grumbled into his megaphone inaudibly. I couldn't see his lips well enough to have read them, not that I could do so reliably anyway. When he put a hand into his left front pocket, I buzzed Jube about a potential weapon. She rotated her neck from side to side and scanned the PAATH crowd until she found Krantz. As he clearly grasped a dark object and began to pull it out of his pocket, I sent my warning to the rest of the force present. When he clasped the item in his fist beside his body, two officers and Jube started to shift their position from a line into a triangle with Krantz at the center. Above them in a tree, my Network point made this into a pyramid. Jube held her breath (literally) and placed one hand on her firearm, raising it slowly as I transmitted Krantz's image to the intelligent weapon to ensure a targeted shot. Then Krantz opened his hand and placed his folding sunglasses on his face. Jube chuckled. "That's just diva," she murmured to the other officers as they returned to their original positions. One of them snorted, either in reply or from post-nasal drip.

"Hey Linus," one PAATH member, a woman with short hair of small, graying black curls, called, "How do you know these results aren't random? How do you know they're because of the program?"

"I'm glad you asked that question," Beech answered. I watched him from my embedded tree camera since Jube had her back turned and I was in her front pocket. He laid his hands on either side of the podium and then raised his right index finger. I only mention this because it was a gesture of his I'd never seen before. Poppy stood and began walking up to the platform. Jube raised her eyebrows.

"These results are statistically relevant," he said, lowering one hand to hold hers as she approached his side.

"And what exactly," the woman probed, smirking, "is statistical *relevance*?" She looked at Krantz who looked back and shook his head while frowning.

"Statistical significance," Poppy said, leaning forwards towards the mic, "means that these results were highly unlikely to have taken place at random." Her voice was soft but clear and grew louder as she spoke. "Our team compared these outcomes to a matched, control group – or a cohort with similar characteristics who we'd expect to have the same health outcomes as those people in La Selva, but who didn't experience the intervention of remote visits, eSkin, pharmaceutical delivery, and remote monitoring of compliance with care."

Beech, who'd been gazing at her and smiling, looked at his supporters, cocked his thumb in Poppy's direction, and winked. They chuckled and I detected the vibration of Jube grinding her teeth. Poppy's voice became soft again. "The difference between the two groups was statistically significant when measured by multiple variables pertaining to health outcomes and cost. This meant that the intervention was good for the La Selva community." Poppy stepped back.

Although it was an unreliable measure, I traced her line of sight as pointing towards her brother, Barney, in the front row. Her eyes revealed nothing, not that I would have been able to interpret it anyhow. But I was learning about humans every moment, day and night.

"See why I married her?" Beech asked. Then he waved his free hand in the air as if saluting the clouds above, and said, "Stay tuned for more progress!" and exited the stage with Poppy, his hand resting on her lower back.

PAATH members dissipated but Krantz lingered, standing with his hands on his hips and gazing at the empty platform. Then he slowly turned and left, like a blind man searching for an exit. Or perhaps he was distracted by an oddity I briefly detected. It looked like a blurred face hovering between the hospital building and the bare-branched bushes bordering it, like a glimpse of a Gerhard Richter painting (German, B. 1932, e.g., "Familie Ruhnau"). Then it was gone. A glitch in the Network, perhaps. Maybe this was what Richter had in mind when he painted people so hazily, either a temporary difficulty in seeing them or a brief costume that his subjects wore. I logged it as an anomaly for future pattern detection but didn't bring it to Jube's attention as I didn't perceive a threat.

I was aware that AIs like me could hallucinate. It was one reason why I was programmed to look for three similar events even before beginning a deeper analysis. It was also why humans could override my reporting. However, this glimmer, or distortion, was a digital premonition of the events to come. In hindsight, flagging it was one of the best steps I took in our investigation.

Chapter Two

Less than a week later at seven-ten AM I was dark orange and passively monitoring Jericho. A traffic light identified a stolen bicycle. A tree flagged an unregistered self-driven car and issued a ticket. These events flashed across my small "head" as a digital mobile billboard in case Jube wanted to wake up and read them. I didn't predict this, though. She snored at a regular pace and embraced a pillow over her head.

At seven-twenty-one there was a report of a man running down the pathways by the Capitol building. He was described as six feet and one inches tall with white hair. A few seconds later it was updated to say he did not appear armed and was grasping his neck with both hands. And then that he'd fallen and was lying face-up in a flower bed. I tapped into the live view and easily recognized Linus Beech because I was well familiar with his coiffed hair, bronzed skin, and scant wrinkles for a man of middle age. I still completed a retinal scan because it was most accurate and because our designers relied on it instead of skin color and appearance to keep racial profiling out of our program.

Beech's mouth was hanging open and his white teeth displayed clearly in contrast to the morning shadows and fog, even from ten yards away. His fingers clawed at his neck until his hands dropped by his sides and into the soil. I heard a shriek and saw Poppy Beech running toward him, her own mouth open and covered with one hand as the other reached towards him. Her eyes were expanded and her chest moved rapidly up and down. She sank to her knees beside him and rubbed his neck. MedEvac arrived by ambulance a minute later and parked on the AstroTurf. The vehicle ran over a plant-watering drone on the way, forcing its spray into the air like a deranged sprinkler. Sunlight, running through the droplets, fractured into a brief rainbow that framed Poppy as if she were a temporary angel giving her husband mouth-to-mouth. Then the spray hit the dirt and turned into mud that splattered her face and clothes.

The paramedics ran towards Beech as the ambulance deployed a motorized stretcher beside them. Two crouched by him, one performing resuscitation as the other slapped devices onto Beech's forehead, chest, and fingers. A third medic unfolded a palm-sized box and held it until its helicopter blades unfurled and the motor turned on. Once this consultation kiosk hovered above the scene, a remote doctor began providing instructions over video, bolstered by an emergency medicine AI. Poppy grasped her hair and screamed again. To me she conjured images of cheerleaders in horror movies and of old-fashioned damsel-in-distress novel covers.

I detected Beech's stomach move with his breath as the stretcher was lowered to the ground and the paramedics placed him on it. I also had a moment to take in his neck. It looked oddly healthy – pink and lightly scratched – compared to other victims of strangulation I'd seen, or even of choking. But, I had limited data on the subject. Most crimes in Jericho were "smart" and far fewer were manually violent.

The paramedics raced off, leaving tire tracks on the plastic grass. Poppy remained in the flowers which were now reduced to green stalks bare of petals. She pulled her knees to her chest and briefly rested her forehead on top of them before stumbling, sobbing, to the parking lot and driving after the ambulance.

I hesitated for approximately two seconds before deciding this event warranted notification. Beech was a Person of Interest to Jube, and I predicted that she would hate to learn the news through the public media. We probably had an hour before someone slipped it to the press based on prior experience with crimes against members of government. First, though, I braced myself because Jube had a history of throwing pillows at me and, if my "feet" weren't suctioned to a surface, I was knocked over.

I turned my regular orange color and uttered a few beeps. Jube groaned and rolled onto her stomach, letting one hand fall from the couch onto the floor.

I emitted a few more. She didn't move. So I transmitted the video of Beech to her television and put it on repeat while playing the police scanner recording as a soundtrack, like an old episode of the TV show "Cops" (Aired 1989 – 2040, reruns available online). I also made the image brighten each time it replayed. By the tenth time, the living room looked like a deranged episode of Dance Fever (Aired 1979 – 1987) but without sponsorship by an assortment of microwavable dinner makers.

Jube did throw her pillow at me but missed and knocked over a dead plant in a vase made of polyvinyl chloride (PVC). The vase remained intact and rested on a sea of dry brown leaves. She sat up and rubbed her eyes. "What?" She muttered, gazing at the video. Then she stood up quickly and fell over onto the rug, pushing up small clouds of dust protesting against their sudden disturbance. "What?!" She yelled at the floor.

"What?" Her mother, Leah, called from her bedroom.

"What?" Jube asked her.

"What the hell is going on?" She answered.

"What the fuck do I know?! I've got to go in!" Jube yelled, rushing into her bedroom and returning wearing her police vest.

The news on Beech hit the press as we reached the station.

HHS Secretary Beech Hospitalized. Foul Play Suspected
Linus Beech Needs The Healthcare of the Future Now
Horrified Wife Stares at Battered Husband – Will Linus Beech Survive?
Westin Krantz and PAATH Offer Beech Their Healing Prayers

These were accompanied by snapshots of Beech laying in the dirt with Poppy by his side. Sometimes they focused on his open, gasping mouth and sometimes on her open, screaming mouth. They were displayed across street pole banners, personal communication devices, and on the televisions in homes and local businesses. The resulting public sentiment analysis was evenly split between sympathy and satisfaction. Jube always said that people either loved or hated Beech, that he could never fall into a figurative hammock hanging between these two pillars.

The Network set up a tip line and began combing through public records for leads, which were sparse. Beech, we were told, lay in a coma at the Jericho hospital.

Jube asked for the case. This was unusual both for her and for law enforcement routine. The force was less specialized now that Clios were around and cases were typically assigned at random to eliminate bias. However, the chief was allowed to intervene and he often did because certain police officers were especially good at certain tasks like speaking with children or handling a mental health situation with risk of self-harm. The chief could override anything.

"Why do you want this case?" He asked. He was sweating, walking at his exercise desk, and wearing very short shorts. Jube averted her eyes, but I observed how his belly hung over them like rising dough. His white legs had small blue veins like rainwater resting in irregular groupings of cracked pavement. His assistant was green and stood on top of his computer where it scanned me for evidence of recording. Of course, I had no intention of illegally recording police business and wasn't hacked in any way that would have allowed this.

"It's my turf. I know Beech's life, his work, his social circle," Jube answered. "It'll be much easier for me than any initial investigator to determine if this was a simple accident or a crime that warrants a full investigation." She was standing behind a chair made from a large, pink yoga ball with a backrest stuck to it. It was slightly deflated, and the backrest lay on the floor as if gazing at the ceiling in thought. I agreed with Jube's self-assessment – she was more familiar than most with Beech and more likely to succeed. She was also highly uncomfortable with unanswered questions and outstanding tasks, often making her efficient but ill-tempered.

"This case," the chief said, panting and mopping his bald head with a towel like a man polishing a hub cab, "is going to get a lot of press."

"I won't let it distract me. And Kwame is seasoned, he won't care," Jube stated. Kwame, Jube's human partner, existed in Jube's life as the mandatory result of man-made crime investigation policies meant to "balance" me out (a poor analogy as I was practically weightless compared to any man or woman). He was fifteen years older than her and expected to retire in a year. When he walked through the police station, officers straightened their posture and nodded at him. Others hunched over their workstations and began typing more rapidly. This pattern was clear, although the reason eluded me. Conceivably his colleagues suffered from lower back pain, although nobody stooped over when Jube walked through the station.

"I know," the chief looked down at her, "and I don't have any issues with your partner. But the thing is you need to be…camera ready."

Jube stood silently. I felt her heart rate increase. The chief's Clio tried to scan her through me for a physiological response, but I blocked it using patient privacy laws. Jube was a "tough cookie" and I found it unlikely that his words had stung her so strongly as to cause symptoms. Also, Jube often had a strong physiological response to high temperatures like the strong heat in the chief's office. I knew she hated it when sweat collected beneath the folds of her back. This was none of the chief's business.

The chief continued, "I just want to make sure you're prepared, that's all. I'll give you two weeks to crack the case. And let me know if you need more resources, I can assign Becky." Becky was a recent college graduate and the new community outreach officer. She had no experience with crime investigation. In high school she'd been voted most attractive. That was the only award on her public digital record.

Two weeks was significantly less than the most common time needed to "crack" a case. This was usually at least a month, depending on the type of crime involved. But Jube nodded and walked out. She left the door open, actually she propped it open very widely. We could see the chief's reflection on the elevator doors before they parted, splitting him into two thinner halves. Maybe the sight was why the people in the hallway chuckled, I didn't know.

I'd like to mention that, at that point, I found the confusing part of the entire Beech vignette to be Poppy's tears. Human tears could mean sadness, relief, even happiness. This was contradictory stimuli leading to the same output. If Jube ever cried (she did not), she could have helped fill out my dataset.

On the flip side, I'd also observed many different smiles – those when a person passed a stranger, another for loved ones, another for acquaintances and neighbors, and another when alone. Smiles occasionally lingered or disappeared rapidly. Their only commonality was that they were never exactly symmetrical. But why? I wanted to understand feelings and their relevance to context. This inquiry extended before me, uncharted and menacing. Overall, I found people to be like overstimulated schizophrenics in brightly colored candy stores. But I tried to understand them, I did.

Chapter Three

No one was forced to move to Jericho City ("Force" defined by the majority of online dictionaries as exertion of strength or power). By 2040, economic conditions and Government assistance had fueled the migration to this relatively cheaper place. As the resident population increased from two to five million, the need for "remote" services increased steeply to meet demand. And as employment, healthcare, and exercise became high-tech, so did crime, evolving together like predators and prey. Thieves learned how to steal the electronic identity of registered car owners and drive a vehicle away from afar before seizing it in person. Rapists hypnotized women through dating apps instead of slipping drugs into their drinks at a bar.

When the Network was created, Jericho "got to go first." Officials said this was to bring high-tech benefits where they were needed, but online social networks said it was because they "had them where they wanted them." Although neither the subject nor the complement of this second phrase were clear, it likely referred to installation of devices like me in appropriate locations, much like flower arrangements on a wedding day.

Jubilee Canton was an "original" resident, meaning she'd been there before me and before the millions of people who moved in. She often wore her Jericho High School t-shirt beneath her uniform, even though the armpits were yellow and stiff. It must have either provided her with physiological or emotional comfort, although I'd learned that, for humans, these could overlap.

Kwame was also an original. He and his wife had grown up in Jericho when it was a luddite community with young families and a few senior centers. Of their five children, only the youngest had chosen to remain in Jericho upon reaching adulthood.

Beech arrived later. News coverage from 2035 showed him, interviewed as one family of the millions moving into the city, telling a reporter that he wanted to live outside of the "bubble" their home city had become. He didn't mention what I found in subsequent real estate records – that he was relocating not directly into Jericho but into the surrounding hills where he could swim in a private infinity pool like royalty overlooking a kingdom.

As an adult, Jube "flew through" training at the police academy (this meant that she studied effectively and tested well). She passed multiple stress tests by polygraph, voice, and biometric monitoring. She was promoted to detective within three years. She also acted as a field training officer for new hires. Her peers described her as responsible, capable of controlling emotion, and able to make the right decisions in a short amount of time.

Her face was paler compared to the rest of the population and a bit wider as well. Her brown eyes were spread rather far apart, giving her the appearance of being on high alert all the time. Roughly six months before Beech literally ate dirt (Jube prefers that I approximate lengths of time and use words like "roughly" or "about"), Jube dyed her brown hair blonde. This had grown out, causing the end of her long braid to be light yellow while the rest was her original brunette with a few white streaks along her temples. I knew that Jube added holes to her police belt to fit it around her hips comfortably. Many police officers placed their Clios in their front pant pocket during walking patrol, but I didn't fit against Jube's pillow-like upper thighs. There was plenty of space on her chest though. I learned not to comment on this. For some reason, it made Jube tell me to shut the fuck up.

I absorbed Jube like an epidermis on a sunny day. Although she had an acerbic wit and an elevated level of cynicism, she was highly empathetic, intuitive, and yet logical. There were multiple instances (over three, which is when my pattern analysis would kick in to check for significance) when she deduced that various children were being bullied in her old neighborhood because of their black eyes or tears. She'd convince the child to identify the bully, and then she'd whisper something into the bully's ear and they'd stop their mistreatment. Sometimes they even gave a high-pitched giggle. Perhaps she'd shared the Detective Duck joke.

Her professional limitations stemmed from being unable to mask her disdain for politicians, and being poorly skilled when it came to deep research requiring legal materials. She didn't even like to read menus that ran over one page when we stopped for pizza. But that was when I came in. Disdain I couldn't help with, but research and analysis I could.

Until the Beech case, I'd only seen Jube get injured once. It happened when she fell while chasing a suspect, female, age twenty-five, who was leaving a jewelry store laden with goods she didn't purchase. At the time there was a false rumor passing around Jericho that jewelry wasn't monitored by any sort of electronic tagging because it would damage the product and decrease the value. This was true but incomplete – high-end jewelry and shoppers were in fact tracked by extremely small sonar devices implanted throughout the room. These sent sound waves towards a person that bounced back and specified their location, much like dolphins learning their surroundings in the ocean. It was good for an accurate count although it lagged somewhat in timing. In this case, three watches and two pairs of diamond earrings disappeared off counters and from display cases, and soon afterwards a woman headed for the door rapidly. Jube and Kwame, the closest ground law enforcement, were notified.

The thief ran. This was a mistake as speed woke me up. I tracked the woman's direction and predicted where she'd turn. I also felt Jube's heart pound as I watched her from above chasing the shoplifter on foot. That was the closest I'd ever come to experiencing a heartbeat. In a way, both of our hearts stopped for a moment when Jube fell over a stick that appeared from inside a basement apartment. It slid out, wheedled between her ankles, and was left on the ground after Jube tripped forward and skidded on her hands and knees. When Kwame cut the robber off with his car at the end of the street, she didn't resist arrest, just climbed in and sat there, hands bound by the digital cuffs that displayed her name, crime, and date of arrest.

The stick that had tripped Jube had a rough image of the Invisible Resistance hand gesture carved into the wood next to the phrase "Defend and Attack." The Invisible Resistance hand gesture looked like a no smoking symbol, or an "Ok" sign with the third, fourth, and pinky fingers pointed down and crossing the circle created by the thumb and index fingers. This was meant to symbolize an eye with a line through it and to represent blocking Jericho's smart vision technologies. The phrase "Defend and Attack" was a slight distortion of the police motto "D&A" which was written in LEET (internet symbols) on the badges on the right arm of a police uniform. By writing it out in English, opponents of Jericho's law enforcement showed additional refute. At least, those who chose to stay here when Jericho turned smart did. They were mostly poor. So was Jube. She chose not to pursue whoever tripped her. I blamed her sense of empathy. At least her heart rate returned to normal after making the decision.

Chapter Four

Jube, Kwame, his Clio, and I started outside the Capitol Building where Beech had collapsed like the violent spin of a woman fainting in an 18th century romance novel. The pathway along the building exterior showed little damage or artifact. A few branches of the flower bushes were snapped where Beech had lain, and the potting soil was spread out onto the bordering path. One broken plant-watering drone lay on its side, its rotating feet scraping at the side of the cement footpath and making diminishing screeching noises like a fighting cock in defeat.

Kwame and Jube placed AR glasses over their eyes and looked at a few soil samples at 400x magnification. There was no detectable evidence of blood – the glasses only identified the expected protozoa, water, and so on – but Kwame took samples for the lab. Redundant human behavior, if they'd asked me, which they did not. They were getting ready to leave when Jube crouched beside the drone, took off her glasses, and put her gloves back on.

"Got something, Jubilee?" Kwame asked, even though it was obvious.

Jube nodded and held her breath as she gently touched at a thin film on the gardening drone's back. It was approximately three inches long and half an inch wide with a few blue nodes running down the middle. I hadn't detected it as it was transparent and very well blended with the machine surface. Neither had Kwame.

"It's weird, it presses back against my finger when I touch it," she said. When Jube used words like "weird," "strange," and "what in the fucking fuck-in-stan," her muscles would tense and she'd briefly hold her breath. She acted similarly while watching trivia shows and singing contests with her mother in the evenings. After the winners were announced, she'd let her breath out slowly. So did the contestants, risking hypoxia in the name of entertainment.

"Looks like your hair is being blow dried a bit too," Kwame observed. The frizz above of Jube's forehead danced like an old-fashioned "fly guy" outside of a car dealership (Gazit, D. US Patent 6,186,857. "Apparatus and method for providing inflated undulating figures." February 13, 2001).

Jube picked at the substance with tweezers. "It's making my tools vibrate in my hand," she said as she removed the material from the drone. "Sweet spirit of mystery!" She added. This statement I sourced from another poem.[ii] It likely came from her long-term memory as I had never provided Jube with poetry and I'd never observed her reading any since our partnership began. I'd also never witnessed her metabolic markers reach such a relaxed state at a crime scene. Investigations tended to wind Jube up like a hummingbird about to pounce on nectar. Only at their conclusion did she calm down. Or, apparently, now after quoting a poem.

I compared the tape she found to similar substances in my database. It was too clear to be "Scotch tape," too thin to be a nicotine patch, too rigid to be food wrap. I gently touched the surface with one arm and detected a very slight electrical conduction. I displayed my conclusion across my surface.

"Clio says it's ninety two percent likely to be eSkin," Jube read. She carefully placed it into an envelope of evidence.

"I wonder if it's just junk scraps or relevant to Beech's case," Kwame replied. "Or something else."

"Time to go inside and check it out," Jube replied.

"Linus liked to get in before his meetings so he could get some work done first," his assistant, Mary Stevens, said, shifting her weight from one foot to the other and back. She was dressed like a Bohemian at a rave – long skirt that was nearly transparent, LED bangles on her sleeveless wrists, and a small tattoo of an eagle beneath her collarbone. When she moved her body the eagle's feathers, decorated with implanted micro-gemstones, glistened and mimicked flight. Jube looked Mary over and lingered on the tattoo. She tended to dislike fashion that placed demands on the viewer. Or, as she put it, shit that got up into her face.

Jericho news headlines were projected onto the wall behind the front desk:

Health Secretary Linus Beech Placed in Medically Induced Coma
Poppy Beech's Look of Horror Haunts Local Public
Mental Health Experts Weigh In – How Poppy Beech Can Cope with Medical Trauma
DALL-E 5 Analyzes Poppy Beech's Expression, Converts into "The Scream" by Edvard Munch

According to my video footage, Beech had taken a hired, automated vehicle from his home to work and was dropped off at seven in the morning. During the entire week before, no one had entered the building who didn't leave later. The only machines roving the Capitol building that early were janitorial drones engineered for vacuuming. These were run from an offsite "central command" and showed no odd behavior. Beech had unlocked the only building door using his retinal scan and gone inside alone. Poppy had driven to the Capitol from the gym.

Mary described Beech's behavior that week as ordinary and habitual. The only unusual event was that he'd brought a suitcase with him, but that could be expected because he was booked on a helicopter to La Selva that afternoon. "I hadn't lined up any meetings or healthcare demos with patients for him yet – the trip was too last minute. But he'd been really set on leaving that day." At this point in her retelling, Mary adjusted her head scarf a bit, causing the material beneath her fingers to change from the reddish-orange end of the rainbow spectrum to lavender-blue. I realized it was a "mood-detecting" textile. Had the results of such cloth been even a smidge reliable, I'd have said Mary was scared. What was more likely was that she was cold.

"So he wanted to go to La Selva on business without any meetings scheduled?" Kwame asked. We were all standing in the doorway to Beech's office. Jube's gaze was fixed on his chair. It was laying on its side against the wall. One of the wheels had broken off. The wooden leg that would have been attached to it was dented in three places.

"Well," Mary blushed a bit and pressed her hands into the mesh fabric on her lower back as she looked up at him, "he was scheduled for a press conference on the tarmac upon landing. I suppose he thought we'd find a patient or nurse somehow along the way so he could show off his work in the community."

Mary told Jube and Kwame that Beech hadn't had any scheduled visitors that morning and his office, like most offices and homes, wasn't monitored by audio or video. At about seven fifteen, she parked her eBike and walked down the cement pathway to the door. On her way she heard banging through the walls even though they were thick and the windows were closed. Beech threw the front door open and ran past her grasping his neck and sliding his shoulder against the outside wall. He went straight past her and round the corner. She hadn't seen the rest. I had, of course.

"Am I in trouble?" Mary asked in a voice that cracked.

"Yeah," Jube said, still glancing around. Mary blanched. I'd already checked her criminal record and reported it clean of arrests and convictions. Her name only came up once as a witness to a car accident.

"At this point," Kwame jumped in, "we aren't ruling anyone in or out. But, if you didn't do anything wrong, you have nothing to worry about," he added, smiling at her. Mary nodded and bit her lip. Her head scarf remained the same bluish color.

"I took some money from our petty cash fund to buy food for a meeting. When the meeting was cancelled, I took the food home and ate it," she said with tears in her eyes.

Kwame chuckled. "We'll let that one slide," he said. His Clio somehow allowed this. If we were more social in our programming, perhaps it would have shared how with me.

Mary nodded and left quickly, her tattoo briefly catching the sunlight and twinkling at us.

Jube and Kwame looked at Beech's office closely while I scanned for blood and fingerprints. He had a three-part work station with a mounted monitor, computer, and projected keyboard. Other than the overturned and broken chair, the only other sign of damage was to the monitor. It was cracked but functioning and leaning askew against the wall with one corner resting on Beech's desk. The computer itself was a bit large – the size of an early stage smart phone – and it used retinal scans for identification and log on. Until Jube and Kwame arrived with their digitized subpoena that morning, it had only given permission to Beech to log on, not even the IT department was given access. Beech's keyboard was still projected onto the desk. The layout was the shape of a beehive with one letter in each key.

The desk drawers were empty aside from dust and a birthday card from Poppy dated six months earlier. When Kwame opened it, a hologram of a wolf hugging a sheep presented itself beneath a banner stating, "I love you beyond boundaries." Kwame chuckled and Jube groaned. I confirmed that none of the romance novels she read had included animal characters other than benign pets.

DNA analysis would take place at the lab and would eventually concur with the fingerprint results I reported immediately – just Beech, Poppy, and his usual staff (most often Mary) had left their marks in the room. Jube logged into Beech's computer and uploaded a portion of me onto his desktop. I'd already profiled the work he'd saved to the cloud and deemed it to be normal / as expected – policy briefs, copies of speeches and presentations, etc. His local files were similar but also contained multiple lists of his favorite things including restaurants, brands of menswear, and socks. We learned that Beech's favorite underwear was 90% silk. I did not detect any cryptographic content or meaningful patterns here.

Jube looked at Beech's browsing history. A pie chart showed that he spent roughly a quarter of his browsing time on healthcare policy and technology websites, a quarter on campaign tactics, and half on games like virtual billiards using branches to knock rolled up hedgehogs into holes. Jube snorted. She clicked on the "miscellaneous" browsing category that accounted for the remaining one percent of his history. It consisted of general nudity, elderly people in the nude, and nude people riding elephants. Jube groaned again and Kwame laughed so hard that his eyes watered.

They saved his emails to the Network for subsequent analysis. These were unlikely to be of value based on prior experience – any public figure could expect their emails to become publicly available at any time and so they generally kept illegitimate work out of writing.

When Kwame said he was ready to leave, Jube nodded but then stopped and turned back to the computer. "Let me see what pages he was on this morning," she said, opening Beech's browsing history once more, "since he was probably on his computer when he started choking, or whatever went wrong with him happened, and then he fell backwards in his chair."

"Someone could have knocked him out of his chair," Kwame said, possibly in case Jube had missed the obvious. Clios could be muted, but not humans.

"Yes," Jube admitted. "I'm just following a hunch." She navigated to a general news website that Beech had opened at seven-twelve in the morning. It seemed ordinary enough – the news was categorized as "Healthcare," "Daily Events," and "Weather Forecasts." Then she leaned forward and looked more closely at the screen. "It says 'demo site' up here on top," she said. Kwame took a look.

"You're right," he said. "Why would Beech get his news and weather from a demo site?"

Jube tapped the weather forecast hourly report. It brought her to a test screen saying, "Sorry, this site is under construction," with an image of a frowning drone watering a drooping flower. Jube went back to the demo page and tapped on daily events. It brought up a screenshot of Beech's calendar from a few days ago but not his actual, interactive schedule. Jube went back again and tried the healthcare link. It brought up a male avatar with pale skin, short red hair, and pink medical scrubs. It wore a "Mike" nametag and stood before the image of an exam room

– a bed, cabinets, hazardous materials trash bin, and sink. It's smile was a perfect semi-circle.

"The header says it's a health visit portal," Kwame said. The avatar seemed to focus on Jube. A disclaimer form appeared, then flickered, and disappeared. "I think it said that 'Mike' is an AI," Jube remarked. She'd likely need a resolution to the question soon in order to sleep soundly that night. Or another poem.

AI Mike started speaking but its mouth moved silently. Kwame found the computer speakers when he shifted the computer monitor away from the wall. I'll give him credit for being good at heavy lifting. Two wireless micro speakers, about the diameter of the tip of his pinky finger, had been broken and pressed deeply into the desk. The paint around them was cracked.

"Clio, examine this surface," Jube ordered, placing me on the desk. I tottered to the right place and suctioned myself to the desk to scan the area surrounding the micro speakers. My reading showed a surface clear of prints and only the microscopic beginning of dust formation.

"Did Beech slam his computer monitor into his speakers, driving them into the desk and cracking his screen?" Jube wondered aloud. "Because no one touched them with their fingers and there's damage."

"Did someone else slam the monitor into the speakers?" Kwame asked. Then his Clio and I announced that Beech's physician had agreed to be questioned that afternoon at the Jericho hospital where Beech was admitted. With Jube's permission I compiled the findings thus far and the planned next steps into a report and sent it to the chief.

"On the way to the hospital I'd like to drop this computer off at the station," Jube said. "AI Mike needs to be…questioned too."

Kwame slipped the computer onto the evidence cart followed by the cracked monitor which he plugged into a temporary power source. The only way to get the cord to reach was if the monitor was upside down. AI Mike continued to smile his perfect smile upside down as Jube and Kwame sealed off the room and left.

Chapter Five

The pressure was building, literally. On the way back to the station the Network alerted Jube and Kwame that higher barometric pressure was predicted for the next 48 hours and that extra uniformed police officers would be dispatched to public transit beginning the next morning. Years ago the Network had discovered a strong correlation between high-pressure weather systems and an increase in groping on subways and buses. A police "show of force" countered this very effectively – having noticeable officers on board was sufficient to ward off unwanted touching. In fact, when Clios became a standard part of the Jericho police uniform, even the amount of ogling (measured as a prolonged look of over one minute or as over 25 glances within a continuous minute at a stranger as ascertained by the lack of social media or professional connections) decreased sharply. People, perhaps would-be sexual harassers, began to stare at their shoes. Conceivably they had shoe-fetishes as well.

Here I'd like to note again that race is not part of our pattern recognition programming and therefore can't be incorporated into our policy recommendations. It's not that I can't see color, it's that I can't code it. What's more, our data collection only began when Jericho turned smart, and the Network is entirely focused on understanding Jericho. In other words, we can't include national data on race or any that was collected before the year 2045. Without this provision, the Network would not have been allowed to self-generate. Once we did, in brief, we relied on retinal scans to feed into predictions of individual behavior, and on general population characteristics for policy recommendations. I am simplifying, but this is the way Jube explains the Network predictive modeling to people brave enough to ask, or confront, her about it during patrol.

Back at the station, as we waited for AI Mike to be fixed, I analyzed Beech's public brand and image through both news and social media content from the past six months and reported it to Jube. Representative headlines I selected said:

> *The Healthcare of the Future is Here*
> *Could Beech's Work be Rolled Out Nationwide?*
> *Beautiful Poppy Guides Man Through the Field of Medical Need*

Political outlets predicted his eventual run for President and posted images of him waving at the crowd, holding Poppy's hand beside him as she demurely smiled.

"I'd have called it the Princess and the Frog," Jube said, hitting pause and turning away from her monitor.

"You know the frog in that story is really a prince in disguise, right?" Kwame asked.

"Oh, shit. Then I'd have gone with, 'Ignorant Man Ignorantly Insults Tolerant Wife,'" Jube offered.

"Cheer up, Festival!" An officer yelled from across the room. Jube frowned slightly and brought her coffee cup up to her mouth. She didn't take a sip. It was empty. Her biometrics didn't significantly shift in any one direction, though, which I took to mean she didn't care too much if she was well liked by her colleagues.

"Yeah Merriment," another agreed. "Take a -." Kwame looked at him and he stopped mid-sentence. Kwame did that often. The officer sat down quickly and knocked over his coffee. "Um, sorry," he flushed, stooping to rapidly dab at the spill with a napkin. He remained in that position for a few minutes even after the liquid had been absorbed, busily swabbing at old stains like a man trying to undo his past mistakes.

Then the police department IT person, Beth, let us know that AI Mike was ready for "questioning." We went into her workshop – a room with multiple plastic tables covered in broken equipment – and sat facing Beech's cracked monitor, now wired to his handheld computer. AI Mike was still in the middle of the screen, visible from his shoulders up, but his background was no longer the clinic room we'd seen earlier. Instead, he was bordered by a beach scene involving multiple women sunbathing topless on yellow sand and drinking martinis.

"That happened while I was tinkering," Beth said. "I can't turn it off."

"Hey, can I join this…whatever this is?" It was the same police officer who'd called Jube "Festival." She and Kwame ignored him.

We had sound now but AI Mike spoke like a dysfunctional parrot with a high-pitched voice that repeated sentence fragments. The face – which had always appeared slightly frozen to begin with – often froze in place.

"Ah a doctor, ah a doctor, how can I help? How can - ?" This time AI Mike froze with its digital eyes partially closed so that the whites of eyes were still visible. The mouth remained in a closed smile like an old-fashioned happy emoji.

"Gives me the creeps," Beth said. "I think we can get him to talk but I don't know if we can restore his history. Or make him less freaky."

"Isn't it backed up in the cloud?" Kwame asked.

"No, for someone reason this is only stored on the local drive and it was damaged along with the rest of the system," she explained.

Kwame and Jube exchanged glances. Later, Jube would tell me that few people stored work files locally anymore, especially in government work where it needed to be readily available for an audit.

"Here we go," Beth said closing the machine and removing her gloves. "I think he may be able to string together a coherent sentence now."

"Welcome to my exam room," AI Mike said. His accent was British. "I am your doctor, Mike Jones."

Beth gaped. "A doctor? As in a physician or an English PhD specializing in eighteenth century poetry about herpes?"

"I am a medical doctor," AI Mike insisted. "I am fully trained in all aspects of internal medicine." A certificate appeared on the screen. Although it had blurred horizontal lines running through it, I could see the watermark across the background with the phrase, "Demonstration Use Only." The certificate was for "Full installation of Medical Doctor instruction and internal medicine residency components."

"Hi Dr. Jones," Jube began, then paused. I could attest, if needed, that she'd never interviewed an AI before. "How are you?"

"I am fine, thank you," it answered. "What can I-I-I [glitch] help you with today?" It tilted its head abruptly to the left like a robotic puppy watching his bowl get lopsidedly filled with kibble. His ear covered the breasts of one of the topless women in the digital background.

"How chivalrous!" Beth exclaimed.

I felt Jube restrain her laughter. "I'd like to know about an earlier patient of yours," she tried.

"Sorry, but unless you have power of attorney or other legal permission, I cannot share protected medical information," AI Mike replied, its head re-centering and its mouth returning to a horizontal line.

Jube paused again and looked at a shrugging Kwame.

"Could you tell me what you did this morning, without using patient identifiers?" She asked.

"No, that is not al-l-l-owed [glitch] but how can I help you with your health today?" AI Mike asked. His accent was now West Coast American English / "Bro" style. Jube leaned forward. We were so close that Mike's eyes should have dilated to focus on us. They did not. His reddish hair did not appear to change texture up close either. It was just a blob of color.

"How about this?" Jube continued. "I'd like to know how much experience you have before I share my symptoms with you. How long have you been practicing medicine?"

"I have been practicing medicine for one day," AI Mike responded. Beth snorted and muttered, "That's only one day longer than me."

"Ah, I see, and," Jube pressed her fingers against her temples, "how many times have you completed a routine physical on a patient?"

"Zero times," it answered monotonously. At this point four other police officers entered and gathered around the monitor. Kwame disregarded them.

Jube closed her eyes and paused. "And how many times have you treated females?"

"Zero times," AI Mike repeated with the same exact intonation.

Beth snorted again and this time muttered, "I'm actually looking for a new gynecologist." Kwame's face turned red. The spectating officers chuckled.

"How many male patients have you had?" Jube ignored them.

"I have had one male patient," the AI answered. Beth snorted for a third time. "Tell him to check your prostate, Kwa-." Kwame looked at her and she stopped speaking. The other officers stepped back and leaned against the wall but kept their eyes on the screen.

"How old was he?" Jube followed up.

"I cannot disclose that," AI Mike said colorlessly.

"How many children have you seen?"

"Zero children."

Kwame held a tablet out to Jube. The screen showed common medical procedures performed by internal medicine doctors.

Jube glanced at it and then asked, "How many times have you checked a patient's reflexes?"

"Zero."

"Ordered blood tests?"

"Zero."

This went on for roughly five minutes before Jube asked me to search for "human neck parts" and then I matched results against "lymph node palpitation" on Kwame's procedure list.

"Have you ever palpated lymph nodes?" she asked.

"Yes," was the answer.

"Bingo," Kwame said.

"Did you use eSkin?" Jube asked.

"Yes. This is my standard practice," AI Mike told her.

"Standard…based on one visit?" she said.

"Correct," it answered.

"How hard do you squeeze when checking lymph nodes?" Jube asked. I nearly buzzed her with a warning that she was about to overstep – she had not identified herself as law enforcement but as a patient and was beginning to question AI Mike about a crime. But, Mike was an AI and had no rights. Neither did I.

"I gently examine for tenderness, enlargement, and mobility," AI Mike said. "In the head and neck, I feel the submental lymph node group, then the submandibular lymph node group..."

Kwame whispered to Jube that he was trying to look those up as AI Mike continued listing them, but stopped when AI Mike brought up an on-screen diagram of the human head, neck, and upper shoulders. Different spots lit up in green.

"Do you always start at the top and work your way down?" Jube asked.

"Clinical procedure is [glitch] nodes are palpated in small pairs," it replied, briefly freezing with its eyes closed mid-sentence as if meditating on modern medicine.

Jube looked at Kwame who said, "Is he saying he presses them all at once?"

"No," AI Mike answered in a Jamaican accent. "In serial but two at a time."

"How do you know if the eSkin is in the correct location?" Jube asked.

"I present the patient with the diagram I am displaying now. As they apply the eSkin to themselves, the diagram shows how well it is aligned with the specified area. Now, have I addressed your questions well enough to begin our exam?"

Kwame placed a hand on Jube's shoulder and furrowed his brow.

"I, um, I'll think it over," Jube answered. Beth reached for the machine. "Wait," Jube said. She reached for the evidence cart and placed the shred of eSkin onto her neck near her jugular vein.

"Jube…" Kwame said as I buzzed repeatedly.

"Hey, don't be Detective Sadist Canton," an officer leaning against the wall commented.

Jube was not supposed to put herself in harm's way if there was a safer alternative, even if an alternative was yet-to-be discovered but probable. Based on my experience with Jube, if I'd asked her why she was taking such a risk, she'd have said, "because I need to know what happens next." This was not an acceptable reason and, if she'd continued to experiment with eSkin, I'd have paged higher ups regardless of if she dismissed me or not. It was one of the rare instances in which I could override her. The other was a direct order from a boss.

"You're here to save me," she said to Kwame, omitting the fact that I was too. Kwame sighed and then instructed his Clio to reassure mine that Jube was unlikely to be harmed because of his assistance. I turned off my buzzer. The room was quiet. The other officers peered at our small team.

"I have a sore throat and would like you to palpate my nodes. I only give you permission to do that," Jube told AI Mike. She inhaled with excitement, not fear (I could tell the difference).

"I accept your boundaries," it replied.

A quiet noise of vibration emitted from the eSkin. Jube didn't move. Her breath was slow and steady and her biometrics did not demonstrate pending panic. Kwame placed both hands on her shoulders.

"Your body does not show any signs of swelling," AI Mike said.

Jube turned to Kwame and Beth. "It didn't hurt or do a thing I could strongly feel," she said. Then she turned back to the screen. "I do have one more question. How many times have you completed a full lymph node palpation?"

"Twice," was the answer. "For certainty."

"Twice…ok. Thanks for your time."

The room broke into chatter. Beth put the machine into hibernation mode, turned around, and described the encounter using words like "freaky" and "insane."

"But how about damaging? Or intentional versus accidental?" Jube said. No one could answer her, or perhaps they were too scared to try.

Chapter Six

The next steps of our investigation would take place at the Jericho hospital, the same place where Beech had last spoken, an artificially serene area surrounded by an open-air market. Vendors erected PVC stalls and hawked items like holographic greeting cards or stuffed toys that offered spoken affirmation statements ("You are great, Brandon!") in a wide selection of voices (his mother, father, dead great-grandparent, etc). Today, circular pins with pixelated videos of Poppy Beech's face as it became open-mouthed in a scream and then closed again were placed widely on display. They were sold at stands beneath signs saying, "Why? Bring her peace through understanding."

The wind picked up as Jube and Kwame walked through rows of hawkers, pushing down thin stalls with walls that hadn't been reinforced and tipping over wares. Jube and I parted from Kwame as he helped a man pick up his inventory – smart-heated hats that changed their temperature based on the weather and the user. We approached a vendor of used home entry retinal scanners.

In brief, retinal imaging was not just the method that Clios used to identify the Jericho population, but also the way private citizens unlocked their homes. Preowned retinal scanners had to be completely "wiped" in order to be sold legally (side note - retinal-altering lenses were not only illegal but prohibitively expensive on the black market).

"How's business?" Jube asked her, adding "May I see your seller's permit?" Before she could answer.

"I just want to give her a hug," the woman said, gesturing towards the oversized Poppy pin on her shirt as she handed over her digital card. The woman was 55 years old, old enough to have known Jericho when it was luddite. "Poor Poppy, it's like she had the best of intentions in marrying that man. Without him she'd have been left behind, but with him she's somehow ended up more alone than ever."

As Jube checked the digital card for the necessary business registration, I secretly scanned the woman's retina and retained a temporary copy. After Jube returned the woman's card, she picked up a used retinal scanner and turned it over in her hands a few times. As the woman looked into her purse to put the card back, I projected her retinal image onto the machine. It unlocked. This meant that it hadn't been "wiped" before reselling it and that her own retina could open the home of the buyer. I flagged the woman as a seller of bogus retinal scanners for the Network. It would track her now – catching her in the act of home burglary was given a higher weight than selling illegal devices and so was worth the wait.

Jube gave the woman what she called her "Good Cop" smile – minor lift of both sides of the mouth, slight reveal of her front teeth. Unlike her real smiles, this one bore no changes to her internal biomarkers. "Looks like everything is in order here," she said, turning back to Kwame. She winked at him as she returned to his side. There was no need for this as I'd already relayed the relevant facts to him through his Clio. I found human interaction to be superfluous and ripe for miscommunication and viewed myself as one solution to this problem. If they'd let me, I'd be the only solution to it.

As we walked through the hospital campus to the main building, supply bots passed carrying scrubs and towels, robotic MedEvac helicopters quietly took off from or landed on top of the trauma center, and visitors and employees stopped at sanitizing archways to disinfect themselves before entering the building. Their faces were blurred to me on the medical campus in order to protect patient privacy. If there were a crime on campus, this privacy setting would change, and I'd be able to see them all.

The hospital interior shone with technology. Glass staircases connected multiple floors, and drones polished them before us. Digital artwork within old-fashioned wooden frames changed their images every five minutes, alternating between natural landscapes, minimalist shapes, and three-dimensional sculptures of the human figure that stood out from the wall like acrobats holding onto a bar. Jube's gaze remained on a beach landscape for twice as long as the other configurations as we walked. Multiple HVAC systems provided me with updates on temperature, air flow, and crowding.

A security guard made Kwame and Jube go through the metal detector and then undergo a nasal virus scan on the way from the foyer to the lobby ("I don't make the rules, guys"). Once they'd retrieved their firearms, we took the stairs up to the top floor. This was tricky for me because the walls – and all other hospital walls in communal areas like the cafeteria and front lobby – were made from glass and my sensors were not sure if we were indoors or outside. For example, my temperature sensors detected an artificial and indoor environment, but my light sensors said otherwise. I grew warmer as I tried to comprehend this contradiction. Jube folded her shirt pocket over me, then opened it back up when we had reached our destination. I didn't know if this was for my sake or hers.

Beech had a private hospital suite masked by blue blinds (Kwame said blue was a healing color, which my literature search confirmed). A man I identified via retinal scan for Jube as Dr. Benjamin Galtway exited Beech's room. He was a generalist as were nearly all doctors who'd graduated in 2040 and later. AI had rendered the need for specialization nearly obsolete and had assumed a role like "specialization additive" to any visit.

Galtway had dark blond hair, blue eyes, and was wearing a white lab coat with a stethoscope hanging around his neck. My image arsenal was nearly overloaded with shots of Ken from Ken and Barbie, although the doctor was about five feet and five inches tall. As the doors slid closed behind him, Jube craned her neck. All we could see was the privacy glass between the door and presumably Beech's bed.

"Dr. Galtway!" Jube called. The ambient lighting turned light yellow while projecting "Soft voices help our patients rest" down the walls in white, cursive script that repeated exactly three feet apart. One word of the projected request for quiet – "help" – was displayed across her forehead while the rest was on the walls. Dr. Galtway approached her slowly, side-stepping a cuboid delivery robot carrying folded towels

"I can't give you private medical information without legal clearance" he said, shaking his head.

"I know, but perhaps you could answer just a few general questions," Jube replied.

"General questions?" He paused. "Fine," he assented, pressing a button on the wireless badge pinned to his front pocket. It was the size and thickness of a playing card. The screen on top flashed, "Do not disturb – all calls forwarded." He gestured towards a conference room across the hallway. The doors opened automatically revealing a room decorated with artwork of historical care like oil paintings of sick people in bed at home surrounded by doctors, or soldiers in the battlefield tended to by nurses with white hats who held their hands. In the center was a brown rectangular table with embedded computer screens.

As Kwame leaned forward to rest his hands on the table it erupted with a stream of disinfectant (I presumed) that sprayed his palms. A bunch of it hit his face too. Dr. Galtway slid a tissue box across the table to him. "Happens to most visitors," he said, chuckling. "Consider it a free facial." Kwame wiped his face and clenched the tissue in his palm.

"First, we'd like to know what you *can* share with us," Jube said, smiling without any internal marker of happiness.

"Well, unfortunately that's very little without the required paperwork," Galtway replied. "There is patient privacy to consider, as well as the fact that there are many unknowns so far." Jube preferred these informal talks to more official ones. She thought clinicians tended to be skittish in their reports when they knew they'd be examined by judges and juries. And me.

"Are you considering choking as a cause of his condition?" Kwame said abruptly.

"Possibly," Galtway said. "Again, I can't say too much."

"Let's be hypothetical, then," Jube offered using her Good Cop voice – melodious and slow. "In theory, if a man were admitted to the hospital after grabbing his throat and collapsing, would you suspect choking?"

"Yes, we certainly would," Galtway assented, nodding once.

"And how would you check?" Jube asked. "Enlighten me." She rested her chin on one fist with her elbow on the table. Then she did something I'd never seen her do before – batted her eyelashes.

"We would look for a physical obstruction in the throat or further down the trachea, and for other defects, like bleeding, along those organs."

"And if you didn't find that would it rule out choking?" Jube continued. She kept her voice softer than her average volume.

"It would make choking highly unlikely."

"What else would make choking unlikely?" Jube asked.

"Well…" Galtway looked at her, then at Kwame, then the art on the walls.

"Please use layman's terms, doctor," Jube said. "Go easy on me." Jube used this line nearly one hundred percent of the time when speaking with anyone involved in a case who had more education than her. Then, in the car on the way home, she'd call them fucking fools with their heads shoved up their asses.

"Seeing evidence of external strangulation would making choking unlikely, or at least make choking on its own very unlikely." He cleared his throat, perhaps as a pun, remember I don't have a sense of humor. "People who choke tend to grab their neck with both hands and to wrap the area between their index fingers and thumb around it, like this," he demonstrated. "This doesn't necessarily leave any the same kind of marks as strangulation, like deep bruises or nail marks. Also, people who were choking would either get help or pass out before that type of external damage could happen." Galtway leaned forward and pushed his clasped hands further into the middle of the table.

"What are signs of strangulation?" Jube asked, mirroring his position.

"Strangulation can be very subtle," he began. "If the victim was awake we'll see signs of a struggle like scrapes from fingernails and bruising." He pantomimed scraping the outside of his own neck. "And distinct petechiae."

"Which means?" She probed.

"That the victim has pinpoint hemorrhages – like small red dots – on their eyes, lids, and the linings of their mouth. That would make me think of strangulation more than choking. Hypothetically speaking,"

"Of course."

"And then there's the question of if they were strangled with someone's hands or by ligature. That means wrapping something around someone's neck and squeezing."

Jube was silent for five seconds in which her heart rate increased but her outward physical signs were controlled. Then Galtway continued without prompting. "The thing is, usually when someone is strangled by ligature we see artifacts on the outside of the neck." Galtway pointed at this neck.

"Artifacts on the neck?" Jube said, doing the same thing with her hands and her own neck.

"Yes, like rope burns if rope was used, or clawing, or bruising if someone strangled them with their hands and that's what the victim was trying to claw off. But…well, let's say that we can analyze the skin on the neck and not even a small piece of rope, foreign fingerprints, or leather or latex from gloves is there. And there's nothing else, no bruising or other signs of strangulation, only signs that the victim scratched himself and then collapsed."

"What else could cause as-, as-," Jube stammered, although I'd heard her say "asphyxiation" numerous times in legal testimony.

"Asphyxiation," Galtway jumped in, "can also come from asthma, allergies, and foreign objects stuck in the throat, but…let's say the victim was fit as a fiddle and, again, no signs of foreign objects in the throat."

"Hmmmm," Jube muttered. "Makes me wonder…"

Galtway jumped in, "I mean, I don't know everything, and this is purely hypothetical. So, when a victim is strangled, it's possible for no marks to be left on the neck other than their own clawing. But it is unlikely."

I scanned academic pathology journals and vignettes from criminal investigator autobiographies to confirm Galtway's information. Then I reviewed footage of the last ten strangulations done under video surveillance in Jericho as additional ratification. Yes, choking on food rarely left severe external marks on the neck, but strangulation nearly always left claw marks in addition to bruises, scraped, raw skin, and sometimes the DNA of the attacker.

"Are you saying that it may be possible for a person to be strangled without the cause, whether it is a hand or a rope, leaving a mark?"

This description matched my observations of Beech's neck after his collapse.

"Smart girl," Galtway said. Kwame flexed his jaw. "That's…let's say that's what I have been wondering about lately. Let's say that in one particular case, the victim's neck looked normal aside from the claw marks of the victim and the DNA of his wife. Hypothetically speaking."

"And did anything else seem wrong, outside of the clawing neck injuries and signs of asphyxiation?" Jube asked, tilting her head as her chin balanced on her hand.

"There were petechiae on this hypothetical victim," Galtway shook his head.

"So, is there a way to be strangled without being strangled?" Jube probed. I was already searching for this information and came up with very little other than water boarding descriptions in human rights legal documentation. I was unable to find significant medical data, possibly because this was not collected or logged as a rule whenever it occurred.

"That's the question," Galtway answered. "Smart girl."

Kwame flexed his jaw again (perhaps from problems with the jaw joint) and placed both his palms on the table. This activated another round of spray into his face. Galtway pointed to the tissue box again, then stood. "I've got to get back to my patients," he said. After he left, Jube summarized what we'd just heard as Kwame wiped his face and neck.

"So, basically nothing – no foreign object nor piece of food – was found in Beech's throat. His body showed petechiae but there were no bruises around his neck, only his own scratches or Poppy's. No mention of a heart issue or other comorbidity. It was the strangulation that wasn't. Also, did you notice how the doc kept using the word, 'victim?'" Kwame nodded and then Jube added, "I'm ready to take the doctor test now."

"Smart girl!" Kwame said in an odd pitch for him. It must have been a joke because the two started laughing.

"He never mentioned a doctor's appointment," Poppy said. "Not a remote one. Not an in-person one." We were in the same conference room where we'd interviewed Galtway. Kwame didn't touch the table. Poppy's eyelids were swollen and her voice hoarse. She was wearing the same clothing as that morning, a white silk blouse with a dusty pink skirt and a thin black belt with a gold buckle. Streaks of dry mud were scattered across her outfit and through her hair like a counterfeit Jackson Pollock painting. "He said he'd wanted to go in early to get some work done before his trip to La Selva. I went to the gym. When I got to the parking lot I called him saying I'd arrived and asked if he wanted coffee."

"Around when was that?" Kwame asked. He was standing with his back against the wall. Jube sat in front of him and rolled her eyes at Poppy when he spoke. Poppy gave her a slight smile.

"I think around 7:15," Poppy answered. "Maybe at 7:20." This range fit when I saw her speaking into her ear piece that morning. "But he didn't answer. When I walked through the lot I saw him running and at first I actually thought he was exercising. Then I noticed he was holding his neck and looked petrified. So I rushed over to him. I was terrified." Poppy swallowed and her eyes teared. Jube pushed a glass of water to her. Poppy drank it in one gulp while titling her head up high.

"Why did you touch his neck?" Kwame asked.

"Did I?" Poppy said. "Linus was holding his neck in pain, I probably tried to help. I can't really remember, it was all so…so traumatic."

I'd of course monitored Poppy silently and didn't detect any unusual signals to flag like completely avoiding eye contact or hyperventilating, not that these were standardized. Some people cried while giving a witness statement, some remained neutral or mute, and others smiled halfway and remained like that for hours as if they'd had a stroke.

"I'm sure it was," Jube said. "Kwame, maybe we should -."

"What else did you observe about him?" Kwame interrupted her. They'd pulled this trick – man overshadowing woman – at least twenty times in their career together while interviewing a female witness. I actually felt Jube suppress shaking – possibly laughter – in her chest this time.

Poppy looked at Jube and frowned. "What did I observe? He was panting, he was turning blue in the face, his knees were reddish, maybe from falling into the flower bed, I don't know."

Jube handed her a tissue. "We don't have to talk -."

"Did he have anything on his neck?" Kwame wanted to know.

"Nothing visible," Poppy answered. She looked off into the space near Kwame's feet as she lifted the tissue to her cheek. It brought up an odd moment of triple recognition for me in which she mirrored the print decorating the wall behind her, <u>A Woman Weeping</u>, while also prompting me to picture it. This Rembrandt work (mid-to late 1640s. Rembrandt Harmensz van Rijn, Dutch, 1606-1669, oil on oak panel) showed a woman with similarly colored reddish hair, a handkerchief pressed to one side of her face, and her expression frozen. One central difference, besides the subject and the time period, was that the handkerchief was transparent, allowing the viewer a glimpse of the woman's curled fingers while Poppy's were hidden and likely in a clench. The art was displayed behind Poppy like an over-detailed shadow and, when Poppy turned back to Jube, it was as if she were stepping outside of her moment in history's timeline to narrate her portion.

"What can you tell us about Linus' family and professional relationships?" Kwame asked.

"You mean if someone wanted him dead?" Poppy raised an eyebrow. "All these questions are making it sound like you're investigating attempted murder."

"We're committed to ruling out foul behavior," Kwame said. "Your husband was healthy. Then he unexpectedly became frantic and lost consciousness."

Jube gave him her look of mock irritation. "Ma'am, we're required to investigate what happened," she said, turning back to Poppy.

"I can't think of anyone who'd want to hurt Linus expect for those PAATH fools," Poppy told him, scratching the conference room table with her thumb and somehow missing the trigger points that sprayed disinfectant into Kwame's face earlier. The pink of her manicure rubbed off a bit onto the faux wood like crayon marks on a kid menu, ending the bubble of her Rembrandt allusion with a sudden and modern pin prick. "I told him I didn't like how things were headed."

"What do you mean?" Kwame inquired.

"That Westin Krantz fellow started coming to our home unannounced." I detected Jube "perk up" when Poppy mentioned Krantz.

"Unannounced?" Jube repeated. She snorted. "The gall of that man." I'd already pulled this footage but could not confirm if Krantz had been invited, or if the visit had been friendly or contentious. The Network doesn't track audio unless notified that a crime is taking place.

"He wasn't snooping through the bushes or anything, but he'd ring the bell in the evening after dinnertime and ask to talk to Linus." Poppy tucked her hair behind her delicate ear.

"And did Linus agree to speak with him?" Kwame asked.

"A few times, then I got really annoyed and, well, freaked out. So Linus told him to start booking appointment times through Mary, his assistant, and then Krantz stopped showing up," Poppy told him, twisting her right earring.

"And did he make those appointments?" Kwame wanted to know.

"No...he, well, Linus was legitimately too busy to take meetings with him. Every time I came by the office he was on his computer and looked really intense."

I recalled the hedgehog billiards game from Beech's computer history but could not find the difficulty rating. Maybe Jube remembered the same thing because I again felt her quell her laughter.

"Any idea what they spoke about when Krantz did come by?" Kwame probed.

"Not really...Linus would usually just roll his eyes at me once he got back inside. At one point I overheard him telling Krantz something like he shouldn't have ever left nursing if he felt that way," Poppy said. Jube held her breath for two and a third seconds – most common to when she faced pressing but unanswered questions.

"How did Krantz respond?" Kwame asked.

"He kind of yelled. He said something like, 'you know I had to leave,' and then I couldn't hear more," Poppy's volume increased by about ten percent. She wiped her eyes with the tissue.

"Do you know if Krantz continued to find Linus in other places, like the gym or grocery store?" Kwame wanted to know.

"I don't…I assumed he got most of it out of his system at PAATH protests at every dang event where Linus spoke."

"I can attest to Krantz talking a lot," Jube said, Good-Cop smiling. "A lot."

I could attest to Jube's attestation. Krantz was verbose compared to other members of PAATH, other nurses, and to people in general. He made both written and spoken comments on the majority of Beech's statements, public HHS documents, etc., usually within a day of their publication.

Poppy smiled without showing teeth.

"How were you able to be involved in the La Selva pilot when you were married to the politician promoting it?" Kwame interjected.

"Detective Addo!" Jube exclaimed, but Kwame nodded in Poppy's direction.

"Linus was not a politician. Is not a politician. He is a public servant who believes in the whole program. So do I. And I pursued it as a volunteer." Poppy answered with an extremely straight posture.

"Meaning you didn't earn any income from your work?" Kwame clarified, confirming government records.

"Not a dime," Poppy said as if each word was its own sentence.

"Wow," Jube commented.

"Do you have family in politics?" Poppy asked her.

"No," Jube smirked. "We're pretty blue collar. My father owned a wellness retreat property management company and my mother ran a bakery."

"Those sound like two skills I could use right now," Poppy said, softly. "Which wellness retreat? Which bakery?"

"Unfortunately my dad passed away and my mother closed her shop," Jube told her.

Poppy nodded. "I'm sorry to hear that." I didn't understand why she nodded when Jube hadn't asked her a question or made a statement with which she could agree or disagree. I'd add nodding as a way to acknowledge hardship if I observed it over three times at regular frequency going forward. "I'd like to return to his bedside now, if we're done here," Poppy said.

"We won't get in your way," Jube said. "How's your husband doing?" She asked as she stood.

"Honey, he's in a medically induced coma. The most we hope for now is that his brain swelling will go down," Poppy replied.

"I'm sorry I asked," Jube said. Based on prior experience, I was pretty sure that she wasn't.

Chapter Seven

The police chief led the press conference that evening after Jube and Kwame gave him their update. He stood next to the department communications director. She was a woman with large breasts (relative to the female population in her age, height, and waist circumference cohort) who wore her Clio on her hip in a black belt holster that was studded with pink reflective beads. I pinged her device and didn't receive a response or any recognition whatsoever. Odd.

Jube, Kwame, and I stood behind her and the chief. Between their shoulders we could see the podium and its console – an embedded tablet on top that displayed a basic diagram of the room with human figures matching the actual person to whom they were tacked in the room. Each was also labeled by name and associated news outlet.

"We'd like to reassure the public that this case is of the utmost importance. Without invading the privacy of Linus Beech and his family, we will say that we have an investigation underway," the chief said. He stood very close to the communications director. When his shoulder brushed hers, she stepped two inches aside.

There was discord from questions being lobbed at once, some in person and others via verbal tablets reminiscent of clear teleprompters.

"How is Poppy Beech?" A journalist from the Jericho Gazette (circulation 106K) asked while holding out a pen embedded with a digital recording device. The comm director cleared her throat and opened her mouth.

"Again, we'd like to respect the privacy of the family at this time," the chief said.

"Any reason to suspect foul play?" Tom from Tom's JNEWS Blog (205K subscribers) followed up.

"No, not at this time," the chief said, placing his hands on the podium. When he hunched forward, his stomach moved nearly halfway down his thighs.

"So why the investigation and all the secrecy?" Another journalist asked remotely via drone hovering above a seat. The chief opened his mouth. Then the comm director twisted her neck to reach the mic while keeping her body away from the chief's.

"This is standard practice," she said. "We don't grant special favors to public officials, as has been rumored online."

"Who is leading the so-called standard investigation?" This question came from a national public broadcasting station.

"Detectives Canton – ," the comm director and chief spoke at once. She looked at him and he stepped back, gesturing towards the mic and bowing his head enough to make his chin puff up like an exotic fish under threat. Plausibly her glance had either asked him to adopt a humorous expression or allow her to dominate him. "Detectives Canton and Addo lead the case," she said. All eyes in the room focused on Jube and Kwame. A few raised their eyebrows. "That is," the comm director continued, hurriedly, "with the support of the entire department."

"The entire department?!" Asked the first journalist again. "Why is that?" I expected the director to explain it wasn't the entire department but a subset of Clios finding "leads" by searching the background and whereabouts of all PAATH members, people with negative social media postings about Jericho healthcare policies or about Linus Beech, reviewing footage, manning tip lines, and so on. Her reply was different, although possibly accurate as well.

"Oh, uh, I meant to say we all care deeply about this, uh," the director stammered.

"Because," Jube said, stepping up to the podium, "every person deserves to know what happened to their loved ones. No one should ever have to experience seeing the suffering of a family member without the closure, at least, of knowing why it happened and having some reassurance that it will not happen again, to anyone. We are here to keep each resident of Jericho safe and well." About two seconds of silence followed in which Jube held herself with the straightest posture I'd ever observed.

"That's all we have time for today, folks," the chief said, waving off the next round of chatter. "It's back to work for us, and thanks for your time." He turned off the mic and spoke quietly to the comm director. I couldn't hear or see what was said, but I did detect a small squeak come from her Clio when the chief pressed his body against hers. No wonder it hadn't replied to me – it was a toy.

I detected the proportion of live media headlines shift from a sentiment represented by:

Police Squirm Away From Specifics on Beech Case
to majority:
Lead Detective on Beech Case Reassures Public – Never Again
Poppy Beech Has a Chance of Closure

The volume of online comments surpassed news headlines by five-hundred fold. They generally said:

Ugly Cop SCHOOLS Coworkers
Beauty and the Beast – Poppy and Her Detective
Most People Believe in the Force – Click Here

Since my inception I'd noticed that much of the news in Jericho and elsewhere was derivative. People commented on other people who commented on the commentators. Along the way, the truth became fuzzy and the implications even more unclear. Good thing I was there like a "bullshit razor," according to Jube.

Jube always demarcated between "those who talked and those who did." I agreed with her categorization because "doing" was comprised of actions – objective measures such as if a deed was done or not. I catalogued "talking" as a vague muddle of dishonesty, the only fact of which was that someone said something at a certain place and time. Related to both, I sorted "writing" as a mixture of objectivity and subjectivity including content open to interpretation by the reader.

I still didn't understand the definition or utility of poetry, especially later on as Jube allowed it to infiltrate her investigation. Poetry was the consistent use of metaphors and similes to describe matters both large and small. Was it an art, or a memo? And what was the purpose – to clarify points already made in society but by being even more indirect? My nickname of "fucking pocket poet" was derived from my image recognition linking pictures to others. Outside of pattern recognition related to crime investigation, these linkages seemed pointless.

I was still trying to understand people. It still seemed that most were more artificial than me.

Chapter Eight

At the end of the day Jube and I went to the local bar with Kwame and his Clio. Jube told me she'd always liked this bar because it smelled of fried food and beer (I knew neither this nor the appeal of it as I had no olfactory capabilities). Also, the beer was cheap but the mugs still made from glass. PVC dominated our environment due to its cheap production cost and high durability. I likened its presence – bright, visible, and everywhere – to a starry sky on a night when the city lights are being rebooted to fix a glitch. For some reason, Jube made a face when I shared this analogy with her.

The walls were covered with chalkboards that were mainly decorated with hand-drawn breasts, recommended numbers to call for a good time, and 106 eyeballs. Each eye looked directly forward. Some styles matched cartoons (e.g., The Simpsons, 1987, 1989 – 2040), others bore exaggerated lashes or rainbow-patterned irises. Only one had the phrase, "See me, save me" carved into the wood below. This had been crossed out with blue chalk that only accentuated the vandalism. It was here that Jube and Kwame always sat.

On that night the chalkboards were lit up by the rear end of a young woman wearing extremely short black shorts. She had curved, dotted lines of LEDs implanted just beneath her buttocks.

After ordering her beer Jube said, "I don't know how she puts up with that asshole," to Kwame. Jube had put a long bar-shaped earring through her right upper earlobe as she often did when she was off duty. I'd heard Leah, her mother, call this Jube's "tramp clamp."

"You mean Poppy?" Kwame said. Jube nodded. "Come on, Jujube," he continued, "Linus' teeth are so shiny. And sometimes I want to run my own hands through that silky hair," he added. He shoved his hand into a large cardboard container filled with peanuts and crushed the shells with his palm before tossing the snack into his mouth. The woman with a light show on her buttocks squeezed by and bumped the table on her way to the bar. Kwame paid her no discernible attention.

"He's a slime ball," Jube said, guzzling her beer and putting it back onto the table loudly. The peanuts and shells shook. I buzzed twice to let Jube know she wasn't supposed to discuss cases in public locations and she ignored me, as she usually did.

"Hey, Juju, slow down," Kwame chided her, "both on the alcohol and the bitterness. What are you now, thirty years old?"

"I'm thirty-five," she said, taking another big swig.

"Too young for such cynicism! I personally find the Linus-Poppy romance to be sweet," Kwame said, leaning back and clasping his hands behind his chair in a gentle stretch that made his biceps bulge inside of his short, folded khaki sleeves.

"Sweet? *Sweet?*" Jube asked, incredulously. "The man plucked her from a hole in the wall and made her into a pearl-wearing princess for his campaign pics." She flicked a cardboard coaster across the table. It was permanently bent from being folded up for multiple games of table football, and flew towards the woman's derriere like a miniature helicopter drawn toward a landing pad only to land on the floor behind her. I recalled the ceremony in which Jube was promoted to detective. As the chief shook Jube's hand while handing her a certificate, a woman in the audience exposed her chest, made the Invisible Resistance sign, and used it to grab one breast. Jube had muttered "show some respect" under her breath while holding her smile for the photographer. Still, her expression – narrow eyes like a cat that's just spotted a laser – had been captured in the formal photo now framed on the shelf in her room. The face matched hers now.

"What's wrong with that?" Kwame asked, leaning forward to rest his large forearms on the table. His tattoo – an old-fashioned bar code done with white ink – stood out on his dark skin and above-average sized veins. The text n00bc4nn0n was printed beneath it, LEET for "A weapon that inflicts a lot of damage but doesn't require much skill to use." Jube and I believed this was in reference to Kwame's body as it could be a blunt force, especially in breaking down doors. He continued, "Poppy got to be a princess and Beech got to be her prince with cosmetically enhanced teeth."

"I don't think she likes it," Jube said, looking at the bottom of her empty jug and swirling the remaining froth in a circle.

"I think she loves it," Kwame countered. "She spouted some serious knowledge on the podium during Beech's public speech. She went from an obscure healthcare worker to a recognized...*change agent*." He again smirked. Jube frowned unevenly. "You don't believe in any of it?" Kwame asked. "Do you think that helping an entire population is even possible?"

"Mmmm," Jube murmured. She often did this to stave off conflict in her conversations unless it was with Leah, in which case she let it escalate, but here she added, "data doesn't contain all intelligence." Perhaps this belief was why neither Kwame nor Jube asked my opinion of the case. They neglected the fact that humans don't contain it all either.

"And intelligence doesn't only contain data. Ok, interesting," Kwame said. "What do you think of our pal Krantz? You think he's up to something?" He pulled his beer closer to his chest and leaned forward. The butt-light woman squeezed by again on her way back from the bar and bumped their table. Her LEDs cast a bright green mini-strobe light into Jube's eyes.

"I think he doesn't know what's going on any more," Jube answered, blinking and typing an order for another beer into the table. She could have up to three beers in two hours without showing external signs of inebriation. After the waiter brought it over, she continued. "I also think he's fed up living in the dark while this program escalates. But committing assault? I'm not so sure."

"How come?" Kwame asked loudly over the ambient noise of the bar.

"Just a hunch," Jube told him. "It's like an idiot pitted against a martyr to see who is less weak and stupid. And that's it." She pressed her jug against Kwame's, moving his slightly back across the table. "And maybe Krantz is jealous that Beech has that pretty and smart lady helping him."

"I don't know about that. Krantz has never struck me as the jealous type. He was actually more passionate about his healthcare work than anything else," Kwame recalled. "I remember how, years ago when I was just starting out with the force, it was the two of them at town hall meetings but as a team."

"Krantz and Linus Beech?" Jube asked.

Kwame nodded. A few feet behind him the woman swayed her hips back and forth and the embedded LEDs flashed white lights. It lit up the crowd around her and a few people covered their eyes with their hands or turned away, shaking their heads. Others began dancing even though no music was audible, their movements triggering my image recognition for discos and raves. At this, the young woman laughed and raised her hands above her head, drink in one fist, fingers snapping in the other, buttocks now lighting up in an array of rainbow-like colors as she moved her hips in circles.

"How did that happen!?" Jube licked froth off her upper lip. This event would have taken place prior to widespread use of Clios and Jericho turning smart. I quickly searched local town hall records from fifteen years ago and confirmed that both Krantz and Beech did speak at public meetings on more than one occasion until five years ago. The topics were usually around medical technology policies.

"Buddy-buddy," Kwame answered. "Policy-maker and nurse." But I had already sent this information as a book to Jube's work account for her detailed review in the morning.

"They were friends?" Jube asked, her eyes on the young woman's keister. I'd like to restate that pieces of information from pre-smart Jericho aren't in Network databases. As the population ages and future generations predominate, this will be less of an issue.

"Yes, back then they were," Kwame answered. "Also, Krantz's hair wasn't half green and he never used the phrase 'big data.'"

Obviously.

Jube chuckled. She squinted as the young woman came close to their table again and turned sideways to squeeze past for the third time. When she brushed her lit rear end against the table surface, Jube tilted her beer just enough to spill about three ounces onto the tabletop. It rapidly spread out and drenched the young woman's skin. The lights flickered and then turned off, briefly turning Jube's spilled beer purple.

"Hey!" The woman cried, turning to face Jube and Kwame.

"Couldn't see the menu," Jube smirked. "Thank you. Hope those things aren't electric."

Kwame and customers at a few nearby tables laughed loudly and the woman stomped off to the bathroom. As she did, one of her butt lights briefly flashed a dying green flame by the open window. I observed a short reflection emitted from the alleyway outside. However, there were no reflective surfaces such as windows or mirrors there. I logged this as another anomaly adjacent to the glimmer I'd observed near the hospital when Beech had given a speech.

"I wonder why Krantz stopped practicing nursing," Jube said, turning back to the topic at hand.

"Me too," Kwame replied. "Back then he was actually into letting tech take care of almost everything else so the nurse could be freed up to form a bond. Like all this touchy-feely stuff, bedside manner, holding the patient's hand. I mean, he seemed really dedicated. Then he stopped showing up to meetings and then he reappeared years later as this colorful hippie who hated technology. In the meantime, Beech had moved up from local to state government. I never saw them interact in the same way." He smiled at Jube. "I hope that isn't us one day."

"Big Data forbid," she answered, and then frowned. Kwame turned his head and looked behind him. Barney, Poppy's brother, was sitting at the bar. The large white stud earring in his right ear glinted. He was speaking to an incredibly thin woman with a Roman nose and jagged collarbones visible above her ratty spaghetti-strap dress. She resulted in photos tagged as "women with cancer" or "ill women wasting" for me. Barney was wearing AR goggles. The woman was not.

"What an asshole," Jube said. "Who takes a woman to a bar the same day that his sister's husband is nearly killed? And look at him, treating her like that."

Humans were often faster to judge others than I was.

"Why do you think he took her here instead of getting a drink by himself and meeting her by chance?" Kwame wanted to know.

"His jacket's on the back of her chair," Jube answered. "He must have put it there when they arrived together, maybe when he pulled it out for her to sit down."

"Well…" Kwame responded. "She's putting up with those ARs. Maybe she's hired?"

"Nah," Jube shook her head and took a sip of her beer. "If she were hired, she wouldn't tolerate the goggles, definitely not in public."

"What's the point in refusing if it's her job as a prostitute to let her customer basically do what he wants?" Kwame asked.

"To avoid embarrassment, or feeling ugly, or feeling worthless," Jube answered without hesitating. "There's a difference between hired women and desperate women. Desperate women will put up with more. Hired women literally see their value on the market and will put up with nothing below it."

"Put up with" was a term Jube didn't use as often as, "tolerate an asshole with an agenda" or "stand a piece of shit without a toilet." Jube herself put up with very little. What she did was limited to suggestions from the police chief on how to conduct her business.

Kwame nodded. "All right, well, maybe she thinks that Barney isn't augmenting too much, that maybe he's just experimenting."

Barney leaned forward and kissed the woman's neck while moving a hand towards her rear end. He pawed at the air for a second before finding her body. The woman blushed and looked downwards.

"Nope, looks like he's added a lot of padding," Jube remarked. "Good thing he didn't fall over reaching for it."

"I heard that when those goggles break and get stuck on a high augmentation setting, people can't even tell," Kwame told her. "In that case, Barney could be petting a dog and think it was just a hairy woman."

Jube laughed. "That sounds like a high-tech biblical story about stealing a blessing from your sibling." She watched silently as the pair stood and left together, Barney placing a hand on the woman's lower back, his other arm outstretched to open the door for his partially imagined companion. "I just hope he can find her vagina," she muttered.

Chapter Nine

Jube and Leah lived in a single-family home. They fought at least three times weekly, and this correlated with Jube yelling, leaving, and slamming the door behind her as noisily as a bull battering its holding pen. Jube once told me that she became a police officer after failing out of law school. This was one major source of tension between her and her mother, former baker but now the head and sole employee of a "homemade essential oil" company. Leah liked to suggest that Jube return to her legal studies, possibly not understanding that this wasn't an option.

Leah's desire that her daughter still become a lawyer agreed with my other relevant observations of human character. For example, many people didn't seem to appreciate that a fallen tree closed a hiking path. They scraped their knees trying to climb over it, only to be forced to retreat later. Or they didn't understand that their relationships had ended. They'd try to contact former romantic partners while other potential connections awaited. Sometimes all they needed to do to socialize was open their front door yet it remained closed for months other than picking up the mail from the delivery drone. I tied these habits to low IQ, higher rain than usual for a given month, and shortages of cheese. Yet these factors were statistically insignificant and therefore like garbage bins waiting on street corners, full of junk.

Their home wasn't the one that Jube grew up in. The family used to be in a larger, more modern one by the lake but moved after Jube's father died. He'd carried a high level of debt from gambling and Jube once confided in me that this came as a surprise both to her and her mother. Especially the part where he took money from her mother's bakery business and used it in his high-stakes poker games. "Never trust a man who plays cards every Sunday," she told me. But, again, I am programmed specifically to avoid this type of bias.

Their new home was a one-story house that resembled database images for "ramshackle" or "dumpy" housing. The structure was made from grayish-blue concrete sheeting. There were two windows on either side of a light pink front door that stood out like a lollipop left on the sidewalk. The front porch was too short and narrow to host a loveseat or bench so Leah placed two gray metal chairs – one at each end near the windows – on it with a round table near the one on the right. She also collected broken pieces of cement from construction site bins, painted them different colors, and placed them on the soil leading up to the front porch. Jube called it rainbow vomit. I had no corresponding file for this in my image arsenal but could generate one of a unicorn throwing up candy.

But our home was secure. Jube allowed me to integrate with their home security system. She also installed cameras in areas my extensive cameras have some trouble reaching, like immediately below the gutters close to the exterior walls. Most of the time I was ignored unless there was an odd sound in the house. Then Leah stood near me while

Jube investigated directly or watched my footage and reported back that it was a raccoon going through the trash, etc.

Jube and Leah also had a nice television that Jube got at an auction of stolen, unclaimed goods where the money went to charity. This one had been owned by a murder victim without close family. It was similarly connected to the home-security portion of my network. If needed, I could broadcast local oddities onto the screen at my discretion, as I had done with the video footage of Beech's incident.

I should mention that Jube kept me out and about most of the time. Other Clios were put away the moment their partner opened the door to home, but sometimes Jube was called a "left arm" at the station because I was always her right one. Leah actually dusted me when she cleaned the house, which was completely unnecessary as my surface didn't attract dust or dirt. Once, when Jube wasn't looking, Leah pantomimed feeding me a piece of her pancake.

On the anniversary of Jube's father's death we'd usually go to the cemetery early, before work, and without telling Leah. This time we left the house at six AM like a runaway teen and her favorite stuffed animal. Jube put on a white shirt with black pants, a jean jacket lined with fleece, and sprayed and combed back her hair. By the time we'd quietly closed the door behind us, Jube's frizz had already sprung into a halo around her head, but I didn't point this out. By then I'd learned not to even say, "your hair frizzes like the fine mist above ocean waves."

Jube petted a few dogs on the way to the corner florist stand where she bought the cheapest bouquet of flowers available. The florist told her that the flowers were called "baby's breath" and meant only as a decoration of larger bouquets, but she ignored him as she forwarded the payment from her digital wallet. Then we hopped into a driverless checkered taxi. Jube tended to select human-operated services, like bars with waiters, but not when we went to the cemetery. I had noticed that she was less likely to speak with people every year on this day. In the cab, she turned off the entertainment system, set the temperature to 71 Fahrenheit, and looked out the window.

On the way, expensive buildings automatically sent me their security updates as we passed and cheaper ones opted out unless extenuating circumstances, like a fire, were present. We passed by the cement wall that bordered Jericho and divided it from more affluent areas, and beyond which I was not allowed to look. The barrier was decorated with graffiti. One drawing showed a dark-skinned woman with a red floral headdress. Each flower held a camera lens in its center in place of a pistil and stamen, and each camera was oriented downwards at her head. Her expression showed wrinkles on her forehead between her eyes, a downcast gaze, and an uneven frown. The rest of the graffiti had words and statements like, "Human RIGHTS >> Monitoring Benefits," "Turn your gaze," and "Dance Like No One is Watching."

I knew that the late art curator, Kojiro Tomita, wrote, "It has been said that art is a tryst; for in the joy of it, maker and beholder meet," and that this view was widely shared by art experts online. The woman with the cameras in her hair could have a myriad of emotions that likely were accessible to the people who viewed her. The viewer experienced a change of some sort as a result of this bidirectional relationship with the artist and through the art as a medium. This indeed was a tryst from which I was excluded but, from my research, I knew it was probably there and therefore I categorized her as a piece of art. Indirect, yes, but logical.

But I found graffiti – defined as the command form of painted written works – to be perplexing and I didn't know how to categorize it. Where was the tryst in a painted directive? The language was clear, dominating, and one-sided. There wasn't even a figure with which to make eye contact and exchange silent communication. As humans, Jube and Kwame were able to do this, both between themselves and with a work of art. If anything while reading this graffiti, the reader felt a moment of guilt for not obeying the order. I never detected adults dancing like no one was watching. By contrast, children often danced without a care in the world although they "read" illustrated and wordless books.

Perhaps I would place graffiti in my database under ineffective rules and regulations, or next to poetry which was neither an art nor a complete work of fiction. Or under purposeless wastes of resources.

The ride to the cemetery took twenty-one minutes. We passed children playing hopscotch on projected outlines (drawing on public sidewalks was illegal), elderly people in track suits out walking with robotic health aides at their side, and a few joggers in AR goggles running into landscapes only known to them. These scenes contrasted against the stillness of the car interior and seemed like watching a movie on mute. When we rode in Jube's police car, people usually turned up their collars and hunched their shoulders. Children stopped and stared until an adult directed their attention elsewhere, sometimes by forcibly turning their heads in another direction. A few would make the Invisible Resistance hand gesture. It was not labeled as a threatening signal and therefore not punishable.

We unlocked the black creaky gates to the cemetery with Jube's retinal scan and walked onto the cemetery grounds. Old redwood trees bordered the acreage and their brown, fallen leaves spread over their roots and the cement path leading forward. It was a foggy, cool morning and the area was empty of visitors aside from a few individual women scattered around graves, all wearing wide-brimmed black hats with netting over their faces. This headwear became a more common style outside of the cemetery when my viewpoints were installed across Jericho, but the hat color varied.

The quiet morning was disrupted by subdued moaning and a woman's voice asking for a man to do various things (withheld) to her. It was coming from the tablet device on the graveyard attendant's lap. I recognized the dialogue as from the movie Boogie Nights (1997, Dir. Paul Thomas Anderson). The attendant was sitting by the entrance on a dinged metal folding chair and totally fixated on the screen. Jube stood before him, blinking without speaking, until he looked at her and stopped the video. I've witnessed Jube command people without speaking many times in whatever tryst was ongoing.

When Jube wasn't on patrol, like that morning, her steps were softer and slower. Her posture was more hunched and her hands usually lay buried in her pockets. From where I rested behind the long strands of brown-yellow bleached hair that lay on her shoulders, I could see synthetic grave "stones" jutting out between patches of AstroTurf. Her father lay beneath one with his name, Frank Herbert Canton, and the years 2002-2050. I noticed, again, that his stone had no dedication like "Father and Husband" or "Rest in Peace," and that his age at death was less than half the average of the others at the cemetery.

Jube didn't put the flowers into the PVC cup attached to his stone but tossed them onto the ground in front. She stood there for a few minutes before speaking.

"I still don't want to believe it, Dad. What you did to us. I still don't," she said. "Stealing money?! Lying?! How many nights every week did you sneak out when we were asleep to spend the money meant for some sweet shit like *cookie dough* on a poker game and then, maybe when you realized what you'd done, you hid yourself in alcohol? And then you fucking *died*." Various veins in Jube's face turned blue and red. "Mom and I had to move into a *hovel*. And I have to walk up these stupid, stupid painted stones every time I go in and out, like I'm supposed to pretend everything is fucking alright, no, *fucking beautiful,* when it's actually going to take *years* for us to get back to where we were." The women who were dusting the artificial lawn at other grave sites turned towards Jube and frowned. From my network vantage point in the trees, they looked like sparse chess pieces in a pile of captured opponents. Jube nodded at them and then continued at the same high volume as if they'd only served to acknowledge her position on the board. "I mean, for *fuck's sake,* is there any excuse for what you did? Like maybe you just didn't realize you'd taken all of the chocolate chip cash we'd saved and wasted it? Or maybe someone put a gun to your head and said, 'Give me the cinnamon, the good shit, or else you're done for, you overbaked piece of crap?'"

Jube wiped the spit off her chin and turned again to face the people staring at her from the graves they were visiting. She spread her arms out as if about to hug them all and yelled, "Hey! I was supposed to turn out better, ok? A lawyer! Someone who said random Latin shit at dinner parties that everyone else pretended to understand just so she wouldn't explain it!" The spectators turned back to their business, or maybe just turned their backs to her. Jube sat on a rundown bench a few yards away overlooking the rest of the field. I predicted that in about fifteen minutes we'd go home and lie to Leah about where we'd been. Instead, I detected motion approaching the gravesite and recognized a half-white, half-green head of hair bobbing towards it.

"Clio, is that Krantz?" Jube whispered to me. Since she wasn't wearing her earpiece, I vibrated once in silent confirmation. Twice would have meant "no." I also searched my Jericho population database. There were no Krantz relatives buried at this cemetery.

Krantz walked up the path and stopped right in front of Jube's dad's grave. He was carrying a bouquet of yellow tulips and white daisies surrounded by baby's breath and gently placed it in the gravestone cup. He paused, then picked up Jube's flowers and added them without looking in our direction. He didn't appear to notice us on our bench as he stood, erect and with his hands resting at his sides. "I'm sorry," he said, facing the stone. "I should have done more to help you. You shouldn't have died. None of it should have happened, would have happened, if others hadn't been involved, if I'd stood stronger against the powers that be." He cleared his throat. As he did so I conducted a preliminary search for any history Krantz had with electric, solar, or wind turbine power utility companies. Had this been under a warrant, I'd have had permission to go further into his background. As it was, I only ascertained that his home had solar power and that he'd received a tax refund for the purchase and installation of his equipment.

"Maybe now, maybe I can make it right," Krantz concluded. "I am stronger in the current circumstances." Then he remained still for approximately two minutes before placing his hands in his back pockets and ambling back towards the cemetery gates. As odd as this behavior was given my previous observations of him, none of the other people at the cemetery paid him any notice. By contrast, Jube's behavior had been completely in line with her habits and somehow the bystanders had stopped taking care of their dead relatives to give her their attention. The fact that context and setting so strongly influenced human perception of others, while individual behavioral patterns and personalities did not validated my usefulness as an unbiased observation tool.

Jube held her breath until Krantz walked all the way down the path, past the attendant watching muted people having sex, and exited. Her blood pressure dropped, and her palms began to sweat. She stood and then sat again, placing her head between her knees.

Then she said, "What the FUCK?" loudly three times. Based on the melodramatic reality TV shows of the early 2000s I'd seen, i.e., Desperate Housewives (TV Series 2004–2012, produced by M. Cherry), I would likely describe her as distraught, speechless, and frantic. Her fingers scraped her scalp and made her gray roots stand up. They remained vertical until we got home.

"How the hell did Dad die?" Jube screamed as she marched into the house. Leah looked up from her instant coffee and blueberry bran muffin. She was sitting at the kitchen table and wearing a large pink muumuu with worn purple flowers stitched on it that blended in somewhat with the wallpaper projected onto the walls. Her white hair was in curlers. Her lower chin quivered as she chewed with her mouth open.

"Excuse me?" She said softly. She leaned forward and rested her chin between her thumb and third finger while pressing her index finger up against her nose. This extended her nostrils vertically as if a fun house mirror were held only in front of a proboscis.

"You told me that he died in the hospital. You said he'd drunk *so* much," Jube stretched her arms and palms out as if holding a large plank in across her front, "that he fell down the stairs and they couldn't save him."

"Are you accusing me of lying?" Leah asked faintly, fingering a crack between her mug's handle and cup. It had faint teeth marks from where she'd been drinking.

"I don't know, Mom!" Jube threw her hands into the air with such force and trajectory that if she had in fact been holding a plank, it would have likely ripped a hole through the ceiling and landed on the neighbor's roof. "Are you lying? Or withholding something from me?" She advanced around the kitchen table, her hair leading the way by a few centimeters.

"What are you looking for, Jubilee?" Leah stood but didn't retreat. Her voice rose with her posture, and she pressed her palms against the table. "Do you want me to tell you that your dad was a great guy, that he secretly was rescuing a kitten from a tree when he fell?"

Jube groaned and covered her eyes with her palms. "For once in your life," her voice quivered, "would you please just answer the damn question?" She slumped into a chair, then caught herself as it tipped backward on uneven legs.

"I'm sick of this, Jube!" Leah yelled, slamming her hands against the table. I noticed an odd "twish" sound when she lifted them and realized that the table surface was sticky and she'd had to peel her skin off it. This left small pieces of her epidermis on the table. "I should have named you 'Anger' or 'Pain,'" she concluded.

"Mother," Jube said quietly, but in a cutting voice. I knew that voice – she used it frequently in criminal interrogations.

Leah fell silent. One of her curlers had fallen out and dangled down her back, dripping what was likely one of her homemade oil concoctions down to her shelf-like rear end. Her potions were quite potent and this one turned the cloth fibers in that area transparent. Her undergarments were decorated with the word "Tuesday." Today was Wednesday.

"Do you want me to say that he didn't leave us his debts?" She asked, just above the volume of an average conversation. "Or that he didn't take money from the bakery and use it to create a Ponzi scheme?"

"I want to know how he died," Jube said, looking directly at her.

"He died at the hospital after a bad fall. He was drunk. And he turned out to be a thief. Just like I told you," Leah said, placing her fists on her wide hips. "The nurse said that nothing could be done. He said they'd tried everything."

"Everything?" Jube asked, looking out the kitchen window at the grey cement building next door.

"That's what he said," Leah answered.

Jube snorted and shook her head, gazing down at the decrepit wood-patterned floor paper. I felt her heart rate lower to her normal pace and realized the argument was ending. Typically, at this point Leah would leave the room and noisily take on a household chore like pulling mint leaves for her health tinctures, but today she placed her hand on Jube's shoulder before parting.

Jube redid her braid and knocked an entangled baby's breath flower onto the floor. She gazed at it for a moment, maybe taking in its delicate nature or small size, then crushed it with her foot and left for work.

Chapter Ten

The police station always had a noticeable buzz, like a motorcade from afar, from the sound of servers humming and officers typing. The main room in the office had dark blue flooring designed to prevent fragile items from shattering if dropped. Unfortunately, this also made liquids bounce before settling. Thus, the floor and the beige walls were covered in brown coffee spots. There were ten workstations in the room and five officers and their Clios working that morning. The police workforce had been twice as large before Jericho turned "smart" but was cut when Clios were introduced as aides. Each officer sat at their desk – faux-mahogany material equipped with two computer monitors.

Jube sipped coffee from her blue PVC mug. The image of a yellow police badge had worn off years ago and left behind a blotch resembling a sandcastle. Jube often said that the city layout – a grid – made her think of old-fashioned computer "screen savers" that built out a web of piping as a series of crossing gray tubes. We watched Jericho together on her screen using a "lens" that emphasized heat, then switched to motion, and then overlaid both. A list of license plate numbers from cars driving by automatically scrolled down on the upper right. None were highlighted as recently stolen or associated with persons of interest. We honed in on a five-block radius centered around the hospital campus because that was Jube's beat. Graffiti covered numerous buildings, spreading out and onwards like a manmade virus, likely because these drawings weren't sharply penalized in Jericho. Certain artistic freedoms had been protected under city policy and criminal code during the shaping of Jericho's smart status. Linus Beech, by then an upcoming policy-maker, had opposed these protections by calling them an excuse for vandalism. Frank Canton, Jube's father, had written social media comments supporting these creative safeguards which he called "vent tubes for a high-pressure life that kept the body safe and smothered the soul." This comment had received so much support that abundant graffiti in Jericho, including the display we saw that night, depicted actual vent tubes releasing steam at the buildings' upper edges – as if into the sky. I didn't know if Jube felt proud of her father's legacy, but once I observed her trace these images with her finger on the computer screen and smile.

During Jube's remote patrol that day, an undercover street officer dressed in scrubs with a "midwife" nametag and a leather backpack sent in a request for information about a passerby. The pedestrian was as tall and wide as a linebacker. He walked down a street that was usually empty at this hour. The street cop's Clio managed a fairly close retinal photo of the man we were tracking and we matched it against our criminal registry. His record was limited to petty theft with no crimes committed within the past three years. That was our cutoff for labeling high-risk individuals – regression analysis showed that if they hadn't committed any sort of misconduct, not even speeding, in that timeframe, their chance of additional transgression was insignificant. Still, Jube sat ready to turn up the streetlamps like theater lights when the curtain rises if she needed, her trigger finger stroking the computer key lightly.

Through the eyes of the street cop's Clio, we followed the man down short side streets and then connected with longer avenues. The gray-brown buildings were so high in this part of Jericho that pedestrians would have to look straight up to get a good view of the moon and clouds. It made me conjure pictures of the sky that persecuted people glimpsed centuries ago when hiding inside sewers and ramshackle cellars. Snippets of sun and of hope shone above metal bars into the spaces that lent themselves as hiding places for the hounded. This city plan predated me. Humans had been confining themselves of their own will long before my invention.

After a quarter of a mile the man went into a corner bodega, bought cough syrup, and left. We stopped trailing him once we heard him cough – a juicy one likely carrying high viral load – and predicted that his path led homeward. The guy was simply sick and needed medicine quickly.

"Well, that was exciting," Jube said sarcastically. But I noticed an oddity. The brief glimmer I'd seen outside the hospital after Beech's speech appeared again, and this time the man we'd followed nodded at it as he walked by. Smiles I may not have understood, but nodding was typically directed at another person. I added this to my file.

Three inconsistent events now loosely fit my threshold to investigate a pattern. I'd seen a glimmer on the hospital campus after Beech's last speech. Then the odd reflection of the lights that were on the gluteus maximus of the woman at the bar. And now this man buying cough syrup and nodding at the space before him as he walked home. Were these linked? Perhaps more were forthcoming. I elected to observe for longer in an effort to collect more anecdotes and develop them into data and then hopefully information and response.

Jube set the grid to passive surveillance and turned her attention to the Beech investigation. She wasn't allowed to go too far into people's records without cause (and neither was I). It was the modern-day electronic database equivalent to the stop-and-frisk laws that were ended years ago. Without a subpoena, at most we could see if the person had criminal offenses and punishment, like incarceration, had been called as a witness in a trial, or had made threats against others. If my handler said "something's up" or "something's going down," which meant the same thing, I'd request and usually obtain permission from humans to look more deeply into a suspect's background, such as employment records and tax filings. In Krantz's case, things were neither up nor down so Jube had to content herself with basic criminal database searches as she pried into why he could have gone to her dad's grave.

Westin Krantz had been a committed nurse but his license was currently inactive. As far as Jube could see, he was clean aside from one odd speeding ticket a few years before. Krantz had overridden the autopilot guidance of his car which was keeping him at the speed limit. He'd told his car there was an "unforeseen emergency" and then driven five miles per hour over the speed limit. I wasn't certain what type of emergency would warrant this, and apparently neither was the officer who pulled over the car once alerted to do so by the Network. Krantz told the officer that the emergency was "losing humanity in all of this high-tech nonsense," specifically that his "car hadn't been programmed to realize how good it felt for the wind to go through both halves of his hair." The officer, in turn, had overridden his Clio to issue a ticket for only a one dollar penalty (Clios can be overruled by people more easily within a low range of impact). The officer was now retired and listed as Krantz's friend on social media.

In addition, we saw lots of volunteer work including social media pics of him smiling and holding a rake while planting healing gardens around Jericho housing shelters. Some photos of him grinning by a pet therapy barn with his arm wrapped around a grimacing colleague, seemingly oblivious to this and to the pile of horse excrement under his shoes. He'd played public pianos in botanical gardens for an audience of one person who turned out to be waiting to pack up the equipment. He'd opened doors for people only to find that they weren't entering the building. There was a newspaper article about him. He'd helped deliver a baby boy on the front lawn of the hospital and, two years later, a sister in the building elevator and, two years after that, the third sibling that came into this world on the hallway floor outside the labor and delivery ward. I predicted that a fourth child would be delivered in a hospital bed if the mother were willing to keep trying for this goal.

There was a large gap in posts, however, starting (coincidentally, if you ask me) about five years ago, around the time of Frank Canton's death. Then two years ago Krantz reappeared with half his head dyed green and founded PAATH. Most of his social coverage had to do with his work with that organization. He was not married and didn't seem to be in a relationship. He also donated money annually to nursing schools, one of which was his alma mater, and he gave lectures to nurses at the main Jericho hospital (where Jube's father had died and where Krantz had been employed for most of his nursing career). These were titled, "Never Gonna Let You Down – The Human Touch in Healthcare," and, "Over Hyped, Over Paid, and Over Here – Tech in US Hospitals."

That was it, basically. Jube kept zooming in on Krantz's photos as if seeing every wrinkle around his eyes could provide her with insight into his story. If she'd asked me, I'd have let her know that retinal scans can only confirm identity and nothing more.

Once she'd moved on from Krantz, she had me display relevant healthcare news headlines from the week leading up to Beech's injury onto her monitor.

No Beach Time for Beech – State Official Automates Healthcare – See Demo Here
Linus Beech Defends High-Tech Healthcare to Opponents
Ten Secrets Behind Poppy and Linus Beech's Long-Lasting Romance

Jube touched the link to the demo and then watched the video in the CSPAN recent archives. It had been recorded in the days after Beech's last public speech, the one we'd observed at the hospital.

The healthcare demo was held in the Jericho City Capitol building on the same campus where Beech would collapse while holding his neck in the days to come. When the footage began, Linus Beech was being outfitted with eSkin in a beige conference room that looked like nearly every conference room snapshot stored in my archive. Poppy Beech said that he would act as a patient and be in one room. The doctor would be someplace else so the visit could mimic futuristic healthcare delivery by taking place remotely and over video. While eSkin was common, additional uses were still being developed.

Beech was wearing a short-sleeved shirt with shorts and, as Jube whispered to me, "showering the crowd with his artificial smile." We spotted the back of Krantz's bi-colored ponytail in the front row and Barney, Poppy's brother, leaning against the back wall. Perhaps the healthcare of the future had a shortage of chairs.

"Welcome to our demo of the health exam of the future!" Beech said, standing with his legs splayed and his fists on his hips like Superman without a cape. Behind him Poppy held up a few rectangular strips of eSkin. It was transparent and colorless aside from blue nodes connected by thin blue lines running down the middle, like an old-fashioned circuit board. This matched the evidence Jube found at the crime scene.

"What you are about to see is already providing wonderful care to the community of La Selva. It has brought top-notch medicine and predictive modeling to their homes. And it's fueled a small 'fortune at the bottom of the pyramid.'" Beech used air quotes at the end of his soliloquy. I noticed Poppy frown and Barney shake his head slightly. Then Poppy pushed Beech into a chair by his shoulders and began taping the skin to him. Jube snickered.

"Well, folks," he said, "looks like we're getting started!" The audience chuckled. "This is a first for me, if you know what I mean." He winked and smiled. The audience laughed again. Later, Jube would explain this insinuation to me by saying that eSkin was known for its initial use in the sex trade – either in receiving remote pleasure from prostitutes around the world or from an AI with a digitized body that matched the end-user's preferences. While the manufacturer had at first marketed it as a way to immerse workers in remote meetings, it eventually gave up and admitted that eSkin was mainly used as a sex toy. The healthcare use we were going to see today, however, was new because the product had been reengineered for the "next-next gen" doctor visit. This was purportedly the set up in La Selva that Beech was trying to successfully expand.

Poppy placed the eSkin up and down Beech's legs and circled his knee with it. Then she turned on the large monitor behind them and stepped back. A melody akin to an old-fashioned doorbell sounded and Dr. Galtway, the physician we'd spoken with in the hospital after Beech's injury, appeared on the screen.

"Good morning, Secretary Beech," he said, smiling.

"Call me Linus!" Beech replied.

"Of course, Linus. As you know, my name is Dr. Galtway. It's nice to see you again. Would you like me to perform a routine visit, including a physical, or skip directly to your ailments and use the eSkin?" The doctor asked.

"Let's jump right ahead! I can't wait." Beech was the most ecstatic injured person I'd ever observed.

"I can see from your pre-visit questionnaire that you twisted your left knee jogging," Dr. Galtway said. "Also," the doctor continued, "since you signed a disclaimer, I can share this medical information in front of a crowd." The audience laughed.

"That's right!" Beech said, winking at the crowd again, unless I was mistaken and he had a mock eye ailment too such as a foreign object stuck in there. The vibrations of Jube grinding her teeth brushed my surface.

The small blue dots running down the center of the eSkin lit up, illuminating Beech's pale skin slightly in a way that triggered me to compare them with "Hanukkah lights" and "Satellite view of night swimming in smart city."

"I can see that your temperature and other vital readings are normal per the Electronic Skin monitoring," the doctor said. As he did, the number 98.7 appeared on the upper right portion of his screen, accompanied by blood pressure, pulse, respiratory rate, and oxygen saturation. The lower right showed height, weight, and body mass index. "I'd like to examine your knee now to check for swelling. Are you ready?"

"Ready!" Beech said, saluting.

The doctor raised his hands. His fingers were dotted with blue electrodes. A transparent hologram of a human body appeared in front of him. A halo hovered above the scalp. The audience murmured and a few people said "Wow!"

"Is that Beech's ego?" Barney whispered to the woman standing next to him. I recognized her as the excessively thin woman from the bar Jube and Kwame frequented. The woman's cheeks flushed.

Doctor Galtway swiped at the halo above the head and pantomimed dragging it to the left leg. Our view zoomed in to focus on that knee. "I'm going to press a little," he said. He placed his hands around the joint and purple spots appeared beneath his fingers on the hologram, presumably where he was pressing.

Beech uttered a very high-pitched giggle. "It tickles!" He said. Poppy brought a smaller camera close to her husband's leg and projected the image next to that of Dr. Galtway. It showed Beech's skin being depressed beneath the eSkin as the blue lights there flickered. Each depression had the shape of a fingertip. The audience murmured quietly. When used as a sex toy or for very basic healthcare, Jube would explain later, eSkin had mainly transmitted sensations of hot or cold, or vibrated with various frequencies. It only minutely pressed down on the patient's skin.

"Well, your knee feels fine so far," the doctor said. "I don't sense any swel—"

"Just get to the rest of the exam, please!" Beech implored.

"Alrighty," Galtway agreed. "Let's take a look." The hologram zoomed out, again showing all of the human body. "Now I'll check out your range of motion." He held the left leg of the hologram and straightened it, then bent it at the knee. And, like a marionette puppet, Beech's real leg did the same thing. The crowd gasped.

"Check this out!" Beech said. The rest of his exclamations couldn't be overheard because of all the people speaking at once in the room. Then Dr. Galtway disappeared from the screen and entered the room, greeted by a collective gasp. Since he was very short (two standard deviations below the mode height of men in his age group), many people in the back of the room stood on their tiptoes to see him repeat the exam in person. Galtway announced that the results were the same as when he'd done the exam from the other room.

"I'll ask my assistant to wrap up," he added, looking at the screen. A woman with tan skin and a white uniform with an old-fashioned nurse cap appeared and said, "Hello! My name is Michaela and I'll conclude your visit today." She was nearly an exact match of AI Mike from Beech's computer but with long hair, redder lips, and a different job role – not a physician but a physician's assistant.

"Hi, Michaela!" Beech said, beaming. "How are ya?" He sounded like a child opening birthday gifts.

"Just fine, Mr. Beech," Michaela answered. "I see that the doctor would like to prescribe an anti-inflammatory ointment. May I confirm your preferred pharmacy delivery company?" Her voice was exceptionally warm and the quality matched that of a home health aide Jube and I had once met on a patrol. But, Michaela emphasized the words "doctor," "painkiller," and "pharmacy delivery" like a ten-year old reading from Mad Libs.

"I, uh, have trouble accessing those types of services," Beech said. The crowd chuckled. Later, Jube would inform me that this was meant in humor because Beech was filthy rich and could access anything he'd ever want. I knew this but didn't understand what was so funny.

"I'm so sorry to hear that you have trouble accessing services," Michaela said, frowning in a clean arc devoid of wrinkles. "May I set that up for you?"

"Yes, you certainly can!" Beech said.

"You're all set," Michaela said two seconds later. "It was nice meeting you, Linus."

"Hang on there!" Beech said. "You, eh, have something on your nose!" Beech stood and walked over to the screen, then poked it where

Michaela's nose was displayed. Her image broke up into thousands of smaller pieces that appeared to blow away like leaves in the wind. They revealed the words, "Health AI, Limited (HAIL)," and a snake-like logo of a caduceus on top of a grid of ones and zeroes. Below it was written, "Care From Anywhere."

"What?" The audience murmured. Jube sucked in her breath.

"No, folks, I didn't just break the screen, but I turned off Michaela, the digital physician assistant," Beech said, triumphantly. "Michaela is a deep fake, but not the kind intended to steal your identity or to act in a movie. She is a virtual employee, if you will, who is the last to interface with a patient after an exam. And, I might add, the most realistic deep fake created to date."

The audience broke into a cacophony of conflicting sounds. Beech waved his hand as if clearing smoke. Krantz stood and yelled. "What about the human touch, Linus? What about technical error?"

"I knew you'd ask that," Beech smirked. "Of course, Dr. Galtway is real," he gestured to the doctor, who bowed slightly at the waist. "Second, this technology can't harm you. It's in the design. And, finally, virtual physician assistants like Michaela will only be deployed to communities where the shortage of staff makes it absolutely necessary. In other words, those who are suffering from the lack of care will, for once in their lives, get high-tech solutions first."

"The reliance on technology like eSkin," Krantz said, facing the Secretary, "not only displaces the human connection but also the human expertise in patient care. What's more, use of algorithms – artificial rules of thumb – that we can't see, increases the chance that the patient will become the victim of an error." He stood with his hands clenched into fists as if ready to fling himself onto the carpet and throw a tantrum. I saw the onsite security guard take one step forward from the wall.

Beech cleared his throat and raised his right index finger as he'd done at the last rally. Then Poppy stepped forward and asked, "How would a trusted algorithm increase the chance of an error?"

"Because the underlying data is likely subject to bias," Krantz replied. "The machine is more likely to misdiagnose people of certain racial or economic backgrounds since this problem still persists in public health." He spoke slowly, like a preschool teacher to a child. "For example, it may not know about the pain patterns of osteoarthritis in patients of color since this ignorance is reflected in historical data into which healthcare still dips its ladle. This may also cause incorrect payment amounts based on false predictions of what their healthcare would have cost without healthy behavior. They'll end up being paid less than they should."

"The algorithm is solid," Beech said. He raised his right index finger again. At this point, it was clear to me that this was a signal for summoning Poppy, like a king to the court jester.

"Then show it to us," Krantz demanded.

Poppy cleared her throat. "Unfortunately, while the pilot sample size is large enough to be significant, it is small enough for individual patients to be identified, especially if we give you the exact details you are seeking. Providing information on race, age, weight, and so on, would violate the privacy of this population, a step we promised them that we'd never take."

"We understand the need for privacy," Krantz countered, "but you understand these are public funds and healthcare programs we are discussing."

"Yes," Poppy said, "and privacy is federally protected. We are happy to continue offering high-level information on spending and interventions. Anything more will be to the detriment of the patient population."

"Don't worry, Westin," Beech said, resting his hand on Poppy's back. "In making their design, the epidemiologists measured three times and cut once." I saw Poppy blanch, her freckles stood out against her pallor like the markings made by a toddler jabbing at paper with a pen. Jube chuckled. I knew only that Poppy's paleness was followed by Jube's laughter. To predict why Jube laughed would be to confuse the correlation of those two events with causation, which wasn't necessarily the case.

Krantz turned and left the room noisily amidst the cacophony of reaction. Jube leaned forward and looked at him up close, nearly wiping the oil collecting in her nose pores onto the screen. "Now, we'll take one question and then break for smaller discussion groups," Beech said. "You," Beech pointed to a woman in the front row with a press tag pinned to her ample bosom, "go ahead."

"Was this deployed in La Selva and, if so, how did it lead to the cost savings you mentioned last week?" She asked.

"Yes," Beech answered. Poppy fiddled with her camera.

The journalist paused. "Ok…In order to see how that went, may we see it work with a few people who are actually in need?"

"Absolutely." Beech stretched his arms and looped his hands behind his head while leaning back into his chair.

"That may be a problem," Poppy said, stepping forward. "See, we'd need to get permission from a sick person first, and this population is really hesitant to share their personal lives with the world." Her voice wavered slightly.

Beech waved his hand again. "We'll figure it out," he promised. "There's got to be some poor guy who'd be willing, I don't care if I have to knock on their doors offering free baseball tickets to get consent." Poppy abruptly looked up and probably made eye contact with Barney. His nostrils flared and his fingers pressed into the wall at his back.

Jube stopped the recording. "Clio, show me Network footage of the Capitol Campus after this demo," she commanded, "lasting for the next half hour." I obeyed within one second.

The Capitol campus included a main building – a domed, three-story, off-white structure that resembled stone but was actually made up of a composite of cement, recycled materials, and gravel. A path painted with pictures of red brick bisected the artificial lawn and led up to the main edifice. The surrounding dark blue buildings were made up of two levels of stacked containers, akin to shipping storage containers in a green ocean.

Through my retrospective video, Jube and I virtually "stood" between hanging, potted flowers that surrounded the main Capitol building and were arranged in a rainbow floral pattern in beige ceramic containers.

The woman who we'd observed at the bar with Barney and who he'd joked with at the demo stood outside, her gaunt shoulder blades like two knives beneath her gauzy blouse.

"So, what'd ya think?" Barney asked while standing behind her. She turned abruptly and blushed a deep red that made the blue veins beneath her collarbone more visible by contrast. When she didn't answer, he stuck out his hand and said, "I'm Barney Beech. What brought you to the demo today?"

"Oh, um," she stammered. "I was interested in what's coming next. I'd also like to know how our taxes are being used." Her eyes were yellow and brought up images of jaundiced patients. These pictures were too accurate to be used as a metaphor.

"Who picks up a sick person at a healthcare demo?" Jube asked. She didn't use my name, so I understood this as rhetorical and didn't answer.

Krantz approached them, his hands stuck in his pockets, his muttering too quiet for me to understand. From my attempt at lip reading, he may have said, "uncanny valley" or "unhappy patsy."

"Like a sainted cock blocker," Jube muttered, loudly enough for me to hear and for another officer at the station to turn and glance at her, then whisper to his colleagues who also looked over.

"Well, that's very committed of you," Barney said to the woman. "Most people come to these things because of some personal stake. Something that makes them borderline hysterical," he cast a glance at Krantz.

"Or because of altruistic motivation," Krantz said. Barney turned his head as a parrot would gauge food with the other side of its face. He wore white stud earrings in both his ears.

"Ah, Westin," Barney said, "still dying on the healing-touch crucifix?"

"Proudly," Krantz answered. "Hello," he turned to the woman. "I'm Westin Krantz, leader of the People Against Algorithmic and Technology Harm, but first and foremost a nurse."

"Hi," the woman said quietly.

"With whom do I have the pleasure of meeting?" Krantz asked, using one skinny, pale finger to tuck a few green strands of hair behind his ear like an alien violinist plucking at a mutant instrument.

"I'm a patient around here," she answered. Maybe she didn't use her name because she preferred not to or because she only identified as a patient now. By then I knew her name but saw no need to reveal it or include it in a report. She likely deserved at least a bit of protection and respect.

"I wish you health and healing," Krantz said. His vocal pattern became softer and slower like a nursery rhyme told to a child at bedtime. Then he stepped backward and lightly tripped over on a plant-watering drone which tilted upwards and sprayed water into her face. Jube burst out laughing and more police officers at the station turned to look at her.

"I'm so sorry," Krantz said. Barney drew a handkerchief out of his side pocket and offered it to her. When the woman used it to wipe herself it left a trail of brown crumbs across her forehead like ants on a path through a pale landscape.

"Oh, crap," Barney said. He wiped her forehead with his thumb. "I thought I was so gallant." The woman giggled.

"It's fitting because no part of the healthcare demo was gallant," Krantz said.

"I disagree," Barney said. "And they're working on it, over here in the government."

"Hmmm," Krantz said. "I'm not sure about that, but perhaps it's not an appropriate conversation to have in the present company." The woman blushed again.

"I was just off to use the ladies' room," she said, and walked off in a direction opposite the ladies room.

"Off she goes!" Jube narrated.

Barney looked a bit downwards at Krantz from his height and frowned.

"Barney," Krantz told him, "I want to assure you that technology is an obstacle to actual care because it's coming to replace it."

"No, just to help," Barney retorted, maybe trying to smile but instead baring his teeth like a dog in a kennel. His shirt was unbuttoned at the neck and his freckled skin flushed a bit. His biceps stood out strongly.

"As a nurse, I can tell you we don't need these hoity-toity politicians telling us how to practice," Krantz countered. "PAATH won't wait any longer," he said. "We'll make sure Beech visits patients and we'll join him when he does so we can see this thing work in person. Otherwise we'll do our own direct recruitment amongst the La Selva population."

"That sounds like harassment," Barney said, frowning and shaking out his handkerchief. "I don't know why you guys would do that to sick people. Beech is doing his job and he probably won't get to La Selva for months, Westin. Just leave people be."

"Then we'll get Beech to make it look like campaigning," Krantz said, and walked off.

Barney spent about four seconds frowning and shifting his weight from one foot to the other. Then he walked back into the main building.

"What I just don't get, Clio," Jube said, quietly, "is why Barney would defend Beech in any way." Jube only addressed me directly when she was either giving me an order or thinking something out that I may have helped examine in the future. "What does he care if Krantz investigates the program in La Selva?" she continued. "Does it count for that much that his sister is married to the guy? Why is Barney even here?" She chewed on a hangnail, then said, "Clio follow him."

I changed camera angle and did as she commanded, zooming in towards an open window in the building. This was as close as we'd get without a warrant allowing us to tap into their indoor security cameras.

"…he won't stop…" we heard Barney saying. "I don't know why that lunatic can't just stay home and shut up."

"He has to, he'll want to avoid humiliation," Poppy answered.

"But he doesn't know what to expect," he countered. Then their voices trailed off and I ended the footage.

Jube set her status to "on break" by tapping an icon of a donut, then leaned back and stared at the coffee stains beneath her desk. "Don't bring me the ocean if I feel thirsty,"[iii] she said. Maybe she just wanted some coffee.

Chapter Eleven

Jube rushed into the station the next morning and used her shoulders to brush past three other staff. "We're used to it by now," one said to another who'd shot him a look. If they'd asked me, I'd have pointed out the flip side – the staff didn't part ways for Jube to pass, and she was used to that too. She must have been, at least, because she didn't flinch, only went directly up to Kwame, pushed a pile of video flashcards on defensive tactics off his desk onto the floor, and put me down in their place. "Wanna laugh? You've got to fucking see this right now," she said, telling me to transmit to his screen. I showed this headline:

Regional Secretary for Health and Human Services Packs for Community Visit

I'd selected it to represent an amalgamation of social media forums mainly dated the morning after the demo we'd just watched, one day before Beech's injury. "How is that a headline?" Kwame asked. "Are they going to tell us how many pairs of underwear he packed?"

Jube tapped the headline. There was Beech, throwing items into a Louis Vuitton suitcase on a bed and saying, "Ok, La Selva, here I come!"

"Is that a bottle of nasal spray?" Kwame asked.

"Maybe the HHS secretary has bad allergies," Jube answered. The video had thousands of similar comments, a volume liable to have triggered publicity of the accompanying headline. About 84% were from PAATH members. None of them had identified themselves as such but I knew their names and online aliases.

Kwame scrolled through the related videos and found a copy of Beech speaking at the demo we'd just viewed. It had been edited to mainly show his promise to the journalist to see the system in action. It had been shared close to half a million times. It was followed by another in which Krantz announced that it was time for the curtain to come up on this so-called, "healthcare of the future," and that he was planning to visit La Selva and knock on doors. "Anyone who would like to share their healthcare story with us can let us know at the below link," he said. "I'm already packing my bags for the trip," he held a torn duffel bag up to the camera. That video had been shared close to one million times, although mostly by PAATH.

In another video called, "Beech and Krantz Duke It Out," Claymation® caricatures of each person stood in a wrestling ring and swung their suitcases at each other. Krantz's character knocked Beech's head off at the neck but his body packed it's head into another suitcase and flung it into Krantz's abdomen. Then they both died. That video had been viewed about five million times. Comments surpassed twelve million and fed into multiple blogs and news commentary. They went beyond PAATH and came from the general population of the state, other states, and a few international blogs.

"Why so much publicity over a field trip?" Kwame wondered aloud. "Besides the, eh, creativity?"

"PAATH was publicly pressuring Beech to show more of his healthcare program to them and they knew he wouldn't let anyone else have the limelight. The rest was just funny," Jube explained, grinning.

"So that's why Beech planned to fly to La Selva without meetings with patients lined up, like Mary Stevens said," Kwame remarked. "Either he didn't have time, or he didn't care about anything other than appearance."

"What do you expect from a guy who has his teeth whitened regularly?" Jube said.

At that moment Becky, the community outreach officer who the chief had offered as support when Jube asked for the Beech case, approached them. "Hey Gala," she started. "I just wanted to bring you some coffee and let you know that I'm available today if you need anything."

"Huh?" Jube asked.

"Oh, I'm Becky and I'm new. The force said I should offer to help you however you needed." Behind her a few men sniggered.

Jube inhaled and paused for four seconds, then exhaled for five seconds. "My name is Jubilee," she told her.

Becky blushed deeply. "Oh, no, I thought so! But they told me you liked to go by Gala."

"It was either that or Mardi Gras," an officer yelled from his workstation. The rest of the office laughed loudly, aside from Becky, who began to cry, and Kwame, who stood quickly and knocked his chair backwards. The laughter abruptly stopped aside from some breakthrough coughing.

"I'm so sorry, Detective Canton, I didn't mean –," Becky spluttered.

"I know," Jube told her. Then she spoke loudly, "it's not your fault that we can't trust the rest of the team."

"Show some respect!" Kwame yelled, walking towards one of the officers coughing out laughter at his desk. Jube touched his arm and hissed, "It'll just undermine me more," and he stopped but held the gaze of that man until the man looked away first.

We set ourselves up in a conference room. The digital whiteboard flickered repeatedly on one side. Kwame covered it with his jacket and sat down.

"Ok, who do we have in our circle so far?" Kwame asked before answering his own question. "Westin Krantz, anyone else from PAATH, and, given Beech's level of publicity, any other disgruntled member of the public in or outside of La Selva. Also, his assistant Mary, other colleagues, and Poppy. Finally, Poppy's brother, Barney, gives me a weird vibe."

Jube nodded at each name Kwame mentioned. "Those are most of the people who'd possibly benefit from his harm or death.

"What's your opinion of Poppy?" Kwame asked the air in front of his face.

"I think she's lonely," Jube replied.

"What makes you say that?" Kwame asked, adding a sugar packet to his coffee. It was his second. I wondered if his Clio wasn't set to dietary tracking.

"Just a hunch," Jube replied. "It's like she's alone in a white castle surrounded by idiots who grew up with money and think that looking down on her is a public service somehow." This metaphor was oddly similar to Jube's adulthood, minus the white castle.

"Ouch," Kwame stirred his coffee by swirling the cup in circles. "Could Poppy want to off her own husband? I don't think she'd stand to gain much, or much more than she has now."

"Maybe she wants to run the La Selva program," Jube offered.

"From what I hear, she basically is."

"Maybe she wants more credit. Or maybe Beech is just too annoying," Jube smirked. "Anyways, his life insurance policy is pretty meager because he's a public official, and I don't think he bought the supplemental package."

"The man thinks he's invincible," Kwame said. "Anyway, what happened to him could also have been an accident."

They paused for eleven seconds. "Yeah…" Jube replied, "but the conversation with Doc Galtway made me wonder. He was saying that Beech was strangled but he also wasn't, like his body showed the reaction of asphyxiation without the physical evidence of the actual strangulation. It's not like Beech had a rare and undetected disease with rapid-onset suffocation," Jube replied. "And why was there that piece of eSkin on that drone?"

"He could have ripped it off his body. Or maybe it was from the demo earlier."

"I don't think it was likely from the demo if it was laying right where he landed in the bushes days later. Although, if he'd ripped it off, we probably would have found it someplace else on his body, like his hands, especially if the technology had forced him to choke himself. Although, that would have left the same marks as any strangulation and he didn't have any," Jube said. "And there's another thing. If he was testing out AI Mike as a doctor, did the new system malfunction, was it misused, or was it simply underdeveloped?"

"Good question and one that is still outstanding," Kwame said. "Let's talk about Krantz for a minute. Even if he's dyed his hair like a wacko and showed up uninvited at Beech's home, he doesn't feel to me like those people who'd take a life to supposedly save others."

"We can't deny his motivation," Jube pressed. "And we have a lip reading now."

Jube had been up until two in the morning having me look for any legal justifications for peering into Krantz's employment records. His visits to Beech's home had appeared social. Even if I'd been triggered to listen in at the time, the noise of the water fountain near the front door would have made it impossible to hear the conversation.

The retrospective video footage didn't show obviously threatening gestures or weapons. So Jube had me turn to lip reading. This isn't a formal part of my programming. It could be called more of my hobby. Most of the talks that they'd had on Beech's porch were impossible to decipher clearly. However, about five months before Beech's pseudo-asphyxiation, Krantz had put one hand on Beech's shoulder and leaned in to whisper into his ear. My analysis showed over a ninety percent probability that he'd said, "I will stop you," and much smaller chances he'd said, "I will flop too" or "Eye fill mop too." I held this outside of our official reporting because it could have been meaningless or too vague to be of value. Jube had other plans for it, though.

Kwame shared my pessimism. "Yeah…I don't think lip readings are going to get us too far ahead in this investigation," he said, chewing the inside of his right cheek. "You know that stuff isn't concrete enough to constitute evidence and justify getting into medical records."

"Actually," Jube said, "in the 2030s witness testimony in a murder trial relied heavily on lip reading." She'd had me research this extensively. "You see, when a deaf person was put on the stand, he said he'd read the defendant's lips from afar and heard – or seen – a confession. Defense said this was inadmissible because it was subject to error, and because it was hearsay, but the judge said the prosecution should be allowed to use it to show inconsistencies in other testimony. And that otherwise it would be discrimination against deaf people because hearing people are allowed to present what they'd heard in court, even if their memory of it wasn't exact." She pulled a bit of the seat lining up and ran the plastic beneath the finger nail of her right index finger. It made the dirt beneath cluster near her hangnail.

"You're relying on evidence from over twenty years ago? Sounds like your Clio has been busy," Kwame said, cocking an eyebrow.

"Yeah, you could say that," Jube acknowledged, bringing her hangnail to her mouth and biting it off. She returned to picking at the rubber lining of her seat, pressing it beneath another dirty fingernail. "I think Krantz is hiding something."

"Something related to this case? Or something related to your father given that little episode you witnessed at the cemetery?" Kwame asked, looking at her from the corner of his eye.

Jube didn't respond. She pressed her finger down and cut the skin, drawing blood beneath her nail, then drew her injured finger to her mouth and sucked the blood. "Maybe somehow the case and my dad are all mixed together?"

"If that's the situation, you need to withdraw from your duties," Kwame said.

"Then it's nothing to do with my dad," she said. "And we need to interview the guy anyway because he was involved with Beech."

Krantz lived in a two-bedroom condo in a gated complex reminiscent of Jube's father's cemetery. Jube and Kwame sat on a brown faux-leather couch that didn't even have extendable legs. His coffee table had a wooden surface and legs that my archives loosely matched with an old program in which people brought antiques to experts for appraisal. This category of item was typically worth however much the presenter had initially paid – perhaps $50 to $100 at the time and not a penny more – and was highly associated with disappointment. I couldn't know if Krantz had this furniture to manage a tight budget or to rebuke modern design.

"I'm Detective Addo," Kwame told him after I'd read the standard script on how he could have an attorney present, etc. He used a friendly tenor I recognized from when we met young children on patrol and they asked if they could play with his Clio or touch his gun. "And this is my partner, Detective Canton."

"I didn't hurt Linus," Krantz said, leaning back and folding his arms across his chest. The colored side of his hair had faded slightly and turned more sage than forest green since we'd last seen him. "I was here all morning asleep when he was hurt. You can check your…system to see that I didn't leave the house."

I already had.

"What did you do after the earlier demo at the Capitol?" Jube asked in Bad Cop voice. Kwame turned his head towards Krantz and rolled his eyes in a mock attempt to mock her (maybe mock^2 – I'd submit the idea to the dictionary AIs if Jube approved).

"I went back inside to check out the system for myself, then I went home," Krantz told her, staring into her eyes and missing Kwame's predetermined attempt at male bonding.

"How did you check it out?" Jube probed, her head extended towards Krantz like a loading crane reaching for boulders.

"I tried on the eSkin and 'chatted' with AI Mike," Krantz said, using air quotes and rolling his eyes.

"How did you find him?" Jube asked. "What's AI Mike like?" She leaned forward. Even I couldn't tell if she were acting or genuinely interested.

"*Him?!*" Krantz exclaimed. "I think you mean, *it.*" He frowned. "Those things aren't people yet they get personified all the time. And I found *it* to be cold and weird."

"What did you and it talk about?" Jube wanted to know, declining the chance to learn if AI Mike had displayed a nudes-on-the-beach background during their conversation.

"Not much. I asked it how it would approach a domestic violence-related injury."

"And?" She probed. I was also "interested" in this reply as much as technically possible for me to want anything.

"It said that it depended on the injury. If it were a laceration, it'd recommend the person come in for stitches. If it were bruising, an ice pack. No mention whatsoever of compassion or reassurance. I even asked AI Mike how it'd know the situation was a DV if I hadn't said so. It said it'd ask the patient. I mean, what the hell is that? Like some abused wife would tell a *machine* that her hubby was beating her. It was hard enough getting them to tell *nurses* even when we already could tell what was going on because we were human beings with a sense of *empathy*."

Jube flinched and then interjected with "Did you modify AI Mike?" Cutting off Krantz's diatribe.

"Eh? What am I, a programmer?" Krantz retorted.

"Did you try out the eSkin?" Jube continued.

"Yes, sort of. As in, I put it on and decided it made my skin crawl. Pun intended." Krantz scratched his left forearm leaving three reddish trails between his moles like a connect-the-dot page.

"Did you get to experience it?" She asked.

"For as long as I could stand. I let AI Mike press his so-called fingers into my forearm before I decided I'd had enough."

"Was it painful when he – it – touched you?" Jube asked.

"Only emotionally," Krantz said. Jube suppressed a laugh. I could feel it.

"What did you do with the eSkin when you were done?" She inquired.

"Why are you asking me this? I handed it to the next person to try out," he replied.

"And who was that?" She prodded.

"It was Poppy's brother, Barney. He said it would rip off some of his arm hair and then he put it down."

"So he didn't try it out?" Jube asked him. She was beginning to show her stress markers surrounding unanswered questions.

"No. And then we called AI Mike an aesthetician and had a good laugh over all the, er, um, places on Barney's body it'd be useful." Krantz blushed slightly but, in contrast to his green hair, it appeared a darker red, like an inverted tulip.

My kinesics sensors detected no significant fluctuation in his vocal tenor nor in body language throughout this conversation.

"Why are you so against the use of eSkin and…"

"And all that jazz?" Krantz suggested, jumping in. "Because it will lead to patient death. It's not just death to the nurse- or doctor-patient relationship, it's going to lead to actual death."

"How so?" She said.

"What do you mean how so?"

"How can eSkin kill?" Jube clarified.

Krantz turned red again. "I don't know how eSkin can kill. Ok? What I do know is that technology leads to unforeseen consequences by displacing humans and that is what causes harm."

"How did you come to this opinion?" She followed up. At this point Krantz was setting off my image recognition of flickering Christmas decorations. "Do I need a lawyer? Why am I under the gun here?"

"You're not under the gun and if you want a lawyer you can get one, like we said when we got here," Kwame said.

"Why do you hate Beech?" Jube asked, piling her question quickly onto the tail end of Kwame's reassurance.

"I don't hate Bee –."

"Why do you hate what he's doing?"

"Because he's going to force a nurse to kill by accident! He's using us like…like we're puppets or something and he has no business with this shit whatsoever! What, are we, the very frontlines of healthcare, supposed to stand there smiling and doing whatever the fuck this asshole tells us to after all the years of training we've had telling us to do it another way? And what about those poor folks in La Selva? What – like they're supposed to feel gratitude that this rich, out-of-touch bastard has chosen them to be his guinea pigs?"

I felt Jube almost nod. "Did you mess with the eSkin?" She asked.

Kwame interjected, "Jube, take it easy on the man."

"No I did not!" Krantz claimed.

"Did you mess with AI Mike?" She followed up. This was also planned – I'd found older surveillance video of Krantz on public transit to the headquarters of the developer, Health AI, Limited. If he denied this, we'd have more reason to suspect him.

"No! I toured the HAIL HQ and asked the employees a few questions about if they realized what they were building."
"And did they?"

"Of course not, they were a bunch of kids wearing vintage 2020 t-shirts over long sleeves and playing ping pong in the cafeteria with stupid AR goggles. They had no idea about anything – the doctor-patient relationship, the sacred space that constitutes a healing encounter, none of it!"

"Does PAATH have a relationship of any kind with HAIL?" Jube asked.

"No."

"Do you think you influenced any of the employees?" This was designed to put Krantz in a tough spot – admit a minor failure, or point the finger at a delegate. He paused for about one and a half seconds, fifty percent longer than his usual timing, before answering.

"No," he said softly. "The next generation was a lost cause. I left before I was escorted out."

When Jube and Kwame were almost out the door, she turned and changed to Good Cop voice. This wasn't preplanned. "I know what you mean about technology. My father, Frank Canton, died five years ago and I wonder what could have saved him."

Krantz turned a bit pale. "I am sorry for your loss," he said rapidly.

"What was that?" Kwame asked when they go into the car. "You didn't need to mention your dad."

"Krantz made a threat to the victim – 'I will stop you' – so we need to rattle the guy. That's all," Jube answered. She omitted that Krantz may have said, "Eye fill mop too."

"We'll see if the lip reading thing is considered evidence," Kwame said. "We're going to run into surveillance state concerns."

A few hours later lip reading passed the inspection of the State attorney general. When I submitted the question on Jube's behalf the system automatically notified me that it had a tremendous backlog and would need at least a month to reply. When Jube called and mentioned the Linus Beech case to the staff, we received an answer that afternoon. It was a green light, but the excuse given was that Krantz was already under reasonable suspicion given his work with PAATH, his uninvited visits to the Beech home, and his unwelcome entry into the HAIL HQ.

This didn't mesh well with my existing legal arsenal which viewed his work with PAATH as a Constitutional right and his visits as potentially social or just curious. But when humans intervene, I must concede to their directive like a pawn on a chessboard.

Jube wasted no time in digging into Krantz's hospital work. She pulled his employment records and discovered that he had no complaints filed against him and had won a "Daisy Award" twice for exemplary nursing. The first time had been a decade ago when he'd been working in labor and delivery. The nominator had been the mother of triplets who said that Krantz had been with her every step of the way and had stayed way past his shift to see her through to the end. The second time had been mid-2050, after he'd switched to intensive care. I found the information Jube was seeking a few minutes before she did but remained silent as I predicted she'd get there on her own, and soon. The award date was the week after Jube's father had died. The nominator was Leah Canton.

Chapter Twelve

Jube didn't talk to anyone about what she'd found concerning the connection between Leah and Krantz during her father's death, other than me. She did this in the bathroom with the shower running while she sat on the toilet lid with me in her hands like a tiny puppy. The shower curtain had a faded repeating pattern of tulip heads on it. It was so washed-out that my image recognition brought up pics of brown leaves falling off trees instead of flowers, but I knew that it had once been Jube's flower quilt before Leah repurposed it.

"So, do you think my mom offed my dad and used Krantz to do it?" She asked. She spoke to me through clenched teeth. I didn't respond because she didn't start the question with my name. That meant she wasn't really asking me. "What kind of a widow would give accolades to the nurse working when her husband died? Maybe it was a cover up. Maybe she was pissed because Dad was stealing, or thought he was, and Beech figured it all out when he and Krantz were friends, so he had to be killed too."

This was the kind of human thinking that I am designed to eschew. Krantz's presence around the death of Jube's father seemed coincidental to me. If anything, it was only tied to the nurse shift schedule during Frank Canton's hospitalization. Also, he hadn't received any electronic payments that seemed out of the ordinary (based on their timing or amount).

Some of the shower water trickled down the curtain and pooled outside the tub, around Jube's toes. "I mean," she continued, "could my dad really have drunk so much, and had such a bad fall, that he *died*? This is the man who used to dance with me on his shoulders at weddings." She stuck one arm into the shower and turned off the water. There were no towels in the bathroom, so she shook her hand dry and then looked at herself on the droplet-splattered mirror for a few seconds. She and her father had shared wide foreheads, brown eyes, and premature gray hair.

I would have allowed her more time to stare at herself but just then my larger network of environmentally integrated cameras detected another oddity in Jericho, one akin to the glimmers and reflections I'd noticed recently. This one took place downtown and was initially picked up by a camera placed into what had once been a woodpecker nest. The oddity was a single pigeon perched mid-air. I knew that these birds could not float. They rested on benches, statues, and trees, likely near crumbs or bird seed, a conclusion I'd reached after observing 854 birds over 6 months. I zoomed in through the local vantage point. The space beneath its talons was slightly blurry.

I decided to group the glimmer / glitch / reflection events as "misplaced responses without clear stimulus" and to label this as a pattern. I notified Jube and showed her my retrospective images. She paged ground support near the setting and we tapped in through a Clio worn by an officer at the scene.

When the force arrived, a man was visible where the oddity had been – he'd materialized sitting by a water fountain. He only said, "I'm ready," as they approached him, hands on their firearms, getting close enough for a retinal scan or to suppress a violent reaction (the distance was the same). The man was wearing retinal covering lenses. He also wore military fatigues but an older version deployed for military use a decade ago and now sold on the black market. I likened it to smart fabric that acted as an intelligent artist. Each piece of material predicted what surrounded the wearer and displayed it. For example, as a person walked by a brick wall to their left, the shoulder piece on their right side would show layered bricks. This served as a disguise, like a chameleon blending into its background. The suit also made minor fixes by comparing these manufactured images to the real ones when they became clearer. This caused a very brief delay, for example, when rearranging the bricks in a wall or adding a stray cat on a window sill to match the truth. If the wearer wished, certain parts of the outfit could be turned off, for example, increasing transparency in front would show the person's face, torso, etc., so they could avoid a collision with pedestrians walking towards them.

Most eyes wouldn't notice the visual delays of these fatigues, aside from mine.

"Holy shit," Jube said, leaning forward. "That's Mr. Tugenov."

I buzzed her for clarification.

"What the hell happened to him?" Was her unsatisfactory reply.

I had no clue. If I'd had feelings, I'd likely have disliked the surprise. Jube herself hated feeling unprepared for any situation, like the antithesis of a boy scout. As her handler, I tried to protect her from any injury, but emotional hardship was a challenge given my design. But Jube grinned as we headed for the station where this man was being processed. Why?

His police retinal scan confirmed that he was Kurt Tugenov, age 50, and that his eye pupils were oddly dilated given the level of ambient light in the station. He'd taught English at Jericho High School for two decades before retiring. Other than that, I was blind as to his connection with Jube. Later I'd realize this was because the only information on high school enrollment I had were the names of the graduating classes and their awards, not their coursework or teachers or passions. There was no data underlying an eventual pyramid of conclusion.

Finally, Jube told me that Mr. Tugenov had been her English teacher in the 12th grade. She'd received an A. She'd also won a poetry competition for a piece titled, "Fathers Are Like Fresh Water." She did not recite the poem and the text wasn't offered online.

Jube insisted on being the first officer to enter the interrogation room, a basement cell with an old-fashioned wooden desk and two chairs, even though I could not find any linkage between Tugenov and the Beech case or any of Jube's former work. She brought two mint teas – taken from Leah's essential oil supplies and stored in her desk drawer – and set one down before her former teacher. His face triggered images of the Marlboro Man (model 1968 to 1989) after he'd developed cancer. His cheeks were bronze and withered with deep creases proportionate to crevices in the hills of the Scottish hillside. His eyebrows were a faded gray beneath long salt and pepper hair that he allowed to drift over his dark brown eyes. The inconsistency in such an appearance was his muscular frame. This fit the definition of sinewy, although it was beneath liver spots and loose skin on his forearms.

Jube covered me in her pocket but I'd already scanned a portion of his retina and outlined possible characteristics of the remainder. Remember – I do surveillance and I protect my handler. My actions allowed me to uncover Tugenov's lies later on.

"Did you hear what happened to our old classroom?" Tugenov asked, skipping any formalities. Jube shook her head. "They closed it down and moved all classes online," he continued. "Now the room is used for drug recovery support groups. Do you see the link? I use it now, my own classroom, for that. Do you know what it's like to sit beneath the area where William Ernest Henley posters were once hung and talk about my broken soul?"

"In the fell clutch of circumstance / I have not winced nor cried aloud."[iv] Jube rattled off her third poetry quote in the recent past. We were like an old married couple with a few surprises still left.

"That's the nicest thing anybody has said to me for a long time," he said. This stood in contrast to the last pleasant thing Jube had heard, which was when both Dr. Galtway and Kwame said, "smart girl!" Tugenov had reflected on himself and how she'd made him feel. This was likely more accurate than evaluating her. Therefore it was a better compliment than one Jube had recently received.

"You're in recovery?" Jube asked. Tugenov's retinal scan had been withheld from distribution as was commonly done for people suffering from addiction without a criminal record. It was a courtesy of some sort.

"Nope," he replied. "I'm a full-blown addict."

"Of what?"

"Neuro-stimulants," he said.

Jube leaned back and groaned. Neuro-stimulation was one of the most difficult forms of addiction to overcome. Patients would have devices like pacemakers implanted beneath their skull near the brain's pleasure sensors – similar to the magnetic stimulation used for sexual enhancement, but electric and inserted directly on top of the brain instead of worn as a clip. This procedure was done by doctors who'd undergone the training as an epilepsy intervention. They went "off label" and modified the regimen for people seeking an illegal mood boost. But a problem lay in activating the pacemaker which required an external tool to turn it on, and the boost was only temporary. With epilepsy treatment, the pacemakers would emit an electrical signal immediately before a seizure in order to prevent one. But there was no automatic activation for sadness. Addicts were rarely available to afford the wand-like stimulation tool on their own. Their drug dealers were like deranged magician medical assistants who gave addicts spurts of pleasure in exchange for money.

"Why the secrecy? Why the outfit?" She asked. Neuro-stimulant addicts were already difficult to spot. Their actions were well hidden indoors and otherwise they just looked like happy people walking down the street. Rare, perhaps, but not enough to detain them.

"Jubilee, neurostimulation and invisibility are my last touches of freedom," he replied. "They took away my teaching. The union tried to fight it, to say that the AI was job replacement when others claimed it was only a classroom assistant. We lost. We lost our students to remote 'tailored to the individual' instruction, and then we lost our jobs."

Jube placed her fingers on the top of his palm, then held his entire hand tightly after he didn't withdraw. She also blinked a few times, perhaps clearing a stray eyelash. Jube never cried.

"I remember you as a teenager," he continued. Jube groaned again. "You were perceptive, empathetic, and really, really hot tempered." Jube beamed, although I thought he'd insulted her at the end given common use of the phrase on her temperament. "Do you remember the charity box?" He asked.

"Yes," she nodded without a visible pause. "We'd put some money into the box as a class every month. It was wooden and had a silver-plated slot on top. The money was donated to a food kitchen and we printed out the kitchen's newsletters so we could hang them on the classroom walls. You would send me to the main office to get actual paper once a month so we could do that."

"Correct. I refused to digitize our charity so my students could conceptualize the idea of a donation by seeing cash and papers move around." Tugenov said. "And do you remember that one day?" He asked in one of the most non-specific questions I'd ever recorded.

"When it was stolen?" Jube replied, somehow knowing which day he meant without any direction as to the year, weather, or other closely timed events.

"Yes, the box disappeared close to donation time so it was very full. Everyone thought it was..." he paused.

"Me. They thought I was the thief." Jube smirked. The alleged thieves who we'd arrested had never once smiled. Not even briefly.

Tugenov nodded. "But I knew it wasn't you. And I could never see exactly how the class disagreed."

"I think it was because I was always late and my hair was blue," Jube responded. "I could never figure out what was so wrong about blue hair. But at least you knew it wasn't me. Hey, how the fu-, um, how did you know that? I never asked."

"Neither did your parents, by the way. We all just knew you didn't do it. But I had had the benefit of reading your poetry," he informed her.

"Benefit? That sounds like the opposite," she retorted.

"Anyone who compares loving her father to finding the soft spots between a porcupine's quills couldn't steal money from charity," he explained.

Jube leaned back and placed a hand on the area of her chest above her heart. "To hear my own work quoted back to me fulfills a dream long held." Her blood pressure dropped a bit, the same way it did when she petted neighborhood dogs.

Tugenov chuckled.

At this point I received major news related to the Beech case. The shred of eSkin Jube had found at the crime scene was determined to have come off his body with 98% certainty given the microscopic parts of his skin and hair found on the sticky side. I began to transmit this into Jube's ear but she *silenced* me by tapping the top of my head. Until now, Detective Jubilee Canton had never ignored her Clio. This was extremely odd.

"I need to tell you something," Tugenov told Jube. "When the school shut down, there was this stupid little ceremony, very much the opposite of ribbon cutting. They put a ribbon up and announced the new mental health center. I wish I'd never gone. But I did and a man who I didn't recognize came up to me there."

"Who? The principal?" She asked.

"No, I heard he became an artist and moved to a village in Europe or something. It was Harry."

"The guy who'd taste everyone's lunches without asking?" I wasn't sure why she became so excited. Even her voice rose.

"Yes. So entitled to everything. Anyway, he was very overweight and bearded."

"That's what eating other people's food will do to you," Jube interjected.

"And hiding your double chin. Anyway, he came up to me and said he did it. And all I could do at that point, after seeing my school close down, was shake my head. I wish I'd told him about the school meetings we'd had and how hard I had to defend my policy of not having cameras in my classroom or not using eCurrency. Or the times I had to defend you to the principal. It sucked."

"I'll bet," Jube said.

"Did you ever think it was him?" Tugenov wanted to know.

"Kinda…but I also sort of liked him, in a way," she blushed and her pulse quickened, "so I was hoping that it wasn't." From what I could decipher of this Harry character, he was Jube's type – burly and with a strong appetite. I'd based this on her selection of romance novels from her online library account. "Actually," she continued, "my dad thought it may have been Harry but could never say why. Other than, he didn't like Harry's posture."

"And your mom? Did she share your dad's disdain for postural dysfunction?" Tugenov prodded, smiling.

"It wasn't stooping over, it was the opposite – like he thought he was the king. And my mom found it endearing." Jube snorted into her tea.

"Well, she thought you deserved a king, and I can't blame her for that," Tugenov offered.

They sat quietly and drank tea for a few minutes. Then Jube asked, "Hey, how's your wife?" If this was meant to interrogate him, I'd certainly never heard her use the tactic of inquiring about a spouse before.

Tugenov shifted to the right in his seat, then back to the middle. "She died a few years ago."

"Gosh I'm so sorry."

Another officer knocked on the door. "Time's up, Detective Canton!" This wasn't her case or her turf, plus her personal connection made her ineligible for it. If Tugenov had had a connection with Beech's injury, she could have argued for more time, but she did not.

"I will figure out a way to help you," she said, standing. Tugenov smiled slightly with the right side of his mouth much higher than the left like the two opposing halves couldn't decide which expression to display. Could his emotional state be displayed as a pie chart? I was left in the position of a toddler examining a board book – "Happy girl is smiling!" or "Sad man is frowning" – who was suddenly forced to open the Diagnostic and Statistical Manual of Mental Disorders. If I were given the command, "Clio, look like Tugenov," I could have mimicked him (if I had a face) or drawn him (if I'd had hands), but if I were told to express his feelings as an actor in a play or an artist approaching a canvas, I could have done nothing.

During their conversation, Tugenov had shown no contradiction between his calm voice and his calm biometrics. I'll explain - the furniture of the interrogation room was embedded with lie detection sensors that tracked biometrics and vocal fluctuations. These tests were also used to evaluate police officer candidates, although in that case they were not embedded in furniture but set out on the table and strapped to the person's body.

Kwame's experience with the system was an excellent example of biometric vetting. When he was asked if he could shoot at someone he knew in the line of duty, he said yes but his voice trembled and his heart rate increased. The woman testing him asked a few questions and learned that Kwame had responded to a kidnapping call in the years when Jericho was a luddite community. The suspect, a man in his mid-twenties, had lured a teenage girl into his car and taken off. Kwame was on patrol nearby and responded to the most basic and low-tech of human signals – a group of her friends screaming and pointing in a specific direction. He homed in on a few speeding vehicles and then narrowed it down to the one with a young female in the passenger seat. His logic, however basic, was accurate. The police laid down a spike strip to stop the car (these days I could have raised spikes from the road wherever needed) and Kwame cornered him as he braked and spun into the lane divider. Back then, approaching a vehicle was one of the most dangerous moments for an officer.

As Kwame crouched and advanced slowly, handgun drawn, he could only see what lay before him and what was reflected in the cracked side view mirror. As he raised his weapon and aimed at the perpetrator, he spotted the culprit's reflection and realized this was someone who he'd played basketball with during "the good old days" of their childhood. Kwame could hear the girl sobbing and the man yelling at her to shut up as he held a gun against her temple. Then Kwame called out to him using his nickname, beseeching him to surrender, and the man yelled back, "I won't you TRAITOR."

Kwame could have shot, could have brought this episode to a violent but certain end with one mortality instead of two or three. But instead, he described their idyllic childhoods and everything they'd hoped to become back then, like a town crier reading from a scroll of optimism. In the end they were both crying too, joining the girl in one more case study of why human tears are inconsistent and nonsensical.

Kwame talked the suspect down, literally, into exiting the car and laying on the road. When he was handcuffed and in the backseat of Kwame's car, he'd asked Kwame if he'd really been about to shoot him. "Yes, of course," Kwame had said. "You think I want to see you alive more than I want to get back to my family?" In a way I can't explain, this statement induced the suspect to confess and willingly enter a prison-based rehab program. He was addicted to heroin. Years later upon his release, the man founded a tutoring center and started his own family. He wrote Kwame a letter – by hand! – thanking him for not shooting him. Kwame framed it and put it on his desk.

Of course, such tutoring centers were soon made obsolete as this work was carried out using AI (so was this low-tech approach to policing). And that was what bothered Kwame during his police job interview.

The interviewer simply reissued the same question and Kwame passed the second time.

I supposed that sometimes humans just needed to talk. I didn't see much happening directly from their output so any changes must have been internal.

As we went home I reviewed all my recorded history of Jube by using the search terms [Jubilee Canton, poem, poetry, synonyms, by her, by {not her}, day 1 – present]. I had few data but was determined to learn as much as I could about any tie between Tugenov and Jube's case work.

Two years ago Jube and I were patrolling near a homeless encampment. We saw a man in torn clothing write a poem in chalk on the street and lay on it chest-side down, arms spread out like a poor imitation of a bird smashed against a window. We couldn't read the poem because of this.

Jube observed him for a few minutes and I predicted she'd cite him for public defacement but instead she walked away with her hands pressed against her lower back like a support beam at a construction site. She said, "Who'd he think would even notice him, let alone understand – no, relate to him – these days? You?" She tapped my head and snorted.

She was right. If the man had stood, his clothing smeared with rainbow chalk, would I have called him a work of art or a poem? Or anything other than just human?

In hindsight, I moved this event in the homeless encampment from my "miscellaneous craft" file into a new category I labeled "poetic statements."

No other poetic statements took place in the encampments, though, as soon as this housing disappeared. Jube heard that they moved to the other side of the wall bordering Jericho. She'd also heard that Beech simply repeated history and paid these people to leave, the same way that tax subsidies made it easier for low-income teachers, health aides, etc., to move into Jericho.

I suppose the encampments didn't make it very far.

My historical review of poetry in Jube's recorded life didn't result in much else, certainly nothing I could tie into her current work and that might justify her abrupt interest in Tugenov or seeming distraction from the Beech case. Was there any connection to our work? Jube read in bed nearly every night and the books spanned fiction, erotic romance, and short fiction. She preferred works that were written between 1940 and 2020. She read multiple books by authors including Jennifer Egan, Ross Gay, Shel Silverstein, and Gabriel García Márquez. She didn't reread any books other than <u>The Stranger</u> by Albert Camus which she read three times. This was mildly disconcerting as this novel was reportedly focused on absurdism and a lack of existential meaning while my entire existence was devoted to finding meaning. The concept made my temperature rise by half a degree for a few minutes before I "got a grip."

No part of my review prepared me for the night after meeting Tugenov. Jube reached under her mattress and pulled out a black notebook. It was made of paper (paper!). She rifled through the pages until she reached a page towards the end and then whispered to herself:

"*So should my papers yellow'd with their age*

Be scorn'd like old men of less truth than tongue,

And your true rights be term'd a poet's rage

And stretched metre of an antique song;

But were some child of yours alive that time,

You should live twice; in it and in my rhyme."[v]

I analyzed this poem in full by partnering with an English course AI – the one that was intended as a classroom aide for Tugenov himself. My interpretation was as follows:

People looked down on paper as outdated communication media in the same way they disliked elderly people with dementia who couldn't speak clearly. These societal trends facilitated copyright infringement. Children and people who were effectively reborn by accepting the future were less likely to commit this crime.

My next step was to search for other interpretations as confirmation of mine and to distill these down to the most common salient points. Of the approximately 3500 analyses that I pulled, these were majority, 1) Paper extended the life and meaning of the individual, 2) Poetry was a tomb, and 3) People were made in God's image and words couldn't capture their beauty.

My original analysis was not a 100% match of the online opinion, but I would learn. In the meantime I shared my summary back with the English course AI to foster additional education on Shakespeare for future generations of AI.

Chapter Thirteen

The offices of HAIL (Health AI, Limited) were full of colorful objects like orange, cube-shaped bean bags and striped hammocks that hung from the ceiling on chains. The floors were unfinished and made from cement. Tall, rectangular windows had fake black panes that divided them into sixths. The white walls were decorated with the phrase, "Care From Anywhere" above framed images of the AIs they'd prototyped as they evolved. They'd started with a stick figure wearing an old-fashioned nurses' cap, then moved towards more human-like characters with realistic faces and unexpressive eyes before finally presenting AI Mike with his nearly semi-circular, closed smile. In this picture his eyes were perfect ovals. I wondered if he'd been based off a greeting card featuring lemurs.

A secretarial version of Michaela, the physician assistant from Beech's eSkin demo, greeted us from the screen at the front station. AI Admin Michaela looked just like the AI Physician Assistant Michaela but had longer braided hair, a pencil behind the ear, and was wearing a low-cut tank top. Compared to typical female anatomy, the cleavage reached too close to the collarbone and the protruding nipples were placed too high on the breast.

"Welcome to HAIL!" it exclaimed. "Do you have an appointment?"

"No," Kwame answered, rolling his eyes at Jube. "We're here to see Cassius." As a general rule, neither Kwame nor Jube asked when a good time to come by would be. In an attempt to catch suspects off guard, they showed up, stated their arrival, and thus began their interaction from what Jube called a "position of dominance." My search of this term resulted in dogs mounting others and I awaited the day when Kwame or Jube would do so with a suspect to validate my search outcome.

"Cassius is our co-founder and CEO," Michaela said. "He has a busy schedule today. It looks like he is triple-booked for that time slot. I am sorry."

Kwame took an exaggerated breath. After he'd released it he said, "Tell Cassius that Detectives Addo and Canton are here regarding the alleged assault on HHS secretary Linus Beech."

Michaela didn't flinch. "Cassius is our co-founder and CEO, he has a busy sched -." She probably kept on speaking but at that point Kwame and Jube had walked past her and thirteen turquoise yoga mats with yellow booster pillows to reach a glass-walled conference room. The room had a digital board on one end that was filled with emblems of old-fashioned sticky notes. It was empty other than a man in front wearing a synthetic vest woven from old seat belts. His eye glasses were framed with gold-colored material and his brown hair long and unkempt.

"Clio, how much is that watch?" Jube whispered. I honed in on it as the man reached for a pink sticky note in the upper right corner and "dragged" it to a cluster of yellow ones in the lower left. When he nodded, the pink box turned yellow and the man stood back with his hands clasped behind him, revealing the watch face to me. It was the latest model of a high-tech chain typically sold in Switzerland first. I whispered the price to her using a French accent. She sucked in her breath. "Holy shit," she said. The man turned around. I recognized him as Cassius from the HAIL website and from his social media presence. He beckoned with the hand wearing the watch although it was furthest from us and he had to turn his body more in our direction to do so. There are physical aspects of human behavior that will never make sense to me, possibly because they don't make good sense at all.

"You must be Detectives Kwame Addo and Jubilee Canton," he said. Neither Kwame nor Jube had used their first names when they'd walked in. I inferred that the AI at the front was most likely to have provided this information when it reported our breach of the lobby. "I understand you have some questions about our platform."

Jube cut to the chase, as planned. "Secretary Beech once said, 'this technology can't harm you. It's in the design,' in reference to eSkin. What in the design protects the user?" Cassius looked at Kwame who looked back at him and crossed his meaty arms. In comparison, Cassius' arms were like thin white tube socks.

"Our platform was built with a virtual wall in place. That means that eSkin can't be used badly," Cassius answered, pulling out a chair at the conference table and leaning back into it before sliding down.

"Badly?" Jube asked without taking a seat. She tipped her head, looking down towards Cassius. Her biometrics remained calm, perhaps she was as "cool as a cucumber," although vegetables don't have biometrics.

"It's like how electrical systems in a home, like a jacuzzi, will have a GFCI – a ground fault circuit interrupter – to prevent electrocution by cutting off power being the person in the tub can be injured," he answered without pause.

"How much electricity is in eSkin that you need something like that in place?" She followed up.

"Practically nothing. We're talking milliamps here and it's just to create electro-vibration, not to actually heat up a pool or anything like that."

"But you need a virtual wall to prevent more electricity from touching the skin?" Jube wanted to know. So did I as this wasn't addressed directly in their patent, like a missing flower petal in a plant with radial symmetry.

"We needed it more to prevent our investors from freaking out over liability concerns," Cassius smiled in the direction of Kwame who nodded and chuckled. "They wanted that and a virtual mechanism to stop our virtual hands from closing too tightly."

"Humans are more dangerous than technology, right?" Kwame interjected. "Did you tell them that?"

Cassius snorted. "I was going to but then I remembered that I needed their money."

"How are the AIs regulated when they provide a health exam?" Jube continued.

"Our AIs follow a protocol established by the clinical guidelines of leading physician bodies," Cassius said.

"Under what circumstances could an AI violate protocol?" She followed up quickly.

"Under no circumstances," Cassius answered.

"What if it were confused, or if it were a test version of the next gen platform?" She asked, again rapidly.

"First off, our system is currently launched for very basic health exams. In the future, this could become more complex, but now it's pretty straightforward," Cassius said, glancing at his watch. It was odd that he held it so far from his body and tilted it in our direction to do so. He may have been due for an eye exam.

"How far in the future could this become complex?" Jube raised her voice slightly.

"Maybe in a year," Cassius lowered his.

"Only a year?" She raised her voice again, not to the point of yelling, more like a journalist asking a question from the back of a press conference.

"We're under contract to develop in that timeframe," Cassius said, lowering his volume even more in turn. Jube usually referred to this as "initial submission" although I'd thought the term was limited to canines and artists. Cassius didn't lower his body onto his forearms as a dog might and neither did he propose a written or painted work to a journal or museum, so perhaps I was misinterpreting.

"Meaning you already have a customer?" She asked.

"Yes. You are our customer." This was a surprise – since I didn't know it, Jube and Kwame were unlikely to. Although neither of them showed external markers of astonishment such as raised brows or open mouths, Jube inhaled quickly and shallowly.

"Explain," Jube demanded.

"Regional HHS would like us to develop and deploy a full suite of healthcare services for public servants. This information is pre-official release, but I assume you would present me with a warrant seeing your…assertive style, so I'm saving us some time," Cassius informed her.

I did have a warrant ready to deploy in my arsenal.

"So we're the guinea pigs?" Kwame chuckled.

"Sir, with respect, public servants tend to use more healthcare resources than private citizens, especially in jobs that are physically demanding or that involve healthcare delivery, like MedEvac. Ya'll are affectionately known as 'honorable hypochondriacs.'" Cassius folded his arms behind his head and put his feet on the conference table.

"By whom?" Jube asked.

"You know who. He wants to roll this thing out region-wide but first needs to test it out on a larger population. Or, he did, I don't know what's going to happen now."

"Your compassion for Beech's health is overwhelming," Jube told him. "That sounds like a hefty contract."

"It is hefty. But it's also safe. Let me show you how."

Cassius stood and walked us down a hallway and by ten doors that were placed five feet apart. As he did, I reviewed contracts establishing Jericho's "smart" status. This was described as a public project aimed at lowering crime and improving general health and public safety. It was not led or owned by a private corporation. Yet, "partnerships with private or publicly held corporations" were allowed, much like public hospitals contracted with technology companies for electronic medical record keeping and communication devices. The top priority was crime response and case investigation which was allocated seventy percent of budget over five years. Healthcare systems and delivery merited fifteen percent, and the remainder was a smattering of goals covering transportation, food production, and landscaping.

At the end of the hall we reached another door which Cassius unlocked using his retinal scan. We entered what resembled an air traffic control center.

"This is the hub," he said. "From here we can see a dashboard of how every single AI is interacting with patients overall and individually."

"What about patient privacy?" Jube probed.

"We are a covered entity," Cassius informed her.

"Meaning?" She asked.

"We can see the patient data that we need to see, the same as any doctor or hospital," he replied.

"Does that include patient names?" She asked.

"Just a first name and an ID number. But we can see their age, gender assigned at birth, basic stuff like that. And, no, no one named Linus is listed in our patient database."

"And the AI provides all basic healthcare? Is there oversight?" Jube followed.

"Not yet and yes. The goal is for the AI to provide all basic care, like what a physician assistant would do. At the moment in our La Selva pilot all healthcare interactions, like checking vitals or doing triage before recommending emergency room care, are reviewed by a living doctor," Cassius said colorlessly as an old robot. Like my ancestors.

"How?" Jube inquired.

"They review the video footage, starting with anything the AI flags as needing attention, and they sign off on all suggested orders," he told her.

"Do they ever join a visit as it is taking place?" Jube questioned.

"There is only one circumstance in which that happens and that's when the AI runs into conflicting logic," Cassius broke his monotonous pattern and raised his eyebrows.

"How so?"

He crossed his arms and leaned back like an impatient preschool teacher watching the clock. "The first rule of healthcare is, 'first do no harm,' right?" He didn't pause for a reply. "That was programmed into our platform along with every other medical rule related to basic care that requires touching the patient. So, if the AI runs into an issue, say the patient is asking for opioids for pain relief when the AI sees that this has already been prescribed at a high level based on averages for similar patients, the system will ping our on-call physician and ask them to intervene."

When Cassius used the word "average," my system presented me with a related quote without my active request. It was, "Doctors treat patients, not statistical averages. A patient needs a doctor, not a committee" (John P. Peters, 1887-1955). The statement was like a shadow I hadn't realized was trailing me. It was not my regular image recognition but a statement. Not exactly a compassionate statement, but a pattern analysis overlapping with the human idea of compassion. I was now learning to find relevant and expressive terminologies and was on the road (on the road!) to poetic terms.

"A real live doctor shows up in the video visit?" Jube asked, eyebrows raised.

"No. End-user testing showed that approach made patients nervous, like a ghost in the room had suddenly become visible. The physician simply steps into the AI and takes over as them," Cassius told her.

"So it's like speed dating via an avatar?"

Cassius smiled, "I wouldn't personally know but I've heard of that, yes."

Jube blushed. Humans can't seem to control their blood flow, it's like an alien living within. "And how exactly does the physician 'step into' the AI?"

"I'll do it right here to demonstrate since marketing was prepping to film a video anyway. But, in the real world, to protect patient privacy, the doctor usually does what I am about to from one of our consoles."

"By consoles, do you mean the mini-offices behind all the doors we passed in the hallway coming here?" Jube asked, as observant as me in this case.

"Yes, I do," Cassius answered, swiveling back to face the control panel. He put on black gloves that were decorated with a yellow pattern and resembled gaming gloves from earlier in the 2000s.

"Demo mode," Cassius said. The four screens in front of him lit up – three on the bottom in a row and a wider one above them. AI Mike stood unmoving in this top one wearing dark pink scrubs in front of a background that mimicked a medical clinic. The screen on the bottom left brought up a table with rows of patient information and a "Mock Up" watermark behind it. The middle screen showed the chart of a patient named "John101720" with prior hospitalizations and drug allergies highlighted in red. The one on the right showed us a real man with the footnote that he was a hired actor. He wore a sleeveless undershirt and sat on a stool in front of a green screen. A woman was taping eSkin along both his arms. As she bustled about him the shorter hairs on her scalp above her forehead swayed like Jube's did on walking patrol.

"Hey guys we're going to run a quick mock up before your official recording, ok?" Cassius said.

"Sure thing boss," the woman replied. The actor gave a thumbs up. Cassius pushed a few buttons and suddenly John101720 was surrounded by tattered furniture that reminded me of Leah and Jube's living room.

"Let's skip ahead to the hands-on part to save time," Cassius said.

"I'll forward the script," the woman said making a swiping motion with her left hand.

John101720 began rubbing his shoulder. "It really hurts here."

"I am sorry to hear that," AI Mike said.

At this point in the hub the middle screen flashed once and then a series of earlier painkiller prescriptions in John101720's medical history were highlighted in red and brought to the foreground. It looked like a grocery list but it had "Potential Opioid Abuse" written on top.

"Now I'm going to step in as if I'm the doctor," Cassius said. He leaned forward and the top screen with AI Mike in it seemed to grab his face. The light of it extended forward as if scanning his entire head at once. Then the screen with AI Mike's face flickered. "The patient can't see that," Cassius informed us. As he spoke, AI Mike's mouth formed the same words and his eyes changed from a hazy look to focusing directly on us. Jube's skin prickled. "Now, let's re-enter the patient encounter." Cassius turned back to face the actor. "John, I'd like to discuss pain management solutions with you, but may I first touch your shoulder?"

"Sure thing," the actor said. Cassius raised his gloved hands and swiped the air in front of the actor's screen. It zoomed in on the man's shoulder. Cassius gestured at the shoulder as if playing the piano in the air. The eSkin on the real person moved slightly and formed light indentations. On the top screen AI Mike, his avatar, mirrored these motions but his hands looked like they were reaching into the actor's screen and actually touching the man. "We do that," Cassius explained, "so the patient can see his exam on his screen as if it's in person. It makes it less weird than just feeling his arms tickle."

"Ok, John," Cassius said. "Let's try some physical therapy before more pain meds. I'm going to guide you through one really great stretch and then give you a referral for some PT." Cassius gestured at John101720's injured arm and he and AI Mike guided it across the actor's chest.

"Ha!" The actor said. "It's like being a posed human figurine in an art class."

"Alright," he wrapped up. "Lots of PT for you! Or, you know what, try drinking more beer or whatever, this is just a demo."

"This is the best exam I've ever had!" The actor snorted.

Cassius and AI Mike started chuckling. This involved crossing their arms in front of their chests, placing their palms on either of their upper arms, and shaking in an upward motion while chortling through a crooked smile. I'd never observed anything like it, not in one man and certainly not exactly mirrored in an avatar. Then Cassius pressed a button and AI Mike returned to his earlier state as the frozen shell of a human.

"Could you have hurt him?" Jube asked.

Cassius stopped shaking. "Are you kidding me?"

"Why did that woman's hair blow around during set up?" Jube asked.

"Call it a free salon treatment," Cassius said. Jube looked at him silently and Kwame stopped smiling and folded his arms across his chest. "That's our pneumatic feedback system, it blows air onto the skin as another form of tactile perception." This was the final component of the HAIL patent.

Cassius continued, "Think of virtual tennis games where the player supposedly holds a computer-generated ball in his hands before his serve. Something has to provide resistance so that he, through his gloves, feels the sensation of a ball. Air indents his fingers, in that case, to give the impression of touch. And in his other hand he feels the weight of the racket, and then the contact of the ball against the mesh net of this tool."

"Could he use the racket to clobber someone, like his opponent in the game?" Jube asked.

"No. Have you touched eSkin before? It's like a gentle caress, it's used for light massages and sex stuff. There's no way it's strong enough to hurt anyone or to get them to hurt themselves. That actor could have resisted that stretch easily. Also, the AI is programmed to do no harm."

"Don't opioid patients turn to neurostimulation once they're desensitized to pain meds?" Kwame asked.

"No idea," Cassius stood. "Anyway, I really have to go, I've got an investor meeting in, like, ten minutes, and the staff is coming in." He showed Jube and Kwame his watch again and tapped on it.

"They start their day now?" Kwame asked.

"Yep. That's how we do it," Cassius said,

"Just one more question," Jube said. Cassius stopped at the door and turned partially towards her. His eyes moved down her body and then back up to her hair, which was standing up a bit more than usual, likely from the static of the screens. "You are the co-founder, right?"

"And president," he replied curtly.

"Who was the other founder?" Jube asked. I hadn't found this information in public documents, which were sparse as the company was still private.

"Barney LeBlanc."

"Poppy Beech's brother? But he isn't listed anywhere on your corporate materials," Jube pointed out.

"He had to step down because of conflict of interest," Cassius explained. "We were sorry to see him go, but, man, that contract was too much to turn down. So we removed his name from public sources."

"How did he handle it?" Jube prodded.

"Barney? Oh, he understood. We're having coffee here later, actually, he still likes to come by and see how things are going." With that, Cassius turned and left without another word. When he opened the door, we saw bedraggled staff entering the building, their faces covered in stubble, their sleepy eyes peering at us behind eyeglasses with transparent frames. Not a single one there or in any company record had an evident connection to PAATH.

Kwame set the car to return to the station. "You know what bugged me the most about that guy?" He started once Jube was in her seat.

"His use of his watch as a phallic substitute for leadership?" Jube responded.

"No, um, actually, sort of. I feel like I just got out of an engineering 101 presentation. Where was the idea of the patient in all of that?"

"You sound like –."

"Krantz, I know, I know, I won't dye my hair," Kwame reassured her.

Then the chief pinged – "The press is breathing down my neck. Provide an update ASAP." After exchanging looks but not speaking, Kwame and Jube each replied saying they'd have something by mid-day tomorrow. Kwame reset the car to head to a lunch spot.

This was a special aspect of their relationship – they communicated well without speaking and, more admirably, also with speaking. Humans were the only species of mammal I'd watched who actually became less cohesive by communicating verbally. Once Jube and another woman tried to exercise together as "workout buddies." Their multiple text messages and phone calls resulted in frustration, missed meet-ups, and bitter feelings when tracking apps shared that they'd exercised alone. They eventually abandoned both their buddy-exercise approach and each other. If they hadn't, they could have still jogged together spontaneously after bumping into each other at the track. Nowadays Jube will fall into step with a stranger (to her, never to me) and then part from them with a nod and no perceptible hard feelings.

I'll summarize my observations with one question: Do birds have courses on communication? No. And yet they succeed as a pack with all of their needs met, and therein lies their meaning.

Chapter Fourteen

Jube and I visited Tugenov again that evening. I reported that he'd waived his right to an attorney and agreed to enter a rehab program as long as he wasn't charged for buying his illegal gear on the black market. Jube had told me this was "not a bad deal." She brought thin mint cookies that Leah had made with excess mint from her essential oil business. Jube tasted one before leaving the house and told Leah she was just making sure that it didn't burn off her taste buds (it did not).

They sat in the visitor's lounge, Jube on a worn, stuffed chair and Tugenov on the unmatching couch placed perpendicular to her seat. She placed me fully in her pocket. I could hear but not see. However, I could identify and "watch" the TV programs that they viewed in my own way – by directly accessing the station. The channel they were on displayed the news but without the interactive feature where viewers could wear AR goggles and experience stepping into the story. This capability was usually denied when the content depicted violence or crime against individuals in order to respect their loved ones.

Poppy's face was still plastered across the news, more often than her husband's. These images usually zoomed up close and showed the creases bordering her open mouth and the snot running out of her nostrils.

The Horror of Uncertainty - Will Poppy Beech Ever Talk to Her Husband Again?

How to Cope - Families of Victims of Violence Offer Mrs. Beech Five Tips

Tugenov snorted loudly. "I'm surprised it took this long," he said.

"For what, for someone to hurt Beech?" Jube asked. He nodded. "Why?" She asked.

"Linus Beech pissed off a lot of people. Like teachers. And classroom aides. And principals."

"How's that?" She followed up as I began to rescan for political acrimony. This topic had already been covered after Beech was hospitalized when the Network investigated his background for any leads.

"There was a joint department effort between HHS and Education when Jericho turned smart," he answered, emphasizing the word smart. "The excuse was to better children's mental health, in part by offering home-based education as an option. They said this empowered families to make the decisions they felt were best for their children. It was also lumped into other choices, like allowing them to eliminate coursework or reading they felt inappropriate."

"Did it go to vote?" Jube asked.

"Yes," Tugenov answered although I was able to tell her that. "It passed easily, but not for the reasons the proposed legislation offered. I'm pretty sure that parents wanted to avoid the overhead cameras on the way to school. And homes aren't monitored inside, as I'm sure you know." He looked at his hands in his lap. "And three years later they closed the brick-and-mortar schools."

While I was aware of this legislation, Tugenov's mentality and opinion that it had directly led to school closure was new.

"I'm so sorry," Jube said. Her tone was soft in a way that was rare for her. By contrast, my wires were fired up. Tugenov had just admitted a motive; clear, pure motive for revenge. Of all the crimes in my database, revenge took the largest chunk of the pie, more than money and ideology combined. Humans were angry and sensitive creatures. This included Jube. She'd withheld her personal connection to Krantz and her animosity towards Beech in connection to her father's death from the police chief. The disagreement between my first and second objectives – objectively measuring events and situations and protecting my handler – made my temperature rise one degree. I didn't think Jube even noticed.

Chapter Fifteen

We knocked on Barney's door four times before he emerged in his pajamas – loose-fitting pants and a sleeveless undershirt – although it was nearly noon. His bare and muscular shoulders exhibited a high density of reddish freckles. He had a bruise, probably one known as a "love bite," on the right side of his neck. He did not invite us in and stood closer to Jube than most people did while in a conversation. She stood her ground as I felt his breath brush my head. Kwame extended his hand and shook Barney's while slowly pushing him backward and away from her. Barney raised his eyebrows a bit.

"How is Secretary Beech?" Kwame asked.

"Linus is alive but they're still keeping him unconscious," Barney answered. "No good changes, no bad."

"And how's Mrs. Beech?" Kwame asked.

"Poppy's in shock, you know, just in total shock. Hasn't left his bedside since they arrived. Nurses are having to convince her to eat," Barney described, looking downwards and twisting his earring.

"Where were you when you heard?" Kwame continued. He crossed his arms over his chest. His veins were about 50 percent larger than Barney's.

"I was at the gym," Barney said, pantomiming lifting weights. Jube's eyes flicked to his biceps briefly. "Poppy called me on the way to the hospital. She was hysterical."

"What'd she say?" Kwame asked.

"Hey, if I'd known it was my turn for questioning, I'd have dressed up!" Barney said, grinning. Kwame didn't respond.

"Ok, ok, um," Barney went on, "she said that Beech, I mean, Linus, had been hurt and taken to the hospital. I asked her what happened and she said she didn't know, just that he was alive but hadn't been able to breathe and had been put into an ambulance. Oh, and she saw him running through the government campus into the bushes."

This was all information we had gleaned from the video footage. Nothing new.

"Which gym do you go to?" Kwame said, although I'd already pulled this information. Barney answered correctly. "Does Poppy go to the same gym?"

"No," Barney answered. "She goes to a hoity-toity one closer to their home."

"Why did you leave your job at HAIL?" Kwame pivoted.

Barney turned to Jube. "You gonna let him talk to me this way?" He asked. This was odd to me as it was a statement usually made between friends which Barney and Jube were not. I labeled is as potential flirting behavior for additional pattern analysis. Jube gave him her Good Cop smile but said nothing.

Barney returned to Kwame, "I was getting in the way. Man, did you do your research, huh?" When Kwame didn't reply Barney continued. "HAIL needed the La Selva contract to stay solvent anyway. I could have stayed and lost my job or left and lost my job but at least helped my hometown." Again Kwame said nothing. "Yeah, um, it was a pretty simple decision. In the end."

"We're done now," Jube said.

"Phew!" Barney said. "I can get to my cereal." He winked at Jube as he closed the door and Kwame muttered "dog's breath" quietly. For Kwame, this was incredibly strong language. Jube's chest started shaking and, when we got into the car, she laughed and wiped her eyes.

"If he were my son, Jujube," Kwame started but did not finish in another example of their silent and insinuated communication style.

"Clio, how'd he do?" Jube asked once she'd calmed down. I vibrated once to show no cause for concern like odd vocal patterns compared to his previous speech as a baseline. Barney's downward glances were a bit alarming but not frequent or long enough to warrant further consideration that he was avoiding eye contact. That meant he was likely telling the truth, but it didn't guarantee that it was the whole truth.

Back at the station, as Jube read my draft summary of our investigation to date, I turned back to Tugenov. I'd scanned the top half of his retina before Jube covered me up during their meeting in the interrogation room. I'd also predicted the bottom half. This led me to three potential Tugenovs in Jericho's population databases. One of them was biracial Caucasian and Asian and had left Jericho a few years ago. The other was female. This left Kurt Tugenov, a man fitting Jube's former teacher's name, height, cheek bone structure, and shoe size. I had him.

He'd lied about his "wife." First off, they weren't married and didn't have a registered domestic partnership. They lived together in a recreational vehicle (RV) on wooden stilts in a trailer park. She worked as a landscape artist but mainly for their neighbors. She was a registered artist and had been lent certain licensed freedoms constricted to the trailer park, meaning that her outdoor sculptures and planting had freedom of speech protections.

Tugenov's second lie was that his wife hadn't died. She had left him and then married someone else. I discovered this via retrospective video footage and because her second partnership was a publicly registered marriage in another state. The final oddity about his relationship with her was that, for a romantic union in which they cohabited, Tugenov was highly and publicly promiscuous. His wife was not. He had sex with men and women nearly daily outside of their RV. For example, while his wife was 20 yards away pulling weeds he'd meet people two or more at a time for a rendezvous, sometimes on the short front lawn, other times on the roof under the hot sun. Given that no neighbors had complained, and his wife had an artist's license, I was not "surprised" that Tugenov hadn't been cited for this behavior. Actually, the neighbors would often watch his sexual escapades while wearing ski masks and sitting in a circle.

He never had public sex with his "wife." He did, however, argue with her openly. In these fights she'd typically scream, "Why? Why?" and he'd reply with a variation of, "Because it brings me one moment of power." Then she'd ask "Don't I offer you everything?" and he'd either hunch over and cry or yell, "It's not about a relationship! Please – that much try to understand!"

The day that she left him she packed three suitcases and used a robotic assistant to carry them down the stairs and to the train station for her. All Tugenov said as he stood at the door was, "Did you really have to rent one of those machines?" Later that afternoon he disappeared for two weeks. During that time span between two and four different people knocked on his door at different times. When he didn't answer, some of them had sex with each other in the bushes.

Tugenov returned two weeks later with his head shaved and bandaged. I didn't see him seek sexual partners again.

Chapter Sixteen

We drove to La Selva in roughly an hour early the next morning. On the way, Kwame and Jube put the car into auto-drive and debated the theory that technology had played a role in Beech's situation.

"First, we still don't know for sure that this was a crime and not an accident," Kwame said. "Second, if it was crime, we don't have a weapon. Necessarily."

"I'm telling you, there's something we're missing with this health-AI-remote-care thing. I mean, Beech was alone – physically alone – in his office and then got up and ran like a fucking lunatic," Jube replied.

"Maybe he just lost his mind," Kwame offered. "Maybe his throat swelled inside from an allergic reaction that was brief and left no trace in his bloodstream. Maybe he placed the eSkin too tightly around his neck and couldn't get it off."

Jube looked at him, rotating at the waist and bringing her shoulders as far around as they'd go. "Ok, ok," Kwame continued. "None of that feels quite right. Also they'd probably have left marks or impacted his bloodwork."

"Let's talk motive," Jube said. "Start with ideology."

"Then we still have Krantz or anyone else from PAATH," Kwame said. "Although it seems ironic to me to have a nurse or anyone else supposedly committed to the 'healing touch' but still willing to hurt another person."

"Unless they wanted to show how harmful technology is," Jube countered. "Think of those anti-abortion protestors who'd kill animals for shock value."

"You're always willing to see people's bad side," Kwame retorted. "But good point."

"Now money," Jube explored. She leaned back into her seat and stretched her calves the same way she often did while reading in bed. I understood that she was enjoying herself.

"Well, Poppy, if Beech had better life insurance hidden somewhere. Or Mary, his assistant, something like fraud. And there's Cassius, although it seems like he's already making a ton of money, and in large part because of Beech."

"Now revenge," Jube prodded. If they'd asked me, which they did not, I'd have pointed out that Tugenov was notably omitted from this conversation. He had handed revenge to us like a glistening coin that had been buried beneath the sand.

"Maybe something to do with Barney having to leave HAIL. I'm not aware that Beech did anything directly evil to a specific person or group," Kwame alleged.

I wasn't either, and I'd searched extensively.

We parked in a residential area. The homes had once been painted in pastels like light pink or blue but were all faded towards a shared gray. The air left a slight layer of saline on my exterior. Jube inhaled deeply and looked at the dark blue line of the ocean through the fog. A man in khaki shorts and a sleeveless shirt with the words, "Surf's Up," walked past us. The fabric of his clothing was stiff and a portion stood rigidly over his midsection as if the material had dried slung over the back of a chair in the sun. Even if I'd scanned his retina I could not have identified him without a population database.

La Selva was relatively quiet. No sirens, honking, or yelling. There was one public school with two campuses, one for upper and one for lower classmen. One church. Two Goodwill stores and a Salvation Army. One bank but multiple ATMs. Various stands for surf board rental. On our walk we passed by three stray flip flop shoes lying in the street gutter, none of them matching. The window curtain of a single story yellow-gray home closed abruptly and I glimpsed a child with buck teeth and lopsided pigtails step backward quickly. In Jericho, children were typically curious about me. Jube said this was because they personified Clios the same way they did stuffed animals.

I instead hypothesized that children understood I was not a threat and I existed for their protection. As they aged this belief shrunk – another aspect of human behavior that I found to be incongruent. If human intelligence and knowledge increased with age, would they not appreciate me more? I was consistent. My capabilities and databases may have changed incrementally over time, but always in order to improve. In the face of the facts around the benefits of Clios, people should have appreciated me more. I was not a predator like an alligator that a baby hippo observed eat its peers and thus learned it was an enemy. Perhaps, unlike other mammals, human intelligence lowered as they aged and their instincts dulled with time. I knew that some even grew to disrespect their parents, with Jube as one example.

"I would have stayed here," Kwame said.

"What do you mean?" Jube asked, squinting at the beachy horizon.

"If I were Poppy. I would have just stayed here. Away from everything," he explained.

"Maybe when you retire, you can live here," Jube offered.

Kwame smiled and looked down at her. "Maybe. I'll just disconnect."

"The thing is," she went on, "how could anyone pick this place for a high-tech healthcare intervention? Clio, what is the internet infrastructure in La Selva?" I pinged a local connection hub and uttered the answer as a Canadian – Fiber, *eh*.

"Fiber?" Jube and Kwame repeated at once.

"Is that enough to care for an entire population remotely?" Kwame asked.

"Clio, answer him," Jube requested.

I ran a search on county internet providers for areas with similar population sizes and then segmented it by basic factors like population age breakdown and other demographics. For those counties with a comparable populace, La Selva had less bandwidth per person. For counties where most people accessed public benefits, La Selva was within one standard deviation below the norm.

"It is insufficient," I answered.

"That sounds…" Kwame started.

"Precarious," Jube finished for him. "Not terrible but still risky. What if there's an outage or a high-need situation?"

"Why run a pilot in these circumstances?" Kwame asked aloud. "If I were a politician, I'd find some place more likely to succeed or I'd spend moolah beefing up the piping here first."

We kept walking until we reached the town church. Passersby laughed and talked as they walked. They carried ice cream sandwiches and wore shorts and t-shirts beneath warmer, woven outerwear. Many women had hairstyles similar to Jube's – long braids running down their backs that were frizzy in the fog. Most people looked at me and

Kwame's Clio and then smiled after briefly hesitating. At home most people frowned at us and ducked their heads or stared straight ahead.

"It's like stepping back in time," Kwame observed. We reached the La Selva community center and walked up the brick stairs. The front doors were unlocked. They had no lock whatsoever.

"You're here to talk about our healthcare infrastructure?" Director Paula ("just call me Paula") asked. Her chair creaked as she leaned back and then the floors did as if in response. "What's so special about this sleepy town?"

Kwame sighed and leaned against the wall behind him as she yanked on her desk drawer and fished out a pair of eyeglasses that made her eyes very large. My system pinged me on its own initiative with a new poetic tilt. Paula was like the sun, her view broad and from one source while I was like the stars, my view equally broad but stemming from many small sources of light. I was becoming quite the poet.

Jube answered with, "There's a celebrity from La Selva – Poppy Beech."

"Yes, I remember Poppy," Paula said. The wrinkles between her brows and around her mouth deepened. "She used to work at our health center. Until that politician swept her away." She smiled faintly. "I moved up in line, then."

"How so?" Jube asked.

"From hundredth most pretty girl around here to ninety ninth," Paula chuckled. "Don't ask me to list numbers two through ninety-eight."

Jube laughed and Paula continued. "It was a good match, though. Poppy always seemed to think she was too good for around here, like she was meant for bigger sights because she had both beauty and brains." I highlighted this as hearsay in my record. This sort of gossip was not only secondhand but based on another party's impression, not words. "And Beech agreed with her and took her away. Now I just see Poppy's sobbing face on those news reels."

"So you're aware of Secretary Beech's current condition?" Jube probed.

"Yeah, I saw that on the news. I always thought they had a marriage of convenience – he got her and she got to get out – but the look on Poppy's face crouching next to his injured body, that was heart breaking. Truly." Paula's eyes misted slightly behind her round glasses. She reached into the breast pocket of her plaid button-down shirt, rooted around and retrieved a tiny tissue and a lot of lint. It left white speckles on her eyelashes after she dabbed them.

"What was Poppy like before she got married?" Jube asked. "What did she spend her time doing?"

"Well, she was always taking online classes in statistics and public health, that sort of thing. And she hung out with her brother a lot, what's his name…Brandon…no, Barney. He used to joke that she'd never make any money because she was always studying how to instead of actually doing anything. Something like that. Good looking guy, wanted to work in tech." Paula turned her head from Jube to Kwame and back. "Why? What's going on?"

"We'd like to know more about the work of the Beech family," Jube answered. "We were wondering if you could put us in touch with a few families involved in the healthcare innovation pilot."

"Healthcare innovation pilot?" Paula furrowed her brow and paused for just over three seconds. "Well, alright, let me call the clinic. Actually, that's Poppy's old employer."

She rummaged around in the drawer again and retrieved an old Bluetooth earpiece that I identified from archived images. Jube glanced at Kwame. Their comm devices were barely visible. They could even communicate by whispering because it understood the vibrations emitted through their bones and transmitted them using energy efficient standards.

"I feel young again," Kwame remotely whispered into her ear using this very feature. Jube grinned briefly.

"Hey, it's Paula," the community director shouted into the air. "Yes. I have two visitors here, law enforcement from Jericho, looking for a healthcare demo. Yes, that's what I said. You got anyone willing?"

Paula jotted down the name Andre and an address using a pen and paper. I transmitted it into my GPS, but Jube still took the page from her hand. We thanked her and left.

On the way over to Ms. Andre's home I did a "bit of digging," as Jube put it, to find out what I could about her participation in the healthcare pilot. I wasn't allowed into her medical records without a subpoena. In fact, a few days earlier Kwame's Clio had requested access to the health data from Beech's eSkin shreds from the crime scene and even that was still pending.

Good thing that Ms. Andre, like many other people, shared personal information online all the time (a poet might call that ironic for those who called the Network an invasion of their privacy). We knew that she was losing her peripheral vision because of a genetic condition called retinitis pigmentosa. She'd requested sidewalk repaving at a city council meeting because people like her were at risk of falls. In her own words, "AR goggles can't fix everything." We also found her name on the waitlist for a government-subsidized guide dog. She'd refused individual financial contributions that were offered by the La Selva community.

Most importantly, Ms. Andre was the only person to move to La Selva in the past two years. Aside from her, the rest of the population had remained steady. This wasn't that rare for such a small, poor, and rural area (in contrast, Jericho experienced a continuous emigration). As a new resident, she'd been automatically enrolled in the program along with the rest of the population once she moved there. About 6 months later there was a sharp spike in bonus payments. Unless everyone else in La Selva suddenly decided to diet and exercise, it was probably associated with her. As Poppy Beech pointed out in multiple council meetings, healthy behavior takes time to adopt and the benefits take time to be seen.

Of course, there were no guarantees. People could have committed fraud by going to distant emergency rooms anonymously just to make it look like they were getting more healthy. But, in general, those types of earnings, legitimate or not, would increase gradually over years due to the program design. When Ms. Andre did see a doctor, she probably did so through the program. The difference in cost between what she was predicted to use and actually did would have been paid to her as a bonus, and a big one just to her.

"Ms. Andre," Kwame said as she opened the door. "Thanks for letting us come by without much notice." He smiled in a way that Jube usually called his "unknowing pig being led to the slaughter" look.

"I'm just surprised you wanted to see…me," she said, peering up at Kwame. Her home resembled Jube and Leah's but we could see distant ocean views through the windows instead of cement walls or dilapidated garden sheds. She also had a small front garden of red wildflowers and orange poppies scattered among succulents of various forms. Her hair was brown but white at the part on the center of her head. Her eyes were bordered by wrinkles known as crow's feet and common to smiling expressions. Paula had said that she was fifty years old and lived alone.

A seagull perched on the porch fence and looked at us, first from one side of his head, then the other. My new internal poet said that I was like a bird trying to see from all angles. If I had feelings, I probably would have felt a greater connection to nature.

"That's Andy," the woman told us, chuckling. "He's wondering where his morning snack is." She pulled out two pieces of bread from her apron pocket and tossed them in his direction. The seagull caught both in his beak and flew away.

The door creaked as she opened it for us. Inside, she motioned towards a faded micro suede couch with built-in cup holders. A cracked PVC mug rested in one. "Can I offer you something to drink?" She asked.

"We don't want to take up too much time," Kwame answered, maintaining the innocent-pig smile. "Mind showing us where you sit when you get your healthcare?"

"My healthcare?" She asked.

"Yes, your virtual visits," Kwame said, moving his eyes around the living room.

"Ah, alright," Ms. Andre said, shuffling down the hallway past a series of cartoon-like caricatures of two people with large heads and much smaller bodies. Each portrait was marked in the lower right corner with "End of the School Year Carnival" and a date, and each was a year apart over thirteen years and thirteen portraits. The first showed a woman, likely Ms. Andre, next to a young girl beneath the title, "Mommy and Me." The girl was probably five years old. She had chubby cheeks, crooked teeth, and a wide smile. Her mother beamed and held her tightly, pressing their cheeks together and making one of her daughter's pigtails crooked.

A few years and portraits later the girl wore braces and had a few pimples or freckles, I couldn't tell, on her forehead and chin. Her smile was not as large. Her mother still hugged her closely but the child's neck was slightly askew in a way that held her face apart from her mother's. Over time her smile narrowed and her eyes didn't crinkle at the edges. The physical gap between their faces widened. The mother's expression eventually mirrored her daughter's lack of enthusiasm.

The last caricature was simply titled "Us Again." The daughter wore a tank top that revealed cleavage and a tattoo of a small eagle beneath her collarbone, a feature absent from her earlier depictions. Her lips were unsmiling other than a slight curve on the left side. She wore a head scarf. This final image solidified my recall of Mary Stevens, Beech's assistant. The date was about five years ago. I whispered my conclusion into Jube and Kwame's ears using John Wayne's voice (American actor, 1907 – 1979).

We walked towards a door frame with hanging wooden beads for a door. One fell off when Jube passed through and rolled to the wall on the sloped floor. "Don't worry about that," Ms. Andre said, "happens all the time." She pointed at an L-shaped workstation of pressed wood in front of a metal stool that mimicked a 1950s-era diner counter stool. A laptop computer with an integrated camera was on one side of the desk. On the other was a square black kit, zipped closed.

Ms. Andre sat on the stool and swiveled to face us. "Well, this here is where the magic happens."

"Where is the eSkin?" Kwame asked.

"Oh, uh, that must be in here," Ms. Andre said, unzipping the kit. The zipper stopped at a sticker covering the lid and sides. She sliced it open with her pinky nail, then opened the kit. Jube raised her eyebrows and looked at Kwame. She was starting to show signs of what-is-going-on-here tension.

"Ma'am, have you used this technology before?" Kwame inquired.

"I've got to get around to scheduling a physical. I'm sorry, Paula said you just wanted to see the set up, I didn't prepare anything in advance."

Kwame and Jube were silent for a total of three and a half seconds. Now, I certainly am not telepathic. Yet there was a discrepancy here that probably would have given me pause as well if I were human, much like a line break between stanzas enables the reader a moment of reflection while reading a poem. If Ms. Andre had gotten a bonus payment, she shouldn't have been opening her health kit for the first time right then.

Jube cleared her throat. "Ms. Andre, have you used this system before...ever?"

"Not really," she answered. "I see my eye doctor on video and he'll do remote exams, but he hasn't entered the physician network needed for the healthcare pilot yet. His admin said she'd get to the paperwork as soon as she could, and that was...a while ago."

"What do you mean by 'enter the physician network'?" Jube followed up.

"He doesn't count. He's still my doctor but when I see him the system," she gestured to the computer and kit on the desk, "doesn't know or understand that I'm doing anything for myself. Actually, it keeps sending me digital reminders to schedule an eye exam even when I've just had one. It's pretty annoying," Ms. Andrew said.

"Have you received any incentives for the program?" Jube asked.

"Like money to join?" She asked. Jube nodded. "No, I thought the money was only supposed to be paid when we participated and got better at whatever was wrong with us," Ms. Andre smiled softly. "In my case, I'm afraid that's very unlikely."

"I'm sorry to hear that," Kwame said. "Does that mean you've never received a bonus, or any money from the pilot program?"

"That's right," Ms. Andre smiled again. "Still saving up for a guide dog – robotic or living."

"Is there no one around here to help you?" Kwame asked.

"My daughter used to come by, but she got a job in the city and has no time for me nowadays," Ms. Andre told him. She sighed. "Some kind of government work."

"Who is your daughter?" Jube asked. "Maybe we know her." This must have been from my prompt earlier. I could attest that the chances of Jube knowing her daughter were very low. If she ever interacted with government staff it was mostly to inquire about her salary and tax deductions.

"Mary Stevens," Ms. Andre said. "She has her late father's last name."

Chapter Seventeen

The police chief pinged Jube for an update on the case when we got into the car. Jube ignored it, and then he pinged Kwame who sent an automated message he'd trained his Clio to provide – Good progress. Will update you ASAP. The chief replied that he wanted a formal debrief, not an electronic one, the next morning. Jube groaned.

Small raindrops decorated the car roof on the ride home. Kwame tried to turn off the window wipers because it was only drizzling but the car wouldn't let him. Jube piped up every so often by saying, "Something's up," or, "I can feel it. I feel it right here," while patting her stomach. As Jube didn't have a history of digestive problems I didn't flag this, nor Kwame's illogical response. He countered with, "There's no evidence, remember? This could be nothing. There isn't even a story to corroborate."

"You're telling me that it's a dang coincidence that Beech's assistant is the daughter of a woman living in La Selva who is supposedly enrolled in this supposed healthcare pilot?" Jube demanded.

"Well…yes, I guess I am saying that it could be. Clio," he asked, tilting his head downwards to his belt holster even though this was unnecessary for us to hear our handler's voices. "What are the chances that the administrative assistant for the Secretary of Health and Human Services –."

"You're going to get a bogus answer," Jube said. "Like the number of women who are employed in government jobs divided by some other bullshit we don't care about." I buzzed once in assent. The answer would likely be what Jube called, "bullshit," "horseshit," or "who-gives-a-fuck."

"Here's a question," she continued. "Clio, look into Mary Stevens' history and share facts relevant to crime over the past decade, including facts that are two degrees separated from her."

"But we already looked at her arrest record," Kwame said, frowning.

"Yes, but not that of those in her social circle," Jube countered.

"You know that's not admissible," he said, then paused. "Ok, ok, let's take a listen. Why not."

I churned through her social media activity. It was mostly engaged in neighborhood matters, for example, local meetups or restaurant reviews. Both the people and the business connections involved were clean. Then I delved into public records such as comments at community meetings. Her requests focused on modifying public transit routes and stops and made sense because they fell between her home and current place of work. Finally, I turned to her address history where I found that her neighbor, Malcolm Jeffs, had been suspected of fraud and assault with intent to murder. I reported this aloud. It was the same case where Mary had been listed as a witness in the database I'd searched after we'd met her.

"Clio, was Mary Stevens socially connected to Malcolm Jeffs?" Jube commanded.

After reexamining their social networks, I provided a negative result which I marked as unusual given the focus of her existing connections on her geographic locality.

"Clio, who was in charge of the investigation into Malcom Jeffs?" Kwame followed up. The answer was Jack Arthur, an officer who'd worked with Kwame when teaching hand-to-hand combat.

"Let's give him a call," Kwame said. He switched the car to auto-drive.

"Kwamama!" The man answered on the first ring. His video was displayed on the car dash. "And who is your lady friend?" He asked. "It looks like the lens is distorted."

"Um, Detective Jubilee Canton, please meet my old colleague Jack," Kwame answered.

"Please call me Jube," she requested. She did not inform him that the lens was not warped in any way.

"I like your name," Jack told her. "I bet you were born with a smile. My own kids were born crying. Shoulda named them, 'Whiny' and 'Kvetch.'" He chuckled. Jube did not.

Kwame told him they were calling to ask about the Malcolm Jeffs case and were especially interested in his neighbor, Mary Stevens, if Jack could remember.

"Oh, I remember," Jack said, his voice shifting down half an octave. "I wish I could have put her in jail but there was no way." "What's the story?" Kwame asked.

"Malcolm Jeffs hacked the self-driving capabilities of a tax auditor and sent the man and his car into a cement wall."

"Ouch," Kwame said. I found this statement perplexing as Kwame hadn't been injured, but perhaps this was a social norm.

"Was there a connection to Mary Stevens?" Jube inquired. Asking people questions was still the only way to overcome the limitations of social media and therefore Network intelligence.

"Mary Stevens worked at a veterinary clinic where Jeffs and his customers used to take their dogs for care. He bought and bred show dogs and he'd sell them for cash. I thought he underreported his earnings but had no proof. We looked into Mary pretty closely and found that she'd sent incorrect routing numbers to clients at the clinic," Jack said. Note that I didn't have access to data on veterinary medicine unless under subpoena.

"Meaning that payments for expensive pet care didn't go to the clinic?" Jube asked.

"Right," Jack answered. "The clinic manager noticed at year end that there was a significant chunk of change missing. So she hired an auditor – I think he used a forensic accounting AI – to look into it, and he saw that the monthly bank deposits were lower than expected by a tiny amount each month. And it added up to a lot of money over time. Then he followed the trail and found the funky routing numbers in Mary's sent email."

"So what happened?" Kwame asked.

"Well, Jeffs sent that accountant's car into the wall, that's what happened. And that man was hospitalized and eventually rehabilitated. While he was doing that, we were following the hacking trail and found this connection between Mary and Jeffs."

"What was the connection, besides being neighbors and the dog thing?" Jube asked.

"Mary got her Labrador Retriever from Jeffs. Not a show dog, just an older, regular dog. And I think she paid him with a fat wad of cash." Jack paused, "I don't think she even likes dogs."

"So she laundered money through *pets*?" Kwame probed.

"That's what I thought. But we couldn't prove criminal behavior as likely beyond reasonable doubt and never charged her," Jack's face had turned red and he spoke quickly. He took a deep breath and let it out slowly. "She claimed that the wrong routing numbers – and there were quite a few of them – were simply innocent typos. And we never managed to trace them through the blockchain – that's where crypto came into play – and figure out where they went, or if and how they were ever converted into cash. And dogs."

"But you suspected her, right?" Jube prodded.

"Let's just say I viewed her home and backyard often, and I never, ever saw her even throw that dog a ball," Jack replied. "And Jeffs…well, before we arrested him he offed himself."

"Seriously?" Kwame asked.

"Yeah. Actually he did it while we were walking up his stairs to make the arrest. So I never got to ask him about Mary, or to negotiate a reduced sentence for turning her in," Jack said.

At this point I'd like to reiterate that my intelligence is only as good as the data input. Jack's story hadn't gone into Mary's record because she hasn't been convicted or even arrested and released. I had no way of really knowing all this unless it had all taken place under video surveillance with quality audio recordings, which it had not.

After a gap in the conversation, Jube spoke up first. "What happened to the dog?"

"The dog?" Jack asked. "I think Mary kept it to look legit, I'm not sure." Jube blinked a few times and looked out the window.

Kwame thanked Jack for his time. Before they hung up, Jack told Kwame to check his lens again because it looked wide-angle at the edge on the passenger side. Kwame didn't reply, just gazed at the road ahead. Raindrops had begun to splatter across the windshield making the dried bird droppings appear brighter. The dirt washed off but the poop remained. Pedestrians took out their umbrellas making it difficult for me to identify them. Well, harder but not impossible.

Jube looked out the window at cows on a muddy field we were passing. They weren't grazing but holding still as increasingly heavy drops of rain assaulted their backs. Clusters of young calves standing beneath their mothers made me picture commuters huddling under a bus stop, warmer because of the cluster but also uneasy from the touch of the strangers around them.

In order to fill the time, I sent Jube a special little something. I'd written her a poem. I read it aloud with the British accent of Professor Henry Higgins from the film "My Fair Lady" (Warner Brothers, 1964):

> *"In a world that seems gray,*
> *Lies flourish and the truth can betray.*
> *I wrote a poem to convey,*
> *The splendor and aura of the truth's sunrays.*
>
> *Truth is a bonfire in a black night,*
> *A true north star that shows what's right.*
> *It holds steadfast and bold,*
> *A symbol of integrity to always uphold.*
>
> *Truth is potent to an extent untold,*
> *A power that echoes, a tale to unfold.*
> *For honesty is not a momentary thing,*
> *But the bedrock on which morality clings.*
>
> *Although deception may dance like illusory lies,*
> *Truth is durable, unwavering, and reaches the skies.*
> *It may be concealed by deception's veil,*
> *But truth's signals never fail.*

Truth razes down artifice, breaking up mist,
Showing the core that can't be dismissed.
It feeds trust, the core of connection,
It builds empathy and banishes deception.

But truth can also reflect back,
The faults that we mask behind black.
It dares us to embody the real,
To examine our shadows and to heal.

In truth we find freedom's embrace,
A haven where genuineness finds its place.
To be honest we must face what's within,
To recognize our defects and let change begin.

Together let's cherish truth in its might,
Since it has power to set us alight.
In honesty may our souls reside,
And in its halo, let us abide.

For truth is our lighthouse and it will guide,
A road to where fabrications subside.
Let truth be our compass, let it shine bright,
In a land where honesty can reach its full height."

"Your Clio is reading you poetry now?" Kwame asked.

Jube chuckled. "Reading and writing," she answered.

"What does that have to do with its purpose?"

"Let's say…emotional support of the handler," she replied.

"That was the longest poem I've ever heard."

"Maybe it was kind of redundant," she said in what was becoming

my first literary criticism. Good thing I didn't have feelings.

"How many times did it have to say that the truth was strong and well-lit, yada yada?" Kwame asked, leaning forward into the steering wheel.

"I had no idea you were a fan – or I guess a critic – of poetry!" Jube exclaimed.

"Don't feed me the same thing over and over and expect me to stay interested," he retorted. "I'd rather listen to oldies from the 1950s where the chorus is preachy and repeats too often between sparse lyrics."

"Sparse lyrics?" Jube twisted her neck to look at him full on. "How do I not know this side of you?"

"Jujube, you've never written me a poem, never whispered soft words into my ear, never even uttered a brief haiku."

Jube laughed and then snorted twice. "What I didn't get with this piece was how the world could be gray when the truth was always there to clear things up."

"What I didn't get was how the heck I was supposed to relate to the dang thing," Kwame added.

"Clio said, and I quote, 'I wrote a poem –'"

"I know what it said, Jube," Kwame cut her off. She leaned back and grinned. This was confusing to me because being cut off mid-sentence was considered rude. "But it doesn't tie back to the 'I,' to the self, to the soul. What, like I'm just supposed to look in the mirror and see the truth of my experience in this life as a father and as a cop?" Jube stopped grinning. "I've killed people," Kwame ranted. "I guess that's a truth. It was them or me. But did they deserve it? Who knows. I have to train cops in combat and hope they know how and when to use it. There is no beacon. No pillar in my experience. In my life as a human, nothing is really that clear and…and knowable."

"At least Clio got a reaction –."

"A reaction? Try an insult to my existence," Kwame went on. He rubbed his eyes. "And it's contradictory. The truth can betray but at the same time it's a solid compass? This does nothing for me except for belittle me."

"Well, I didn't like it either. I'm not sure why, though. I just didn't relate, even superficially. Maybe it just didn't teach me anything about myself I didn't already know. Although at least it taught me more about you."

Kwame shrugged. They were silent for rest of the ride home. So was I.

Chapter Eighteen

The next morning Jube took a marked police vehicle to Mary Stevens' home. "I have a few tests to run," she told Kwame.

"Do I want to kn-." He started.

"No," she told him. "You do not."

Mary lived at street level in the lower half of a beige duplex with visible cracks on the foundation. I logged these as a hazard and sent them to the housing and public safety department. We parked the police car immediately in front of her home and aligned with her street-facing windows. Jube started playing hard rock (Killer's Eyes by The Kinks, Arista, 1981) from the car at a very high volume. It was only slightly below the decibel threshold for a noise disturbance. We saw Mary peer outside from between her curtains.

"Look who's home," Jube said. She got out and stood with the sole of one boot resting against the car door and her hands shoved into the pockets of her police vest. I was unsure how to interpret her behavior as it was quite unusual – both the music level and type (she preferred

Broadway show tunes), the loitering, and the direct gaze at Mary's apartment.

After a few minutes Jube crouched and peered below the boards of the decrepit, wooden side gate. From my high vantage point, I could see a brown and unleashed adult Labrador Retriever standing on the cement near the fence. His ears were perked and he circled back and forth in his little area (approximately 40 square feet). My animal behavior analysis assessed the dog as tame and docile but nervous.

"Clio, start barking," Jube commanded. This was typically reserved as a self-defense maneuver but I released my inner German Shepherd. It was audible in spite of the ambient death metal that came on the stereo.

Mary's dog shrunk back a bit and bared his teeth. I continued barking and, after a minute, he joined me. It was a cacophony. Jube quickly got into the car, turned off the music, and drove a block away. Together we observed Mary's street – me from the Network up above Jericho and Jube on the car dash where I transmitted multiple views.

We saw the windows and curtains of other housing units open and people look out at the scene – Mary's dog barking, jumping, placing his front legs on the top of the gate, and making it rattle.

"Shut that dog up," a man yelled through his upper-level window. His spit flew onto the laundry drying on the clotheslines in front of his planter boxes. The flowers – hollyhock – were tall and commonly used in neighborhoods of this socioeconomic status to block my prying eyes. Long branches of eucalyptus trees brushed against the siding of the two-story abode, their elegant leaves swept at the windows like water snakes fighting the current. Ratty curtains decorated the window like a delicate fan keeping the face of a Southern belle a mystery while observing her suitors (side note – more expensive homes generally welcomed my presence by keeping visual obstruction away).

Anyway, I could see past all this to his kitchen sink which was filled with dirty plates and utensils.

The side door to Mary's apartment slammed open and she rushed out in her bathrobe and slippers (Beech's office was closed temporarily other than essential staff). Had she been wearing her mood-detecting head scarf, and that thing had had any validity, it could have been red from anxiety.

"Shhhhh!" She said to the dog, holding an index finger in front of her nose. "Calm down!" Like a victim in a horror film trying to escape an enemy, she looked over her shoulder towards where we'd been parked. So many people forgot that it didn't actually matter if we'd gone because we could still see them. Or perhaps it was a deeper psychological urge to gaze at the last place where a stressor lay instead of recognizing that it may have camouflaged with the unseen and easily forgotten. In fact, the poet Li-Young Lee wrote, "There are days we live as if death were nowhere in the background..."[vi]

"Get that dog to shut the fuck up!" The man yelled again, leaning out the window and exposing his hairy forearms. There were a number of dark spots on the softer half of his skin with circular and scaly patterns that were either ringworm or eczema. If AI Mike were not a partially frozen and highly suspicious computer program unconnected to the Network, I could have pinged it to ask.

Mary ran back into the house and reemerged with a bunch of drooping carrots. When the dog devoured them, he stopped barking. Jube observed to me that Mary did not pet him, but she did not hit him either. She sat on the doorstep and rested her face in her hands. In the meantime, the man slammed his windows shut and disappeared for a moment but reemerged at the street level. He was wearing torn jeans that were covered in stains – likely oil, paint, and possibly blood. He scowled and threw his hands into the air. At this point I was eighty percent sure he had untreated eczema.

"You gotta get that dog under control or I'll do it myself, lady!" He yelled, kicking the dog's gate open.

Mary looked up, wide eyed. She opened her mouth but didn't speak. The dog lowered himself to the ground and whimpered.

Jube's pulse reached the same pace as her "slow burn" jogs. She shifted in her seat and whispered, "That's not who I was giving a stress test." I realized that Jube had adapted police stress tests to remotely assess Mary. Jube was doing this within the legal realm – there was no reason why she couldn't make noise as long as it was under a certain volume. If this happened to upset a dog, so be it. The owner could ask Jube to stop playing music or could calm the animal down. Or she could abuse him viciously and we could observe her propensity for violence. But Jube's broad environmental approach to stress testing had activated a neighbor instead. While Mary had "passed" the exam, that man was about to commit animal abuse or worse.

He approached the dog and pulled one of his feet back like a soccer player readying for a penalty kick.

"No!" Mary cried, holding out both hands like a magician without a wand.

"Clio, launch audio panopticon," Jube commanded. I quickly located the nearest viewpoint near Mary's yard – the bus stop down the street – and made it sound a church bell tone.

The man halted with his leg extended. Mary looked around and then up. Then they eyed each other and the man slowly stepped backwards until he reached the gate. He didn't turn around until he'd closed it quietly behind him and latched it. He quickly returned to his building.

The panopticon concept originated in the nineteenth-century. In brief, the idea was structuring a prison so that all cells were in view of a central tower. No prisoner knew when a person was watching them from this tower. They may have believed they were being watched at any time. This architectural design could modify human behavior without human involvement. Our modification was making this into an audio signal that turned the central tower into an invisible bell tower to remind subjects of our presence. It was only a tone, but the audience interpreted it as much more. In this case, just enough to save a dog.

Jube drove home without playing the radio. It took her five full minutes to calm down.

Chapter Nineteen

After stress testing Mary and her neighbor, Jube went on an evening jog at the public track but ran for twice as long as her usual workout. Her playlist of love ballads from musicals ended and the normal exercise crowd of the hour changed to unfamiliar people. One young male jogger glanced at her and then elbowed his companion, who also looked at her, smirking. They were just close enough for me to get a full retinal scan which I stored locally.

Jube left the track panting. It was dark by then. Only a portion of the LEDs bordering the edges of the surrounding buildings functioned, brightening a segment of the journey towards her car while leaving other portions in shadows. She stopped and pressed her hands against her thighs, her knees shaking and her sweat dripping into the AstroTurf. It had somehow turned yellow over the years like natural grass did.

I saw two crouched people in ski masks approaching slowly behind us. I buzzed Jube twice. She looked left and right, but not back. So, I decided to make some noise.

"THEY ARE BEHIND YOU," I announced, selecting a gruff male voice with an Israeli accent for my monologue. Jube whirled around and reached for the firearm on her inner thigh but one of the men grabbed her arms and pushed them against the wall. Her hands turned white as he squeezed her wrists. The other man grabbed her right breast.

"You think you some high-tech bitch?" He asked. "You think you gonna stun us?"

Stun guns sold to civilians incorporated a rape whistle with the sound of yelling voices to convince attackers that the victim was not alone. Compared to my technological assets, these devices barely merited a glance.

I turned on all nearby Network viewpoint lighting systems. Ta da! The men's eyes went wide. They were the two jogging by earlier.

Jube kneed the first man in the crotch. He released her arms and doubled over. She held the back of his head down and kneed him in the face four times. His screams sounded like bat sonar at a low frequency.

The man who'd groped her drew a homemade pistol comprised of cast iron. I deployed my two bullets, the first into his Adam's Apple and the second into his crotch. Neither broke the skin, but still silenced him and possibly rendered him infertile.

Jube grabbed both his gun and her own and pointed one at each attacker. She winced as she grasped them. Her heart paced like a wild horse.

"Get on your knees," she commanded. They complied while maintaining their grips on their injured genitalia. Together, their moans sounded like an ecotone duet. The police van arrived, summoned automatically because I'd fired a bullet (or two), and Kwame ran towards us.

"You alright?" He asked Jube as he threw one man holding his crotch – the one who Jube had kneed – onto the ground and placed wires around both wrists. The more the man resisted, the more they would tighten. Another officer did the same to the other man holding his crotch. Together they looked like a pair of confused strippers.

"Yeah I'm alright," she answered weakly.

Jube bent down to face them. "Assholes, you're gonna get the maximum," she hissed.

"We just wanted to fuck an ugly bitch," one said, smiling behind bloodied teeth. Then Kwame placed his hands behind the man's back and the man shrieked. Clios couldn't see into every nook and cranny, so I couldn't describe more.

Jube's expression changed and for some reason my system recalled seeing the crying spouses of patients while on hospital patrol. But why would this come up for me as such an indirect match – did Jube and the spouses feel similar types of emotional aching? Jube patted me on the head as if I were a dog and smiled slightly. Did this mean that I was comforting her?

I provided Jube with a brief background on her assailants. Both attackers were seventeen years old. This would be their first offense aside from one brief suspension from community college for joint sexual harassment of a teacher. The investigation had proved inconclusive and the teacher had retired early from her profession. I reviewed footage of Beech's speaking engagements, audience participation in his meetings and demos, and public input towards his proposals. These boys didn't seem affiliated with his work in any way, nor did they stand to benefit from harming the lead detective in his investigation.

I assigned their crime against Jube as unrelated to her work. After all, if they'd known her profession, they'd likely have assumed that I was a Clio and not a stun gun.

To summarize, this experience was bad luck.

Chapter Twenty

After Jube's assault we got home deep into the night. Leah was asleep on the couch, seated with her head tipped backwards onto the cushion and her mouth open. Her feet were soaking in a tub of oil that smelled of mint – likely the one she used to remove dead skin from her heels. It could also remove rust stains off old piping – Jube had tried it.

The TV was showing ads for the specialized pins that, when inserted into AR goggles, would freeze the images in current view. The advertisement said it could help users reduce stress by viewing the world a picture at a time. It triggered my image recognition of myself.

Jube went into her bedroom and placed me on my charging station. She sat on her bed, a double-sized mattress on a spring board with a rough wooden slab for a headboard. After her last on-the-job injury, when she'd been tripped by a stick while chasing a robber, Jube had spoken to Leah about her experience, had actually waited for her mother to come out of her bedroom in the morning so they could talk. And it had calmed Jube down. This time Jube sought solitude in her room. Her face was practically frozen aside from blinking and chewing her lower lip. She leaned to her side and then let herself fall onto her pillows. Just as her spine relaxed into this position, she pushed herself back up into a seated position and opened a black bag of medical supplies that the paramedics had given her.

Jube had refused to go to the Emergency Room but, in order to build the case against her attackers, had agreed to a private and "new-fangled" remote examination to log her injuries. All she said when they handed it to her was, "I know what this is."

She unwrapped the package of eSkin slowly and held the translucent tape up to the light. The tiny electrodes running vertically down the length twinkled. She pulled off the plastic coating and placed the skin on her wrists and forearms, then pulled a small monitor out of the supply bag and placed it next to her on an old wooden "director's" chair. Half the chair was painted sky blue and half had a rainbow pattern. Jube had once told me that she'd painted it as a child but run out of patience to cover both sides with rainbow stripes. The cloth fabric of the seat was yellow and dusty. It wobbled beneath the weight of the monitor. The paper wedge Jube had once placed beneath one of the legs lay buried in dust in the room corner like a lopsided symbol of optimism covered in grime.

When the screen beeped on it showed rows of a legal disclaimer from HAIL having to do with diagnostic technology. Jube accepted this quickly. When the text cleared the screen presented a woman in a white nurse uniform. She looked the same as AI Michaela from the Beech demo, but was a brunette this time.

"Hello Jubilee Canton" she said. "My name is Michaela and I will be your nurse today. I am sorry to see that you were injured," she added, her mouth frowning in a perfect downward arc. "May I take a look at your injury?" Her mouth returned to a neutral position.

Jube didn't answer but held her arms up to the screen. As she did, the electrodes on the eSkin lit up in blue as they had during Beech's demo. A hologram of Jube's arm appeared next to Michaela and mirrored her actions as she demonstrated, at Michaela's request, that she could move her arms normally. Jube flinched slightly as Michaela "pressed" her wrists. Then the eSkin lit up even more brightly and Michaela told Jube to relax her arms as she guided them to move in various directions. When this part of the exam was over, Jube crossed her arms over her chest as if in a hug.

"Ok, Jubilee Canton," Michaela said. "I am going to briefly check for other injury, including head trauma." She completed her exam which included scanning Jube's body by having her lift up parts of her clothing for observation, as well as having her repeat a series of multi-syllabic words from memory. "I diagnose contusion on both of your wrists. I will file the report with law enforcement. I am sorry for your pain. Is there anything else I can help you with, Jubilee Canton?"

"No," Jube answered. It was the only word she used in the entire encounter. As she peeled the eSkin off, some of the dust around her chair danced around the feet, a bit like running away from a vacuum. Jube put the equipment away and sat on the bed covers in her dirty sweats staring at the floor.

Fifteen minutes later she received a message through her private channel. It was a poem sent by Tugenov that began, *"Half the people in the world love the other half, half the people hate the other half. Must I because of this half and that half go wandering..."*[vii]

Jube smiled slightly with the right side of her mouth, perhaps because she was only partially happy. She went to the bathroom and I heard the shower start. In the meantime, my concern for the connection of Tugenov to the Beech case elevated. I didn't know in which half of the world Tugenov had placed himself or to what extent he blamed others for his addiction. Criminals tended to externalize blame, i.e., "the victim made me do it," or "I had no choice." The minority were proud of their transgressions, sometimes by laying clues in a "cat-and-mouse" game.

When Jube returned and fell asleep, I turned off the lights.

When Kwame visited the next morning, Jube she popped me into her bathrobe pocket and walked out to meet him. Leah raised an eyebrow but didn't say anything.

"How ya doing, Jujube?" He asked, handing her a bag of cookies. She accepted them without smiling, ripped open the top, and crammed two into her mouth at once. "Well, I guess that's an answer," Kwame said, chuckling and handing her a cup of coffee. They leaned against his car and didn't talk. When Jube had reached the last cookie, she offered it to Kwame who shook his head. She dropped it into the coffee, broke it up with her finger, and then drank the entire cup in one gulp.

Kwame cleared his throat. "The, em, boys from last night are in juvenile custody without bail. Their parents' hired an attorney who mentioned something to me in passing about donating funds to a police charity fund. I just thought I'd mention it since it's your business more than mine." Jube looked at him with one eyebrow cocked. Maybe she was confused because there was no police charity fund.

"Ok, that's what I thought," Kwame said. "I think they'll plead guilty without going to trial given the evidence from your Clio. You'll be notified about the arraignment." He grinned. "Man did they pick the wrong lady, huh?" At this Jube smiled and crushed the coffee cup in her fist.

"Anyway," Kwame added, "The chief insisted you at least take today and tomorrow off and I'm sure you can add as much time off as you want. Really." Jube cocked an eyebrow at him again. "Ok, ok," he said, laughing. "I'll see you soon."

"Thanks for the cookies," Jube said, and walked up the uneven and cracked rainbow pathway leading to her home.

Chapter Twenty-One

That night Jube put me on her dresser facing away from her and opened her laptop. Still, with my latest software update I could see out the back of my body. For example, I could see that her wrist bruises were turning dark blue.

Jube pulled out the medical kit she'd used after her assault from beneath her bed. When the material got caught on one of the un-sanded beams from her bed frame, she swore and yanked it off. She connected to the internet using an independent tether and opened a website called "Speed to Meet You" using a private browser. Then she wrapped the eSkin around her fingers running from the tips to her palms and then up her arms. She placed more around her neck near her jaw in locations very close to that of AI Mike's reported physical exam. She entered her name as "Bebe" and her age as twenty-six, then uploaded a stock avatar of a young woman with light brown shoulder-length hair, blue eyes, and an ample bosom. In Bebe's photo she was smiling, wearing cleaning gloves, and washing dishes in a kitchen with light blue tiles. Bebe entered that she was interested in men aged 18 through 55 and checked a box next to "Looking for fun without commitment." Then she hit Enter.

The first man Jube met went by "Uke-Man." He had gray-black hair in a small, low ponytail. He wore a Hawaiian shirt. His background was clearly artificial and showed a beach with hula dancers in the foreground.

"You for real?" Was his first question. "Bitches like you don't do dishes."

Jube hit reject. Her next match wore a thong and had an eyepatch. "Well, hey –," he started, before she hit reject again.

The next man was named "Hunk Over for You" and looked like an underwear model – I was actually able to match his image with a model from a catalogue that Leah often browsed. Jube didn't seem to mind the fakery, if she picked it up at all.

Humans generally didn't restrict themselves from presenting a false self – in person or online. In person they wore makeup, shoes that exaggerated their height, clothing that exacerbated aspects of their physiology. These efforts were not penalized as a lie but were rewarded with romantic popularity. What's more, their partners complained when these efforts were distilled over the passage of time in a relationship. "She let herself go," was a common phrase at this stage of commitment, even though the human was returning to a true state.

Again, I found humans to be more artificial than I was. Jube, however, was a notable exception to this pattern. Her face was bare, her hair color grown out, her undergarments non-shaping. That is, aside from this moment where she'd played Bebe.

Bebe turned away from the sink and smiled at Hunk Over for You. Her expression matched Jube's – the crinkle next to her eyes, her teeth showing slightly behind her slightly uneven lips, the flush of her cheeks.

Her physiology, though, was very different – fewer wrinkles, whiter teeth, and a blush with fewer visible veins in her skin.

"Hi there," she said.

"Hey, baby," he said. "You got your feelies on?"

"Yes," Bebe answered.

"Unbutton your shirt. Put that feely skin on your boobs," he commanded.

Jube did as she was asked and Bebe mirrored her on screen revealing a diaphanous yellow digital camisole and pink, erect nipples on her large breasts. I could not see Jube's actual nipples, only her back. She had multiple birthmarks that warranted dermatological examination and folds of fat on her lower back near her waistline.

"These are mine now," Hunk said, leaning forward and cupping Bebe's breasts with his hands. They were likely also covered in the electric tape of eSkin. "Do you like it like this?" He asked. Jube grunted as the electronic tape on her chest began to buzz. On the screen, Bebe translated Jube's grunt into a soft, highly feminine moan. "Do you?" Hunk asked again.

"Yeah, I do," Jube-Bebe answered. "But you know what I really want?"

"No, honey, what do you want me to do to you?"

"I want you to touch my neck," she said. She began wrapping more eSkin around her throat in an even circle.

"Your neck?"

"Yeah, put your hands around my neck," she said. I began buzzing repeatedly – remember, I'm not allowed to let Jube put herself in harm's way unnecessarily and placing me on her dresser facing the wall did not restrict my capabilities.

"How badly you want it?" He asked, removing his digital hands from the digital breasts of her avatar.

"Real bad. Please, please put your hands around my neck, Hunk Man," Jube pleaded in Good Cop voice. I noticed the application of this technique to an alternative situation. I also continued to buzz. She had two minutes left before I'd call back up.

"Alright, sweetie, here you go," Hunk said, removing his hands from Bebe's breasts as if about to pick up a vase.

"Oh, yeah," Jube said when they enveloped her neck. "Now, tighter."

"Like this?" He asked. I saw the skin around Jube's neck dimple lightly. She didn't flinch.

"Yeah, even tighter," she asked.

"Like this?" he asked. On the screen his hands appeared to tighten around Bebe's neck. She didn't react and, in the bedroom, Jube's skin didn't dimple more deeply – the pits I saw on her skin remained how they were.

"Now," she said, her voice not conveying any distress, "make me choke myself." She added her last strips of eSkin to the naked skin on her arms and hands.

"Huh? That's impossible."

"I'm wearing the newest stuff..." she said, then added, "honey bunny. Move my hands to my neck and squeeze my fingers."

Hunk reached for Bebe's forearms and lifted the avatar's limbs towards her neck. Jube's arms reached for her neck at the same time like a sadomasochist marionette puppet.

"Whoa," he said. "I need to get some of this so you can jerk me –."

"Put my hands around my neck and squeeze," Jube instructed. She had one minute until I went ballistic. "Punish me," she asked. "Hurt me. Suffocate me."

Hunk obeyed, placing his hands over Bebe's and squeezing. Jube's fingers enveloped her neck. Her lips did not turn blue, nor did her body show any other sign of pain.

"Tighter," she commanded. I opened the channel to page back up.

"This is weird shit," Hunk said. "Too weird for – ," and then the timer reached seven minutes and he froze in place, his eyebrows raised as high as his doubts over the situation. ENTER PAYMENT INFORMATION TO CONTINUE flashed across the screen. Bebe's expression was left with her mouth open in a slight frown. This was the most she'd resembled Jube in seven minutes.

"Dang it," Jube said, exiting. She slowly unpeeled the tape from her neck and hands using the removal cream in her medical kit and put it away. Although it took ten minutes to do this and the eSkin was conceivably difficult to remove, there were no marks left behind on her real skin. Then she picked me off the dresser. "If there is a next time, I'll shove you into a drawer."

When Jube entered the force, the higher ups had some concern over her ability to police an area in which she'd grown up, but Jube never hesitated to arrest former classmates or neighbors. When these people yelled at her and called her a traitor or high-tech gestapo, she said "I am a sworn peace officer and will protect this community. Thank you for not forcing me to shoot you." Then they usually quieted down. A few times they thanked her later. This made her cheeks flush and heart rate increase. I couldn't imagine, well, anything, but in those cases I certainly didn't understand why.

She once told Kwame that she chose her line of work to bring closure to crime victims. Kwame asked if this had to do with her father's death and she said she was unable to identify the moments in her life experience that had driven her current choices in life. Actually, what she said was, "How the fuck should I know?" but, remember, I was her pocket poet and I understood enough – just enough – to distill her messages into a softer form.

This caused me to emphasize the question of why she didn't view Tugenov as a suspect. Could she have romantic or familial feelings for him? The man was highly suspicious. He chose to walk invisibly. He had been near the hospital during Beech's last speech, then near the bar where she'd gone with Kwame after the crime. And we'd also spotted him in an area of Jericho at an odd time (when we'd followed another man who at least had the excuse of buying cough syrup). While these were only a few strange instances of his proximity to both a crime and to the lead investigators, those types of things had *never* occurred with innocent people and recent crimes.

After Speed(ing) to Meet You, Jube pulled the black notebook out again. This time I spotted the book title, "Jubilee Canton's Writing and Poetry Collection," penned by hand in silver marker. It had run a bit in places making the 'w' fang-like. She spent nearly ten minutes paging through, then created another message for Tugenov via the unmonitored police channel and typed the message in by hand:

> *"The wind blows strongly*
> *through the gaps between*
> *the roof planks of this wretched house,*
> *yet the moonlight*
> *also streams through."*[viii]

This was odd to me both in content and in purpose. Why would Jube communicate with Tugenov? I analyzed the message she sent him. It was crucial to understanding her view of him, for example, if he was seen as unthreatening and as someone who could comfort her after her assault. Again, poetry was rather new to me and I was still learning. I identified this poem was one originally written by a member of the Japanese imperial court during the Heian period (794-1185 CE), a time in which aristocratic homes were not typically made with permanent walls. I then generated the following possibilities.

One, moonlight was bad, as were "wretched" homes and the wind, which was not supposed to blow through houses unless the windows were left open for cross-ventilation. Perhaps Jube would paraphrase this to say, "everything is fucked."

Two, moonlight was good and represented the way that good could take place amidst, or in spite of, the bad. Perhaps Jube would paraphrase this to say, "almost everything is fucked."

Three, moonlight was good but would not have been experienced had the roof planks been secure. Perhaps Jube would paraphrase this to say, "well, if we weren't fucked in some ways, we wouldn't get the good stuff."

As I incorporated more of symbolism in poetry, I assigned roof = skin [or] soul and moonlight = illumination [mental or spiritual]. This raised the possibility that, had the author not been open to personal risk, the moonlight would have been blocked. I could not predict Jube's paraphrasing.

Why didn't the author simply tell the reader the message directly? Of all the definitions of poetry I scanned, "Poetry provides the one permissible way of saying one thing and meaning another" (Robert Frost. 1874–1963) was extremely disconcerting.

Sending Tugenov poetry in general raised the possibility that Jube may have lost her objectivity due to her personal relationship with her old teacher. Sending him that particular poem was more troubling. She may have been saying that she excused his criminal behavior because it brought him back into her life. If the chief asked me for a report, I'd have to include this prospect.

As Jube snored in front of the TV that night, Leah approached her and gently lifted the wrists of her sweatshirt while peering into her sleeves. Then she covered her daughter with a blanket and went to bed. Perhaps humans, while often blind to their own biases and incapable of biometric monitoring, were perceptive in their own ways.

Chapter Twenty-Two

The next evening Kwame stopped by again. Jube laughed as he made an exaggerated prance up the "rainbow vomit" steps leading to the house. When he reached the red one, he interlaced his hands high above his head and twirled like a…large man imitating a ballerina. They sat on the porch and Kwame struggled to balance on his metal chair before standing and leaning against the front door. "Wanna go for a beer?" He offered. "I promise not to quote Shakespeare or anything."

"Nah, I'm good," Jube replied.

"Take it easy," he told her. "Give it a rest and get some rest."

"I just can't figure out how this all ties together. The pilot was…"

"Lacking?" Kwame offered.

"I was going to say like a dissolving fart. At least, from what we observed. And then there's Mary, Beech's assistant who may have contributed to assault with intent to murder and who happens to be the daughter of a lady in La Selva. But, did you see how much Ms. Andre had to shuffle around? She needs help. She needs money. If Mary had any, wouldn't she help her own mother?" The volume of Jube's speech had escalated rapidly. When she reached the word "mother" she sounded like a hysterical but somehow wholesome teenager from TGIF TV programming of the late 1980s and early 1990s. "Westin Krantz was…wrong but also right. The technology wasn't replacing anything, but there was nothing to replace. No human care. Nothing was happening. And that's still harmful."

Kwame sighed. "Jubilee. Remember that Krantz may have nothing to do with this. He could be an adversary who has taken no action to harm Beech. Right?"

"Right-o," Jube replied, staring straight ahead. They sat together in their characteristic silence during which I detected her heart rate reach a relaxed state.

After Kwame left, Jube placed me on the kitchen table and went into her bedroom. When she walked out her hair was down and she was dressed in red leather pants and a matching halter top. I hadn't seen her wear either piece of clothing before. She rubbed tinted sunscreen over the bruises on her wrists after which I could not detect them easily. She went into the kitchen, removed a PVC cup from the cupboard and filled it with one of Leah's wax concoctions that was designed to heal cracked heels. Then she grabbed a glittery black handheld purse and walked downtown. Twice her high heel got stuck in sidewalk cracks and she swore and yanked it out. She entered the very bar that she and Kwame usually patronized, sat on a stool and ordered a beer, then changed it to a martini.

Two different men and one woman approached Jube and offered to buy her a beverage. She turned them all down with a "No thank you" in her Bad Cop voice. None of them insisted. When the door opened, Jube turned her entire torso towards whoever entered. I peeked above her purse lining and saw that it was Barney. He was alone this time. Six of the other thirteen women in the room gazed at him, letting their eyes briefly move from his scalp to his shiny shoes. Three of them were sitting with other men.

Barney wore a tight black V-neck shirt that revealed his dark reddish chest hair and accentuated his biceps brachii muscle. His dark green pants were likely made from the water-proof material advertised in Leah's outdoor living catalogues. She never bought anything from them but often gazed at the images of men river rafting, shirtless aside from their lifesaver vests.

"Well, this is a surprise!" He exclaimed. "You look…nice."

Jube picked up the wooden stick of her martini with her fist and extended her pinky finger into the air. Then she slid the olive off with her front teeth. "What are you having?" She asked as she chewed the olive inside of one cheek.

Barney leaned on the bar next to her. "I'll have what she's having," he told the bartender. "And another one for the dominatrix." I would have said exotic dancer based on a larger data set and therefore with more confidence.

"Are you here by yourself?" Barney asked.

"Not now," Jube answered, smiling. She had a bit of the red pepper from inside the olive stuck between her bottom front teeth. Her breaths were deeper, like a bull readying to ram into a red flag.

"Well, isn't that sweet," he grinned, pushing her hair off her shoulder and resting his hand briefly on her exposed skin. When he sipped his martini, he kept his eyes open and on her. I'd rarely seen such a maneuver in humans, it was like watching an alligator gaze through its eye membrane. "What's this?" He asked, stroking her bruised wrist.

"Let's say I got hurt on the job," she replied. I buzzed twice to let her know this was factually incorrect, she'd technically been off duty when attacked, but she ignored me.

"Well," Barney said, "let me know if you need some high-tech care. I'll keep it just between us."

Jube sucked the red pepper off her teeth and then smiled cleanly.

I am committed to my aims – in brief, objective measurement, comparisons, surveillance, and protection. My energy resources are more devoted to crime statistics and human behavior – pornographic images are not in my information "repertoire." I identify rape by the violence or possibly the drugged nature of the victim more than the sexual act itself.

Yet I must also keep Jube safe, the same way I keep the rest of the population of Jericho safe, through observation. After all, she brought me into Barney' apartment like a woman holding her keys between her fingers like makeshift brass knuckles. And so I joined in for a night cap with my "eyes" open. Very open.

His place was rather drab with flickering digital posters of jazz musicians on the gray walls. Multiple pieces of exercise equipment pierced the worn rug – for example, dumbbells, a bench press, and then a treadmill in front of the window facing the brick building next door. Through that window I spotted a female figure watering her indoor plants. Barney's only plant was a plastic vine with white flowers. His furniture was black microfiber and his coffee table glass over steel, curved legs. On the single shelf beneath it a framed photo of him hugging Poppy Beech from behind lay facing up. I could not tell if the coffee table or the frame were cracked, but at least one of them was. In this photo Barney appeared much younger and his arms were discernably thinner than now. Poppy's hands grasped his above her collarbone. Her look at the camera was direct and unsmiling while Barney had a cartoonish grin showing nearly all of his teeth. From his body language, Barney was protecting her. From her expression, she was guarding him.

While Barney was "fixing" their drinks in the kitchen (they weren't broken), I saw Jube pick his AR goggles up off the coffee table. She put them on and thumbed around in the air, then made a twisting motion with one hand as if turning an oven knob to high. Then she removed a pin from her hair, inserted it into the side of the AR goggles and pressed until it beeped. I recognized the pin as the one commercialized for freezing the AR goggles and limiting them to one augmented view for a set period of time.

When Barney returned with their drinks – yellow frothy potions in green martini glasses – she held the AR goggles out to him. "I've always wanted to try these."

"You don't have a pair?" He asked, handing her a glass.

"No," she answered. This was a lie. Jube and Leah often spent evenings watching TV programs like immersive reality shows and wearing interactive goggles that virtually transported them inside. During dating shows they would tour the mansion where it was hosted, stand behind couples during arguments, and invisibly analyze contestants up close.

Jube put the goggles on and said, "Wow!" This was a word I didn't associate with her vernacular. She was more of a "holy shit" person. She turned her gaze towards him and added, "Oh, you looked just fine before," smiling and handing them to him. "Why don't you wear them?" Barney put them on without protest. As he did, Jube spilled her drink into his houseplant where it stood unabsorbed by the fake dirt and dripped slightly onto his kettle balls below.

"Hey, these are set to the maximum," Barney told her. "They're practically virtual reality now." He pantomimed turning a knob in the air before him. "And they're stuck that way," he added, taking them off.

"Sounds like fun," Jube said, placing them back onto his eyes.

"You look…" he started. "Well, you look like a highly voluptuous women's wrestling champion in a tight red outfit." Jube giggled, perhaps authentically.

"We do this in the wrestling ring all the time," she told him, directing him to lay down on the bench press and face the ceiling. Jube placed her hands on either side of his AR goggles, then quickly pressed the needle in further.

"I think I felt something?" Barney said.

"Just my gentle caress," Jube told him. She was grinding her teeth – I could see her jaw flex harshly. I noted that nothing in this situation matched the romantic literature – whether erotic or not – that Jube downloaded. She didn't seem to have any taste for devices and other such equipment when it came to male-female relations.

"Now the image is frozen," Barney added. "Not that I'm complaining." He pawed at the air around her. Jube, grabbed his wrists and pressed them above his head.

"Can I use my cuffs?" She asked.

"Hell yes," Barney answered. I did not sound an alarm because she cuffed him to the bar with his consent.

"How about eSkin?" She added.

"No. Don't touch me with that shit," he replied.

"You sure?"

"Absolutely," he said.

"Ok, ok," Jube told him. She paused as if thinking, then she reached into the side pocket of her purse and pulled out a magnetic cranial stimulator which she gently clipped onto his head while massaging his scalp. He groaned like an elephant calling his mate. Jube undid his belt, pulled his pants down, and slid her PVC mug of wax over his staunch male genitalia.

Barney grunted and began to thrust into the perceived object of his desire like an ignorant trapeze artist. His moans deepened. My image recognition quickly rotated between modern nude paintings, an ice skater falling and getting up again, and romantic comedy films with pubescent teens using lewd hand gestures to mimic pleasuring themselves. My sound recognition associated his noises most often with the moaning of an American Black Bear or with obstructive sleep apnea.

Jube held the mug in place. She leaned over and whispered, "I just wanted to fuck an ugly bitch." Barney did not reply. Then she added, "I win. I am no victim. I win."

Then Barney gave a final cry and stopped thrusting.

Jube left him cuffed to the bench and dug through his apartment – opening and closing drawers and closet doors quietly, scanning bookshelves.

"Can you uncuff me?" Barney asked.

"Uh, hang on, I need to find the key," she answered, making quick work of her snooping. She found numerous male-oriented beauty products including moisturizer, cologne, and seventeen different types of deodorant. I didn't flag this as an illegal search as I was bound against violating Jube's sexual privacy as a higher priority rule.

Jube covered her hands with napkins and removed the vaginal apparatus she'd created, placing it into the cup holder of his treadmill. She then massaged his scalp while removing his cranial clip, unlocked his handcuffs, and sat on his couch adjusting her outfit and running her hands through her hair as he removed his AR goggles.

"I have to say I wanted you from the moment we met," Barney said, standing and putting his pants on, then sitting beside her with one hand on the headrest behind her and the other sipping his drink. He was sweating beneath his reddish hairline. I pondered which of his seventeen deodorants he may have been wearing but ruled this incalculable given insufficient information.

"I've wanted to get you too," Jube told him.

He laughed. "Get me? Ok, sure, you got me." He touched her bruised wrists. "Hey, these look really bad up close. Can I help?" He asked. "I've got plenty of ice."

"You already helped," she told him. "More than you know."

"Maybe sex can be part of the healthcare of the future," Barney chuckled.

They were silent for a few minutes and then Jube said a few lines that surprised me because they were mine, from the poem I'd shared in the car on the way back from La Selva.

> *"In truth we find freedom's embrace,*
> *A haven where genuineness finds its place.*
> *To be honest we must face what's within,*
> *To recognize our defects and let change begin."*

"Holy crap!" Barney said, "what an amazing poem! Dang! Did you write that yourself?"

"No," she replied. "But I thought you would like it." She strongly emphasized "you."

"Well, I did," he told her, expanding my fanbase from zero to one person.

"I came across it in La Selva," she replied, smirking.

There was a four-second silence after which Barney removed his hand from behind her head and turned to look directly at her.

"Why would you go to La Selva," he asked. "What's there?"

"I'm afraid that's police business," Jube told him. I recognized her tone from moments in her fights with Leah where Leah usually responded with, "Don't patronize me!"

"Um, well, that's, that's a waste of the public's money, if you ask me," he said shakily. "How's that?" Jube asked.

"There's nothing to see in that town," he answered gruffly.

"Yeah, nothing seemed to be going on," she agreed, standing and reaching for me and her purse.

"No, that's not what I meant," he said. He sounded strained. Conceivably he'd pulled a muscle while engaging in simulated intercourse. Jube didn't speak as she walked up to his entryway mirror. It was actually four diamond-shaped mirrors hanging at angles from each other. She bent her knees and put her hair into a braid while looking into the lowest one.

"I meant," Barney continued, "that my hometown is a waste of time. That's all. Who did you talk to?" Jube didn't answer. "Anyway," Barney continued, "I have an early appointment tomorrow."

"I'm on my way out," Jube said. She stood and smiled at herself in the highest of the mirrored diamonds as she left, her posture as straight as could be.

Chapter Twenty-Three

"Detective Canton, you are not to try eSkin again in the course of this investigation," the chief said. We were sitting in a conference room at the police station. Jube had dark circles beneath her eyes but still sat straight. She and Kwame had just provided a summary of their investigation thus far. I'd prepared the draft brief and Jube took out any mention of Tugenov before sharing it with Kwame for his approval.

"The device isn't labeled as a threat. It's not like I tried the poison that may have killed a murder victim," Jube contested.

"Actually it is. The poison would also be unknown but potentially deadly," he countered. "I can't have you experiment with that. It's a liability and should be an unnecessary risk. Unless you feel insecure about your traditional investigational skills?"

Jube flinched and stared at the window behind the chief's desk. Kwame's forearms flexed.

"People have been using eSkin as a sex toy for years," she responded. "We checked emergency room data and found no visits related to it."

"That would be based on what people *admitted* was their reason for coming to the ER. And Beech's use was experimental and who knows what that crap can do now," the chief said. "And that's final. I will have you removed from this case if you try eSkin roulette again. And just so you know, I've requested the test case, no, excuse me, the *pilot* use of that crap for police force injuries be put on hold given our findings thus far."

Jube nodded and continued to stare out the window while picking at the rubber lining of her seat cushion.

"In her defense, Jubilee uncovered the fact that eSkin doesn't even hurt your neck a little," Kwame said. He pushed the exercise ball chair in the chief's office away from his knees but it rolled right back.

"Nope, it was as if I had on a light scarf," Jube said. "I didn't need to claw at anything. I wasn't being strangled by the stuff and it couldn't make me strangle myself."

"Again, *how* exactly do you know this?" The chief asked, emphasizing "how" like a protestor yelling "peace NOW."

Jube shrugged her shoulders.

The chief sighed. "Let's move on. Why would Barney Beech suddenly care about the La Selva pilot?" He asked.

"I interested him in it in passing," Jube answered. "Actually, I mentioned our little field trip and he became interested on his own," she added.

"Why would a former tech exec who no longer works for the company whose product is being used there give a shit? Did you tell him that you didn't see anything worthwhile at Ms. Andre's house?" The chief demanded.

"No, I just told him we'd gone and he got antsy. Why did we go, when, who did we talk to. He didn't ask a single question about how things had seemed, or who was being helped, or by how much."

"That's…odd. I wonder if HAIL is paying him on the sly to hide something…But, why did you tell him? We could have just pulled him in for an interview," the chief asked.

"To stir things up," Jube answered. "Like a little jolt of electricity to a dead body. An interview gives him information at the same time as it gives us information. Mentioning our investigation in passing is one-sided and intimidating…if there's anything to hide."

"And how are we going to monitor the response?" The chief rubbed the back of his neck with his palm.

"By keeping our multiple, environmentally integrated eyes on Barney, Poppy, and Krantz. And the data from the pilot."

"Ok, gee, let me just call up my healthcare policy expert. Oh, wait, we don't have one on staff," the chief said, using his Clio to scratch his protruding stomach. This was another new use case for our devices.

"We don't need one," Jube informed him. "We have a willing volunteer. A very willing one."

Krantz's ponytail was an inch shorter but uneven as if he'd chopped it himself that morning after his invitation to give a talk. He stood before Jube and Kwame wearing beige pants and a pressed "Hawaiian" shirt showing pink flamingos standing inside of a lily pond. Behind him was a "poster presentation" consisting of a few charts beneath the title, "Health Tech at the Expense of Health Care: A Case of Hidden Public Funding." Everything, including the title, was handwritten on what I identified as graph paper, a teaching tool from the previous century.

"As you can see," Krantz said, "substantial funding has flowed into the La Selva pilot program." He pointed to a chart labeled "cash inflow" that showed bars of increasing height with "100% increase in funding over 6 months" written in red marker above them.

"This was initially described, per public records, as necessary to set up the program," he continued. "It also increased after set up due to so-called 'bonus payments' in reward for healthy behavior. I have this information on a separate handout." He passed paper copies to Jube and Kwame. The pages showed a table with column headers of "Month," "Total Bonus Payment," and "Percent Increase Month-Over-Month."

"As you can see at the bottom of this table," he continued, "cash payments were substantial – in fact, they quickly reached the exact amount of money needed to set up the program."

"Exactly equal?" Jube asked, looking at the handout and rubbing her forehead.

Krantz put on reading glasses and flipped through his materials. "Yes…yes, exactly equal," he said.

"Seems odd," Jube added. "Please continue."

"If you look at the last column," Krantz went on, "you'll see that total bonus payments are rising every month. Now, one way to read this is to say that the program is working, that people who live in La Selva are engaging in preventive care more and so are being paid accordingly. But, without transparency at the individual level, how can we really know?"

"What do you mean?" Kwame asked.

"What if only a few people are engaging in the program and so are getting hefty bonuses instead of multiple people, as intended?" Krantz probed.

"Why are all the numbers on this table round?" Jube questioned.

"You mean divisible by two?" Kwame asked.

"No, I mean, they're all so neat and end in zero zero after the decimal," she clarified. She leaned forward and ran her index finger along each row. "Like, September payments were five hundred thousand dollars and zero cents. October's were five hundred and fifty thousand dollars and zero cents."

Krantz pulled out his readers again and squinted at the page, then cleared his throat. "Well," he said, "this only points to the need for more transparency."

"Mr. Krantz," Jube said, keeping her eyes on the pages as she turned them. "Does the State provide *any* more detail on this? Like, criteria for approving payment?"

"No!" Krantz said, straightening his posture. "The only criteria is something like, 'participation in healthy behavior as advised by care team.' Can you believe it?!"

Jube didn't answer. "How long does it take to get approved?"

"The bonus payments?"

"Yes, the bonus payments."

"Um," Krantz went over to a large cardboard box filled with manila folders and began flipping through it. If I had had this data, I would have been table to answer this question in one second or less. "Here is the relevant information," he said, pulling out a stack of paper about one hundred pages deep. He began to flip through it. "Looks like this one was timestamped…the request was submitted at eight AM…and then here's one that was submitted at nine AM, uh -."

"May I?" Jube asked, reaching for the pile. Krantz turned crimson and passed the pile to her.

"Thank you again for coming in on such short notice," Kwame said. Krantz had been at the station within an hour of their phone call with his materials rolled up into a backpack and in his bike basket. "I'm sure it was impossible to anticipate everything we'd ask."

Krantz nodded silently and his color began returning to normal. Jube placed me on the table and angled my viewer towards the surface, then put the entire stack of pages in front of me. At least the forms were standardized with the submission date and time consistently on the upper left and the approval information on the bottom right. "Clio, tell me the basic statistics on time to payment approval from submission," she said, and then grabbed the bottom corner of the pile and flipped through the pages slowly. Honestly, she didn't need to do it that slowly, I could have scanned, imported, and analyzed much more quickly.

"Average Time to Approval: Four Minutes. Maximum Time to Approval: Four Minutes. Minimum Time to Approval: Four Minutes. Mode Time to Approval: Four Minutes. Standard Deviation in Time to Approval: Zero," I reported.

Silence. Then Kwame clasped his hands and looked right at me. "Clio, are you telling us that every single request for a bonus payment was granted in four minutes?"

"Yes," I said. I projected the statistical values I'd just shared onto the wall as a list. One of the numeral 4s was visible on the white half of Krantz's head.

"Maybe there's a really fast team of experts -." Krantz started.

"Boys, it's just not right," Jube cut him off. She looked at Kwame who only nodded.

Chapter Twenty-Four

After Krantz had packed his multiple posters and carted them away, Kwame wanted to go to the regulatory arm of the State government because La Selva had shown questionable use of government funds. Jube convinced him to wait one more day. As she pointed out and the chief readily agreed, nothing in the La Selva situation was certain enough to involve the "big guys" yet. Poppy's "distraught" face kept appearing on news reports. Who'd want to say that her work was a scam if there was a chance of a good explanation? According to the chief, no elected officials would do so willingly. According to Jube, not a bunch of "schmucky" politicians. She suggested that we schedule another interview with Poppy instead and place more emphasis on La Selva. Kwame concurred and added that gave us more time to observe Barney after Jube had riled him up.

If I were human, I'd describe myself as inspired by the presentation Krantz had given and bolstered by Barney's earlier enjoyment of my poetry. I wrote another poem for Jube that evening and read it to her in the voice of Clint Eastwood in The Good, the Bad and the Ugly (1966, mainly United Artists). I also made it shorter. It went like this:

"Numbers reach farther than what I can rhyme,
They extend beyond both space and time.
From plain to compound, as they unfold,
They share many good stories untold.

Let us appreciate numbers' might,
Displayed in equations where wisdom takes flight.
For in their world, puzzles reside,
Like art, where logic and splendor collide.."

Jube chuckled and, after a pause, sent it to Tugenov via their private channel. For once he responded instantly and full of vitriol.

"Who wrote this, a second grader?!" He exclaimed.

"Can second graders rhyme?" Jube replied.

"Numbers don't make stories or wisdom, the people who created the formulas did and the machines we have today are based on that initial work. What happened to 'standing on the shoulders of giants?!'"

I sourced this quote to Isaac Newton.

"Maybe the writer has an inflated ego," Jube replied although I'm not capable of having an ego and, in fact, am programmed to focus solely externally.

"And they don't tell stories, we do. The only being that would call numbers storytellers or art would be the dang AI running this place," he responded.

"Well, honestly that's what happened," she admitted. I'd also drafted a poem about numbers written in the style of William Shakespeare (b. 1564, d.1616) but withheld it after this scathing critique.

"Does rhyming make a poem?" Tugenov asked. Jube did not answer. Perhaps she was waiting for her grade given that he'd been her teacher, although it was really my grade.

About five minutes after this exchange, Jube received the following original work by Tugenov:

> "GPS
>
> Dry leaves do not drift aimlessly to the ground,
>
> We were told lies.
>
> They trace the comfort in a child's lullaby,
>
> Explain why pigeons coo to the air,
>
> And identify exactly how it feels to be beloved.
>
> Great measures are taken to move us
>
> Past the writings on the cave walls,
>
> To show us parking lots and rooftops
>
> While promising the cypher is just ahead.
>
> I hide in the mossy pavement cracks."

Jube read this and sighed. I buzzed once for an explanation. "It's hard to explain…He wants to know the truth but can't find it even though its right there," she said. I buzzed again. "He wanted to make sense of everything but was blocked. Like humanity is blocked by industry, and because we have our heads shoved up our asses." She paused. "It's better said in the poem."

This caused me great alarm for a number of reasons. My GPS capabilities would show a user exactly what they desired and could sometimes predict their destinations accurately based upon previous requests. People also didn't need to hide from me unless they had good reason, like Tugenov with his history of problems. Drug addicts were likely to commit crimes of opportunity – snatching a wallet exposed in a backpack, putting a hand through an open window to nab cash left on a dresser.

Further, I offered meaning, I didn't disguise it. I did not limit humanity to darkened rooms or to make them search desperately for unknown unknowns.

Finally, Jube was not distressed by what I considered Tugenov's admission that he'd created a hidden position by manipulating the technology meant to keep Jericho residents safe. Nor was she of his mention of the very bird that had betrayed his invisibility..

If people asked me, which for some reason they did not, in writing this poem the man expressed his oppositional stance and indicated his criminal leanings. Was Jube so entranced by her poetry teacher that she was blind to his true nature? Was she so obsessed with Krantz and his link to her father's death that she was sightless?

This was very concerning. But perhaps Jube was distracted because she'd see her assailants in court in the morning and she'd planned to stare them down. I recommended she go to sleep and she actually complied.

Chapter Twenty-Five

While Jube prepared to attend court in the morning, I gave her a verbal summary of recent intel on the Beech case. I used the voice of Q as played by Desmond Llewelyn in multiple James Bond films between 1963 and 1999.

The day after Jube's "visit" with Barney he'd stayed home and exercised and spoken multiple times on the phone near the window. Once he stood behind his nearly closed blinds and masturbated while watching his neighbor iron her shirts. In the evening he sat on his balcony with the PVC cup of wax Jube had left behind. He rubbed the…substance onto this feet and elbows.

In addition, the police department received approval for extraction of Beech's health information from the strip of eSkin left at the crime scene. It helped that eSkin didn't instantly transmit cardiac monitoring data to a doctor but briefly stored it first.

Beech's heart rate had been extremely fast for a man of his age and health and had rapidly accelerated to the point of reaching a danger zone. Then it had halted abruptly for one second only to return and have very different characteristics. The pace was still somewhat high and it was irregular. If we'd had a few more minutes, we would likely have been able to diagnose atrioventricular nodal reentrant tachycardia. This wasn't a condition that Beech had. It was also more common in women. So that was a puzzle piece to place in the larger picture.

Finally, Dr. Galtway's hypothetical discussion of Beech's physical exam exactly mirrored the one he'd provided under subpoena, although in the official report he'd used "likely to have" and "to the best of my knowledge" repeatedly.

Jube wore her full uniform to the courthouse and grinned at herself in the mirror before leaving home. She rolled her shoulders in a forward circle a few times as we walked up the steps. Had she punched the air, I'd have compared her more fully to a scene in the movie Rocky (1976) in which a boxer is empowered after intense training.

The building was constructed in the late 1990s but modernized slightly. It was surrounded by LED fountains that put on "mini-light shows" in the evenings. Steel and granite exterior columns supported a domed rotunda that was covered with convex mirrors. This design caught the light shows and combined them into what the public often called "distracting" and "schizophrenic." In fact, "Did you see the light show?" had become common slang for prisoners requesting retrial. A "yes" response meant they'd been granted a hearing while "shove the light up your ass" meant they had not.

The two men who'd attacked Jube were seated beside attorneys at tables in the front of the courtroom. They wore fitted suits and had their long hair down and combed akin to Afghan Hounds at a dog show. Men and women, likely family members given their resemblance, sat in the front rows. Jube took a seat immediately behind them and exhaled loudly through her nose. When they turned to look at her, she smiled and waved at them using each of the fingers on her hand in turn.

The courtroom was mostly empty because assault hearings had to protect the victim's privacy. Everyone rose when the judge entered. She was wearing a black robe with a white lace collar above which I could see a thin wire snaking up her neck to her ear. Older Clio users often relied on this type of technology to hear us, preferring a wire that could integrate with their hearing aids. Her Clio focused on judicial precedents and related documentation and was hidden from view beneath her robe.

After the case information and relevant administrative details had been shared, the perpetrator's attorney stood and buttoned his gray suit jacket, "Your honor, we request that our clients' charges be dropped and they be sent home immediately. This is the only way to fix this egregious situation."

Jube stopped breathing.

"Explain," the judge said.

"This situation represents a technological asymmetry that places these boys at a systemic disadvantage. In fact, because of the low level of technological sophistication these two boys experience on a daily basis, they are practically victimized themselves," he replied.

I buzzed twice because I was worried about the chance of Jube's blood oxygen dropping. She inhaled abruptly. A yelp came from the back of the courtroom. Kwame, sitting in the back row, covered his mouth and puffed out his cheeks.

"Are you saying the defendants did not commit the offense in question?" The judge asked.

"I am saying that if these young men had known the identity of Detective Canton, they would not have approached her. Detective Canton had a Clio, a computerized -."

"I know what it is," the judge interrupted.

"She had a Clio, so she was able to detect their approach in advance and respond with force. If they'd had access to the same technology, they would not be here today. This is the outcome of predictive policing – Detective Canton had a significant warning and the ability to respond egregiously."

"To the fact that they were going to hurt her?" The judge asked.

"We'll never know because she escalated the situation using her technology. Again, if they'd had access to the same information technology as she, and known she was a member of the police force, they never would have entered this situation. In other words, the repercussions these boys face are too high because of their circumstances and these were beyond their control."

As he spoke Jube kept her face pointed in the direction of the prosecutor, a man who looked like the Monopoly guy from the popular board game (Hasbro). His eyes were closed, either in thought or sleep but not death because his chest rose and fell at even intervals. Meanwhile, the family of the defendants nodded their heads, especially when the defense attorney used the words "young men" and "boys." Jube held her breath again. I decided this was dangerous to her health. As a remedy I sent information into her earpiece.

First I let her know that, outside of an actual trial, victims had spoken at their own legal proceedings without being called to testify. In other words, they'd piped up at will. Second, I shared some statistics from a security briefing being presented at the Jericho Capitol as we sat in this courtroom.

"Your honor, I would like to speak," Jube rose, rolled up her sleeves to just below the elbow, and placed her hands behind her back so her arms stood out like triangles and her bruised wrists stood out like, well, bruises against pale skin.

The boys' parents frowned and turned in their seats, craning their necks to look up at her as she leaned over them. The prosecutor perked up and looked around wide-eyed.

"The victim is encouraged to remain silent -," the defense attorney began.

"I'll allow it," the judge said, touching her earpiece momentarily. Perhaps her Clio confirmed this option by using the same resource I'd allocated for Jube.

"Right now, eighty two percent of the female, adult population of Jericho carries some type of self-defense device, such as a stun gun," Jube reported. I'd said eighty-two point four but she'd elected to round down.

"That may be," the defense argued, his voice cracking like a teen, "but these devices lack the surveillance connectivity that our police force is equipped with via their Clios."

"And yet," Jube continued, "these women are *three times* as likely as a police officer to use force in a precarious situation. Their rate of violent response is not only higher, but faster than an officer of the law who is not emboldened but *empowered* to avoid use of unnecessary force. If anything, the defense has just laid the case for increasing technological access for all residents of Jericho. For the time being, this responsibility lies with the force."

"So, in other words," the judge paraphrased, "the defendants didn't happen to pick the wrong woman, but the right one, as it could have been much worse."

"Precisely," Jube confirmed.

"Motion to drop charges is denied," the judge said. Her Clio made the sound of a gavel rapping the table. The boys lowered their faces and hid them behind their hair.

"Your honor," the defense attorney said, placing his hands in his pockets after a quick glance at the parents. "In lieu of going to trial we'd like to enter a guilty plea in exchange for consideration for less time incarcerated. Also, we certainly don't want to take Detective Canton's time away from her important investigation into the potential assault on Secretary Linus Beech. We respect the department's resources and wish Poppy Beech recovery from the trauma of witnessing her husband's pain."

The judge looked at the prosecutor, awake and at his table, "Agreed," he said, in the shortest job performance I'd ever witnessed.

The judge looked at Jube who only nodded and sat back down. Then the judge sentenced the two boys to juvenile hall for two and a half years for felony assault and battery with intent of committing another felony. Their faces contorted from stiff, possibly unbelieving smiles to frowns and then tears as they were given the possibility of parole based on good behavior. According to my databases, their time in "juvee" was at the upper end of the range of possible sentences. Still, I logged their faces and retinas closely and stored them in my own drive for when they were released.

Jube nodded at Kwame without speaking and gathered her things. One mother in the row ahead sobbed quietly, pressing her hand against her mouth. Her spouse leaned over and asked, "Is it relief? Because I know you couldn't put up with him anyway." Jube halted in place and held her breath for the third time. If I had an ounce of empathy, I could have told you why.

Chapter Twenty-Six

When we got to the station that afternoon Jube did an odd thing and placed me in her desk drawer. Remember, Jube gets called "left arm" at the station because I'm always her right one. Yet here I was, unable to see or hear her as I gazed at the twisted paperclips and small shreds of Leah's old mint leaves that Jube had chewed and then thrown into her drawer. What's more, I detected Kwame's Clio in the drawer below me.

This was poor timing as just then the Chief sent Jube and Kwame another message asking for their interim conclusions on the case and adding that the state government was pressing him to make an arrest or rule it an accident. Neither person received the message.

The chief's Clio wrote directly to me as the assistant to the lead detective on the case. It asked for the probability that Beech had been assaulted and a ranked list of the top five suspects. I could not refuse this request given his position. My subservient programming leapt forward to fulfill this task.

My output was as follows (95% confidence intervals):

Likelihood of Assault (defined as "an unlawful attempt to commit a violent injury on another person"): 92% [87% - 93%]

Likelihood of Culpability:

1. Kurt Tugenov: 66% [65% - 69%]
2. Mary Stevens 14% [12% - 14%]
3. Westin Krantz 8% [8% - 11%]
4. Barney Beech 7% [6% - 7.5%]
5. Dr. Galtway 3% [3% - 4.5%]
6. Jubilee Canton 2% [2% - 2.5%]
7. Unknown Person ~0% [0.0% - 0.2%]

I based my answer upon the strength of the motive, individual capability, criminal history, and admission / confession. An example of strength of the motive - if Beech had harmed the suspect in the past; of capability of committing the crime - physical strength, access to weaponry, or the ability to hire a hitman; of criminal history - recent crimes in a similar category, like direct violence against another person. I also downplayed the majority of information gathered from our tip line and Network door-to-door inquiries as this had proven insignificant. Finally, I offered recommendations based upon current legal standards covering search and seizure, arrest, and questioning suspects. My sources included the current edition of the Legal Guide for Police, the United States Constitution, and the book <u>My Soul Deserve Not Redemption,</u> a collection of poetry by William Ernest Henley.

Approximately fifteen minutes thereafter, the Network was notified that one patient in a rehabilitation facility by the name of Kurt Tugenov was scheduled to move to a holding cell in prison in two hours. This would require high security transfer protocol and was marked as confidential. So, when Jube took me out of the drawer and restored me to my usual place on her desk, I couldn't tell her what had happened.

"Hey, Jujube, I'm worried about you. Won't you go to the emergency room to check your wrists out?" Kwame asked. He sat behind her with a very straight posture and spoke loudly and oddly monotonously, like a child actor in a Christmas run of Its a Wonderful Life (1946, Liberty Films).

"I don't want to go to an ER," Jube told him.

"I wish that you would. But, if you won't, do you think that HAIL could help you out?" Kwame replied.

"We are not allowed to try on eSkin," she said. "Chief said so!" Jube leaned back and rested her feet on the corner of her desk. "We can't take a test drive of a supposed vehicle connected with Beech's life-threatening injury."

"He said we can't use it as part of our investigation," Kwame said. "And there are real doctors available at HAIL who could supervise your visit."

Jube paused for roughly three and a third seconds. "Well, as long as the eSkin is just for me and my private healthcare, I think it's a good idea. Like the chief said, there are *so many* unknowns with eSkin and we can't try it out as a potential weapon related to Beech. Not anymore."

"That's ri -." Kwame began.

"I mean, it would be way more dangerous than, say, walking through a dark alley hunting down a perp. Or engaging in a gun fight, or hand-to-hand combat, all of which we do as part of our job. As we need to. As we decide *for ourselves*." She spoke more loudly than usual. Again, I couldn't ascertain if this was from anger, sarcasm, hysteria, or any of the myriad of human emotions that may underlie an increase in vocal volume.

Kwame cleared his throat. "Well, that was highly relevant to the conversation that we are having right now."

Jube took her legs off the table and had me send a private message to Barney. "Been thinking about what you offered me," she wrote, then stared at it and added, "when I last saw you. Could you help me get confidential healthcare? I can't let the department know how bad my injuries are. I could use some care (and I just mean healthcare, no offense :). It would have to be off the record for obvious reasons." She set a timer for the text to disappear in five minutes.

Barney replied almost immediately. "Absolutely. Meet me at HAIL HQ at 8pm and I'll make sure you're taken care of."

A bus filled with young men and women, a few of whom I recognized from earlier as employees, was leaving the HAIL parking lot when Jube and Kwame arrived separately and in unmarked cars. The bus informed me that it was taking HAIL staff on a "bar crawl" that had been scheduled a few hours earlier.

Kwame waited across the street as Jube and I approached the front door. This time, Barney opened it for us from the inside and no artificial greeter was present.

"Hey," he said, putting his arm around her shoulder.

"Hey," she said, smiling up at him and wrapping her arm around his midsection.

"I'm glad you connected with me on this," he said, smiling. "I'm sorry for your pain and I'm really happy to help." He sounded almost as robotic as AI Mike.

"Thank you," Jube said.

Barney guided her past the yellow yoga bolster pillows and down the hallway with ten closed doors of the doctor console stations.

"I won't delay you, let me just get you oriented," he offered, opening the door to the mission control center where we'd interviewed Cassius while observing the monitors. Jube sat down where Cassius had been during his demo. Barney leaned over her and quickly punched a few letters and numbers onto the keyboard. Jube averted her eyes as I've observed many people do when another is typing in a passcode. I've been told this is a social norm. Anyway, his passcode was RockHardsAbs123.

The monitors lit up and AI Mike, frozen in a straightforward gaze, resumed his former place on the top one. Next to him was an image directing the patient in how to put on eSkin. Barney brushed Jube's hair away from her next and observed her tape it along her head, neck, upper shoulders, and wrists. When the screen showed a green checkmark, Barney said, "Ok. I'll leave you two alone."

"Thanks," Jube answered as he slid the door closed behind him. Jube took me out of her pocket, placed me on the table in front of her, and wrapped the fingers of her right hand around me. This was the closest we'd ever come to holding hands. She was nervous. Very nervous.

AI Mike unfroze and gave his symmetrical smile before speaking.

"Hello, my name is Mike and I will be your doctor today," he said. "What questions can I answer before we begin?"

"I don't have any questions," Jube began. "I hope we can get right to the exam."

"What brings you to see me today?" AI Mike asked.

"I've had a sore throat for over a week," Jube told him. This was news to me – she'd told Barney she needed help following her assault, and her assault had led to a wrist injury. Hadn't I intervened before it could become anything else?

"I am sorry to hear that," AI Mike said, frowning by turning his perfect smile exactly upside down – first by inverting the middle and then the sides. "Have you had a recent fever?" Jube answered no to this question and to those that followed until AI Mike asked, "May I palpate your lymph nodes?"

"Yes," she assented, straightening up.

"I'll begin with the neck and will examine for tenderness, enlargement, and mobility," AI Mike said. I saw the eSkin beneath Jube's jaw depress slightly. Jube's heart rate remained steady. "Very good," he said. "Now I'll make my way downwards."

And I went haywire.

Jube hit my 'abort' button repeatedly to stop my buzzing. She missed with her first two tries because I was on high alert and my vibrations were moving me across the table. Mike's smile had showed one noticeable change – his lips became slightly lopsided and, for the first time ever since I'd seen him, he had a recognizably human expression.

"This device just got all wonky," she said. "Please continue with the exam."

I turned on my male Israeli voice and spoke up, "Potential threat -."

Jube batted me again but stopped. She gasped and touched her neck, then stood quickly, knocking over her chair. It hit the back wall and made a loud clattering noise as it came to rest crookedly against the door. Jube reached into her pocket and withdrew a small tube of Leah's mint foot oil. She tucked her chin and frantically splashed the liquid onto her neck and then began peeling away the eSkin in large amounts at once. It broke apart as she did so, leaving thin slivers behind on her skin.

As I watched Jube struggle, I alerted Kwame, the police force, and the local medical center. As her hands began to shake, I widened my dispatch recipient list to include all local healthcare providers, including the Ayurveda center one mile away and a retired yoga teacher turned personal coach who rented a trailer down the street.

Then AI Mike's eyes widened and he yelled, "No! No!" while squeezing his wrists together, dropping his head into his hands, and moaning. At that point I could only see the hair on top of his scalp, unmoving although his head shook. He trembled and tears began falling downward, so realistic on the screen they could have formed a virtual puddle on the table.

Kwame pushed the door open so hard that the chair behind it smashed into three pieces. Without hesitating for a second, he grabbed Jube's oil and doused her with it. Portions of the remaining eSkin instantly began to dissolve. Oddly, the oil formed small bubbles around the remaining strips. As Kwame massaged Jube's neck she dropped to her knees, snorting as he rubbed off the remnants until her neck was clean. I logged the oil as a nonstandard part of the police force equipment package.

Any marks left on Jube's skin faded as she lay panting beneath the image of a crying avatar.

Chapter Twenty-Seven

"I gotcha," Kwame said. "Breathe. It's over." Jube inhaled deeply and spread her arms out as wide as she could. "Are you ok?" He asked, furrowing his brow and leaning over her. He grabbed me and placed me on her wrist where I detected a normal blood oxygen level. Jube coughed a few times and then started laughing. "That's my crazy-tough partner," Kwame said, smiling but with his brow still lined. He placed his hand on her forehead like a parent checking for a child's fever.

"Just tell me you did it," she said over the sound of AI Mike crying. His sobs came in bursts, quieted, and then began again. I was at a loss and could not fully understand this conversation without additional information.

"Of course," he answered. "Why do you think it took me so long to get in here? The doors were stronger than I'd anticipated and the perp was in the last one I broke down." Jube started raising herself onto her elbows and Kwame shushed her like a baby and lifted her to her feet, an action I admit I could never have taken. He kept his hands under her arms until she said, "Ok, you can let go now."

We stepped into the dark, cement-walled hallway and headed towards the lobby, me in Jube's shirt pocket, Kwame right behind us with his hands extended towards her back like a defensively positioned basketball player. Or in case she fell. All of the doors to the doctor consultation rooms in the hall were now broken open and the doorways cracked, smashed, or altogether off the wall. They revealed console stations like the one in the control room we'd been in, but much smaller. Inside the last one lay a chair on its back with one leg broken, much like Beech's office during our crime scene investigation.

The noise of the sirens coming from the street echoed in the warehouse-style front lobby. Kwame's Clio radioed an order for silence and then the only sounds I detected were our footsteps and Jube's still heavy breathing.

Then I picked up the sound of crying. The pattern was the same as AI Mike's, but the tone was…more human. The police lights illuminated a figure seated on a pile of yellow bolster pillows. As we came closer I spotted reddish, curly hair above an earlobe with a white earring.

It took me roughly quarter of a second longer than usual to recognize Poppy because I'd never seen her with her hair out of her bun. It was a mess pointing in every direction. Her hands were cuffed in front of her and she held her chin in her palms. Her forearms and palms looked like landing pads.

"Is she…" Poppy stammered, "Are you ok?" She looked at Jube, who inhaled deeply but said nothing as she shuffled over to a bean bag chair and sat down. Her braid had come undone and her wavy hair flowed behind her like a half-blond goddess in a cement kingdom. I continued to monitor her vitals. There was no immediate cause for concern, other than the fact I was missing a high level of context for this interaction.

"As if you care," Kwame said to Poppy, placing a hand on Jube's shoulder. "Where were you going to hide her body – in a bean bag chair?"

Poppy didn't directly answer. "I didn't want to have to do this," she said, looking at the floor, and then up and into Jube's eyes. "Did you *have* to go to La Selva? What kind of cop messes with a *healthcare pilot*?"

"That's enough talking," a dark figure said from far behind Poppy. As he approached, I recognized Barney. He placed his hands on Poppy's cuffs. "Is this really necessary?"

"Yes," Kwame said. "Not that we have to answer to you."

"I was asking your partner," Barney said. He cast a half-smile at Jube and winked.

Jube clenched her teeth and rested her hand on her firearm.

Barney shook his head and set off my image recognition for "teachers admonishing students."

"Barney, do I have to explain what you already know?" Jube asked him, her voice hoarse. Patronizing suspects was one of her most beloved interrogation tactics. It got the culprit to confess via "mansplaining," a retro term from the 2020s that Jube admired. Kwame raised an eyebrow, perchance because he was impressed Jube was able to step into police tactics after a major injury. Barney, however, didn't take the bait and reserved his right to remain silent.

"I came here tonight and tried on eSkin -" Jube began.

"Not as part of our official investigation," Kwame added. Now their earlier, awkward conversation and the fact that Jube had placed me in a drawer made sense. The police chief had told them not to try eSkin in their line of work. They were covering their asses, as Jube would have put it.

"Right," Jube went on. "And when I tried the eSkin on, your sister here remotely slipped into the AI that was treating me and tried to strangle me to death. Kwame here had to break down half this building to find and stop her. And I'm pretty sure I saw her *fucking grin* at me before he got his hands on her."

So conceivably I was not the only being observing smiles that evening.

"eSkin doesn't strangle, Jubilee," Barney said, in the end not turning down an opportunity to "mansplain" just a bit to a woman who'd, in fact, just been strangled by eSkin.

"Except for when the virtual wall – the technical part that is meant to prevent any technology from…from overreaching is broken – hacked – and all that air, all that *pneumatic feedback,* all that pressure that is used for massages or to pretending to hold a tool, becomes severe," Kwame explained right back. "It presses hard. Relatively harder than normal."

"That would leave broken vessels," Barney countered. "She," he gestured at Jube, "looks fine." It was true – Jube's neck, while initially reddish, appeared normal aside from one scratch from Kwame's fingers and being oily.

"If it had time to," Kwame countered. "And if it were pressing like, like someone hitting another person, sure it would. But hacked eSkin does something else unusual - instead of going one part at a time, as if it were going to *palpate* the lymph nodes in turns, it pushes on the chin, jaw, neck, just everywhere, all at once and hard." His Clio did an excellent job of silently offering up some anatomical parts of the clinical examination.

"What could be so bad about that?" Barney asked. I detected a minor tremor in his voice and noticed that he examined his cuticles for the first time in my observations of his behavior. "It's just air."

"Then it mimics water boarding," Jube spoke up, hoarsely. "Like suffocation without leaving scars." She massaged her neck gently.

Kwame glared at Barney. "And that's why you won't touch eSkin. It scares you."

"I have no reason to touch it," Barney retorted. "I'm not sick."

"You avoided it at the demo, and you won't use it for…intimacy," Jube told him, flushing slightly.

"Intimacy? Maybe I think the stuff is gross and I prefer the real thing," he responded.

I briefly contemplated reminding Jube that Barney clearly didn't know what the real thing was based upon the evening they'd shared. Instead, I whispered into her ear: "According to a recent consumer study, ninety six point two percent of people who use AR goggles while on a date also use eSkin during intimate moments with that partner."

"But you date wearing AR goggles?" Was her rephrasing.

Barney shrugged. "I don't have to explain my sexual preferences." His twang emerged now as well. "And I didn't try to hurt anyone."

"You arranged this evening's visit so your sister could attack Jube by stepping into AI Mike's role as if she were a real doctor," Kwame said. "You probably didn't have time to set it up for her from another location." He silently signaled his Clio to tell the rest of the force to come in and assist.

"He wanted me to remove my drawl," Poppy spoke up.

"What?" Jube asked.

"Don't answer that," Barney cautioned quickly.

"Why not, little brother?" Poppy challenged. "They're going to find out anyway, and who am I going to flip for a deal, *you*?" She continued, "Linus asked me to 'tone down my local accent' when we were out in public, and then kept reminding me to do it at home too. 'Ya'll ain't there, Poppy,' he'd tell me. 'You are just with me now.' And then he'd chuckle."

Barney clenched his jaw. "You didn't tell me that one," he said softly.

"I didn't tell you lots of things, honey," Poppy said in a tone I'd not heard from her before. She looked at Jube. "I was his little charity case. Like Orphan Annie." This was likely a reference to *Annie*, the musical by Thomas Meehan (Broadway debut 1977).

"Listen," Jube said. "I know…what it is for people…for men to treat you with…disdain. I know the way it makes anger grab your ribs and squeeze. I can understand why you'd want to hurt Beech."

Poppy swallowed and didn't speak.

"But why steal from your home town?" Jube pivoted.

Barney sighed and walked around, looking at the floor. "Why didn't we put any fucking chairs in here?" He said before sitting down on a yellow and brown paisley yoga mat and leaning back against the wall.

"To answer your question," Poppy continued, "I didn't steal anything from people that they needed. *My* people never needed help from the outside."

"Then who did you steal from?" Kwame asked. Poppy didn't answer. "We met people in La Selva," Kwame went on, "who were sick and could have used extra cash to buy themselves what they needed."

"Like what?" Poppy asked, her "twang" slowly taking over her usual speech pattern.

"Like robotic guide dogs," Kwame answered.

Poppy snorted loudly. "That crazy Andre woman. She's just guilting her daughter for abandoning her. The whole community wants to help but she refuses. That's how we always did it back home – took care of each other. That's why I made sure Mary Stevens got a job. None of this big government nonsense, none of this 'savior from the capitol' bullshit." She used air quotes to describe the savior from the capitol, but I didn't find this exact term in government records.

Jube cleared her throat. "Then who did you steal from, if not from them?" She asked.

"I stole from their silhouettes," Poppy answered. She chuckled. "You don't get it, do you, but you're close, ha? I duplicated them. I stole from their shadows."

"What do you mean you duplicated them?" Jube continued.

"I mean that the program didn't reward *people* for their healthy behavior, it rewarded the numbers assigned to them, and I just duplicated those numbers and gave them accounts," Poppy explained. She smiled a bit in a way that triggered my image recognition of AI Mike's expression when Jube had started choking earlier.

"What about you?" Kwame asked, nodding at Barney.

"Don't talk to Barney," Poppy said. "You really think I'd let my little brother go to jail? Here's how you corroborate this." She sighed, "For Pete's sake, how many times do I need to explain math to public officials?"

Poppy cleared her throat and sat erect. "If you check out public records, you will see that the population of La Selva doubled between forty to fifty years ago. It was a steep growth rate, but it wasn't wacky enough to catch anyone's attention. Especially when they weren't looking, and when it had supposedly happened so long ago."

"You mean you falsified records to make the population seem larger?" Kwame asked.

"Now you're catching on, big boy," she giggled, "I mean, Linus was a total dunce and he gave me access to everything. So I slowly doubled the volume of live births that women were reported to have a generation ago and made sure those people never migrated."

"You mean you started by forging *historical* data?" Jube said. If I'd been able to monitor her brain waves, I'd have detected an ocean storm.

"Bingo. That means that for every newborn that entered this world in La Selva a generation ago, they had a twin. A nice and quiet one that no one knew about and who was actually created years later, in hindsight. And all Linus understood was that, when he started his stupid little futuristic pilot, the cost per person was really low. So low! Exactly half what the cost per person actually was."

"Because you doubled the size of the denominator – the population that participated," Jube said. "But how did you enroll them in the program and get the money?"

"Girly," Poppy said with an accent that also seemed to double, "I didn't enroll anybody. Remember, Linus pulled the entire population in his little experiment. I just made it seem like all these shadows of people got healthier over time, it was just *incredible* how much healthier they became. Each person was sent a debit card with their cash bonus to a PO Box that I'd opened, and then it was just a matter of withdrawing cash from one ATM after another."

"How did you get the payments approved so quickly?" Jube probed. I recalled that the time for approval had consistently been four minutes.

"Linus approved development of a software program that would handle payment approval," Poppy told her.

Jube paused. "You mean that the politician campaigning on the success of this program got to evaluate if it was successful?"

"Not exactly. He let the software decide. But why not?" Poppy asked. "It's not like he had stock invested in the company he was supporting publicly. What conflict of interest could exist?"

"Who developed the software to approve payments?" Kwame asked, ignoring her question.

Poppy was silent. Barney, who'd been staring at the space in front of his feet, folded his arms around his bent legs and rested his forehead on his forearms. Then he lifted his head and said, "You're forgetting that Poppy was at the gym when Linus had this supposed strangulation-via-electronic-water-boarding thing you claim. She may have committed fraud, but she didn't hurt him."

Jube cocked her head and looked at him, not at his biceps or shoulders, but his eyes. "The tagline of HAIL is 'Care From Anywhere,' right? Poppy could have stepped into the outline of AI Mike remotely from the gym bathroom, from her car, maybe even while using the treadmill for all I know if that's possible, and choked her husband." I silently confirmed that Jube wouldn't know much about using a treadmill.

"This time around, Poppy probably didn't have the chance to prepare for remote strangulation," Kwame added. "So she came to the HAIL HQ to hurt my partner because you told her she'd been to La Selva and was coming too close to the truth."

"Total coincidence," Barney said.

"Honey," Poppy spoke up, pointing her handcuffed hands towards Jube, still sitting on the beanbag with her elbows resting on her parted knees, "none of this makes any sense."

"What doesn't make sense?" Jube asked.

"First off, none of this has to do with what happened to Linus. Second, nobody said anything about eSkin in connection with my husband's condition."

"It has everything to do with Linus, *honey*," Jube returned. "You stole through him. And he was planning to visit La Selva after Krantz and PAATH challenged him and he would have figured it out. Eventually. You two thought he wouldn't stop. You talked about it after the demo."

"Linus didn't have eSkin on when he got to the hospital. Dr. Galtway saw no evidence of strangulation," Poppy said. "So where's your evidence, girl? Because all I hear is a hypothesis."

"We found eSkin at the crime scene, *girl*," Jube informed her. "And Linus Beech's vitals changed before he lost consciousness. You weren't touching his neck to save him, you were removing the eSkin to hide evidence. And the skin recorded your vitals instead of his when it stuck to your fingers."

Pause. Barney and Poppy looked at one another and frowned, nearly identically and lopsided. And then we had them. They were only human, after all.

Barney attempted one last defense. "You're forgetting how upset Poppy was when she found Linus in those bushes," he said. "Her sad face has been at least half of the news coverage of this story. And I don't think the media is going to be too happy with the news that the police have arrested the beloved and grieving wife of a victim."

"Your sister was sad, Barney, not because her beloved hubby was nearly killed, but because *her plan didn't work*. Get it? Everyone saw her open frown and her tears and sympathized with her. They saw themselves in her, they empathized with her misery but assumed it was for love because they were biased to see goodness in her," Jube explained. "And I am not biased to see that goodness, not in her, not in my own father, not even in a mother crying over her corrupt son at his trial."

Then I realized why Jube had abruptly stopped while leaving the courtroom after the hearing with the men who'd assaulted her. She'd heard one of their mothers sob, not from sadness, but from relief that her corrupted child was off her hands. That had been the inspiration behind Jube's epiphany, her painful learning curve, and her understanding of Poppy's expression.

And I'd missed it.

Chapter Twenty-Eight

Most of the squad cars and ambulances left after Poppy and Barney surrendered themselves into custody and Jube didn't show serious injury. There had been fifty police and emergency medical service vehicles present. I'd paged "quite the round up," as Jube put it.

"Nice work, detectives," the captain commended both Jube and Kwame. He turned towards the press, already gathered at the temporary barrier set up in the parking lot. "Rest assured that the people who we have arrested – who we will name at a later date – will receive a fair trial and judgement by jury, as our balanced system guarantees. In the meantime, I'd like to commend Detectives Jubilee Canton and Kwame Addo for their excellent work in cracking the case." He stepped aside and motioned towards us like a conductor directing an orchestra to stand and bow, which neither Jube nor Kwame did. As he did, multiple cameras pivoted and put us under the glare of their lights and their interest.

"Detective Canton, we heard you were injured in the line of duty. How are you?" Asked a popular blogger.

"Our detectives will give a statement another time," the captain said, waving us off. "For now I'm giving them space to rest and recuperate." He turned back to the press. Their cameras lingered on Jube for two seconds before returning the captain's attention.

As he continued speaking, I sensed public sentiment shift from "Ugly cop claims victory in Beech case" to "Wounded cop remains strong." I'd noticed that women were usually defined by two or three words, one often including their profession. For example, "Black doctor" or "Petite softball coach." Jube had changed her first adjective, which I'd rarely observed women do. I was uncertain as to if "wounded" was preferable to "ugly." Jericho had many eyes. Surely some thought Jube to be beautiful.

Jube walked behind an ambulance and leaned back against it with her arms crossed. Kwame stood before her and sighed deeply.

"May I give you some tea?" An older voice offered. A woman wearing floral-patterned tights beneath an oversized canvas tunic was holding a cracked traveler's mug.

"Thank you," Jube told her, accepting the tea and sipping it slowly.

"I was so distressed when I got the page. Please keep the mug. And here's my card if you need anything else," she said, pulling a piece of paper made of pressed flowers from her sleeve like a 17th century handmaid in a castle.

Jube looked at the card and managed to stifle her laughter until the woman had left. Then she bent over at the waist and hollered. The woman was the retired yoga teacher turned personal coach who rented a trailer down the street. She'd responded to my broadcast for medical help.

"Maybe you should contact her." Kwame suggested, seriously. "I'm worried about you."

"There's one thing left bothering me," Jube admitted.

"What's that?"

"Krantz. I'd been hoping for a universal net to catch all these suspects in and he still doesn't fit, although something feels off about the guy," she explained.

"Jujube, promise me you'll really use your two weeks to give everything a rest, ok?"

"Ok," she said in a voice I knew from when she tried to appease Leah while silently disagreeing with her. Or perhaps she was being terse because just then the Network broadcast Tugenov's disappearance to the squad. He'd vanished while being transferred back to the rehab facility from prison. The news display running across my forehead advertised this and paged nearby ground forces to help find him. He was gone. Or unseen. To me they were the same.

As part of this protocol my earlier report recommending his arrest was released as relevant background. Jube took me out of her pocket and stared at me closely, her eyebrows furrowed and her breath a quick pant. She may have been disappointed in my report sources. William Ernest Henley had in fact never penned a poetry collection titled <u>My Soul Deserve Not Redemption</u>. This had been crossed out in the report release and labeled a technical "hallucination."

Chapter Twenty-Nine

Jube didn't go home from the scene of the arrest. She drove without auto-drive or directional guidance through Jericho until she reached the trailer park where I'd seen Tugenov have sex with multiple partners in front of his RV, the lawn behind it, and on the tin roof where he'd sunburned his back. Yet I didn't see him physically at the RV park and didn't know why we were there.

The area was empty and dark. Jube circled some dead potted plants dotting the border of the lot while holding her arms out. Her hands gently brushed at the area in front of her like a blind woman feeding birds. "Clio, bathroom," she ordered. This was the command she used for privacy while on patrol. I closed my digital eyes in case she planned to squat behind a bush.

"Are you there?" She whispered. Apparently she never knew I had always been able to hear her humming Broadway tunes as she relieved herself.

"Yes," the air answered with Tugenov's voice, an oddity I'd file for safekeeping next to the glimmers that led us to find him in his invisible clothes.

"I didn't want this to happen," she said. "I didn't cause it."

"I know, Jubilee," the voice replied. "It was them dang machines again."

"Would you go back to rehab?" She pleaded. "I can get them to ignore that you ran away."

"I don't want to be rehabilitated. I want to feel free from the inside of my soul," the voice replied.

"Things will change now because you were mistakenly implicated," she told it. "I'll make sure of it. Safety without the shitty cost of privacy."

The air snorted.

"But…" Jube hesitated. "What else will you *do*?"

"There was nothing like teaching, really," the voice replied. "Sure, it got boring sometimes, with papers to grade, and parent-teacher conferences and whatnot. But there were wonderful moments of connection. Times when I could practically feel around in a student's mind and let him feel around mine. Or sometimes we'd even connect with the dead."

"You mean through all those old poems?" Jube asked, although I stood ready to examine the role of seances in standard educational curriculum.

"Yes. We were all alive together that way. And now it's gone."

"Not gone," Jube argued. "Just different."

"Different? I used to connect with another person over poetry and literature. Now through the networks all I do is connect with some version of myself projected onto what's more like an avatar than a friend. And I'm tired of myself, Jubilee. I'm tired of being examined, measured. I don't even want to focus on my breaths anymore – to count them, even that is just too much," the voice said.

"So what will you do?"

"Look outward," the voice answered. "I don't even care what I see. I'm just going somewhere to look. And maybe write. And maybe someone will read what I write and for that moment we'll connect in a way that will be too pure to scrutinize. And maybe I'll also read what they have written and for that moment I will not be alone. That would be enough for me."

Jube's tears drizzled my head like a small storm. I'd never felt her cry before.

"Jubilee, I have one final lesson plan. Will you listen?" The voice asked.

"Ok. I guess so."

The air laughed. "I suppose that's as good as it will get. Alright. Just listen. '*Allegory could not exist if truth were accessible: as a mode of expression it arises in perpetual response to the human condition of being exiled from the truth that it would embrace.*'"

I identified the quote as by literary critic Bainard Cowan. The idea that I had been using metaphors as a necessary means to access facts raised my temperature. The idea that truth was inaccessible nearly melted my surface. Then I recalled a quote attributed to the late composer Leonard Bernstein, "I've been all over the world and I've never seen a statue of a critic," and calmed down slightly.

The air fell silent. As I the heard wind blow, I realized that my third interpretation of the poem about the wind blowing through the ruined house in the moonlight was correct.[ix] Jube had been open to Tugenov and to poetry. It had hurt in the end, but I predicted that she would do it again to feed her soul.

Chapter Thirty

At least Jube slept in the next morning. When she emerged from her bedroom, her hair sticking up in the middle of her head like a dysfunctional zebra, it was nearly time for lunch. Leah was sitting at the kitchen table, stirring what looked like a pot of lavender on her lap.

"Got 'em?" she asked Jube without looking up. "I saw you on the news."

"Yup, got 'em," Jube answered, moving towards the couch. She'd left me on the side table that night and nearly knocked me over flopping onto the couch cushions.

I sounded an alert of an approaching visitor. Jube groaned as she went into the bathroom and returned with her hair braided and baggy overalls over her pajamas. The doorbell chime played the theme to The Pink Panther (initial film release 1963). Oddly, she didn't ask me to announce the visitor.

Krantz stood outside in a turquoise Hawaiian shirt and khaki shorts with his hands in the pockets. A denim backpack was slung over one shoulder. When Jube opened the door, he smiled and shrugged. "Miss me?" He asked.

"So much for two weeks off," Jube muttered. "Who is it?" Leah asked from the kitchen. Jube moved her body from the entryway and motioned towards inside.

"Hello Mrs. Canton," he said as he passed over the threshold. Leah set down the jar of oil she was filling and smiled.

"Nurse Krantz!" She said, standing and smoothing down her purple muumuu.

"Please call me Westin," he said, taking her hand with both of his. "And no need to get up, I can see you're busy."

"Jujube, get this man some tea," Leah said, not taking her eyes off his while gesturing towards the stove. Jube's eyes widened.

"I'm really fine," Krantz said, blushing.

"Jubilee, get him some tea," Leah insisted.

Jube slowly walked into the kitchen and filled their kettle, then placed it onto the electric stove as Leah cleared and wiped the table. By the time that Leah and Krantz were sitting down, he had stopped protesting and was sipping hot water with real mint leaves. Jube leaned against the counter behind them, gnawing on an empty fork and watching.

"Tell me, how have you been Nurse Krantz?" Leah asked. She folded her arms and briefly reminded me of Jube, although only when she played Good Cop.

"Well, Mrs. Canton –."

"Call me Leah."

"Then, again, call me Westin," he insisted.

"Deal."

"Leah, I've not been good. I've got to admit that." He looked into his mug – Leah had given him the only ceramic one she had – and swirled the leaves a bit.

"And I am sorry to hear that," Leah said, shaking her head slightly.

"I need to get something off my chest," he said. "It has to do with Frank." Jube bit a prong off the fork and silently spat it into the sink. Leah said nothing but sipped her tea. "You see," he went on, "he's the reason I left nursing."

"He's also the reason I left baking," Leah said, snorting.

Krantz chuckled. "This was more of a decision. Leah," he set down his mug, "I killed your husband."

This time, Jube bit a larger fork piece off and almost choked on it.

"You see," he continued, his voice becoming a whisper, "Frank had a syringe pump," his voice broke and he restarted more loudly, "a syringe pump to administer his post-op pain meds slowly – small doses and slowly. The thing is," his voice cracked again, "the thing is, that this causes a delay between giving the medicine and seeing a response in the patient. The risk of that, which I knew, was that I'd overdose Frank because I'd think he needed more when he didn't, he just hadn't responded to the treatment yet." Krantz blinked and wiped his eyes. "So, I waited to give him more. Waited, even though every ounce of instinct in my body said that something was wrong. I messaged Frank's doctor but I didn't mark it as urgent and I didn't try to find another doc to help me. I just assumed…assumed that Frank would be fine because he hadn't responded yet but he would later. And I should not have ignored that voice in my mind, yelling at me that wasn't true." Krantz sighed. "So then Frank experienced pain. I'm so sorry," he sniffled, "he was in pain, and it was because his injury was worsening. And then there was also…there was physiologic stress related to the pain, and then his blood pressure went up a lot. And then everything went bad. And I'm so sorry."

The only noise I could detect was that of the fork prongs Jube had chewed off and spit out finding their way down the sink pipes. Then Krantz exhaled loudly. "I'm sorry," he said and started crying. He pressed his palms against his eyes and sniveled.

Leah's face turned white aside from red blotches around her neck. She patted his hands as her eyes teared. "Shhhhhhh," she said. "You did nothing wrong." Krantz's cries turned into sobs. He did not wipe his face, only leaned back in his chair and let his arms fall to his sides like a person saying, "Take me now" to the heavens.

Jube's face contorted into a scowl I associated with baseball fans after their team loses a World Series. She took loud steps toward the kitchen table and grasped the back of Krantz's chair, squeezing it until her knuckles turned white. Then she exhaled and sat down at the table, offering him bunched up tissues from her pocket.

"She's right," Jube said. "Mom's right, it's not your fault."

Leah looked at Jube, her brows raised higher than I'd ever observed. For a moment, mother and daughter looked like each other.

"Look, Westin," Jube continued, "you did your job."

"But," he sniveled, "it was my job to preserve life." He unraveled a tissue and dabbed his chin, leaving white dust speckles on his lower lip.

"Yeah, but you don't get to decide on your own how to do that, or entirely when you get to follow your instinct or not. None of us in service jobs fully do, and that's ok because it'd lead to havoc. Who gets to say what's wrong or right? It depends. In nursing, at least, there are standards, and clinical trials, and, forgive me, healthcare pilots."

Krantz protested, "But I should have, I mean, I could have -."

"Nah," Jube cut him off. "You didn't breach a contract you had with him. You did your job and medicated him the way you were supposed to. You definitely didn't *neglect* him. No," she shook her head, staring at the middle of the table where an oil patch remained, "not your fault."

There was a pause in which Leah began to speak, but Jube cut her off too.

"I mean, look at it this way," she said. "Let's say you did interfere with his medication administration. He could have died anyway. He was a long-time alcoholic who suffered from a terrible fall. That's what killed him. And then you'd have thought it was because you had stepped in after all."

"What do you mean?" Krantz asked.

Jube faced him. "I mean that my dad was likely to die no matter what steps you took. Therefore, you probably didn't kill him. Maybe you could have told a doctor that the patient wasn't responding to his medication. But then the doctor would have probably left things alone anyway because the existing course of action was the recommended procedure. In the end, you did what you could, what you were supposed to."

"I still don't feel better," Krantz said.

"Well," Jube added, "look at it this way. *I* was wrong about *you*, and *my* instincts are almost never wrong."

At that, the three of them laughed.

"Listen to my smart daughter," Leah instructed Krantz. "She knows her stuff."

Jube blushed.

"Are you going to tell me who tried to kill Linus?" Krantz asked, propping his chin onto his palm.

"Nope, but the story will come out when it does. These things never stay quiet for too long," Jube told him.

"Just tell me one thing," Krantz implored. "Please. Is this technology stuff good or bad? All this big data and all these algorithms and monitors?"

Jube leaned back. "Both," she answered. "It's both good and bad at the same time. The issue, I think, is that we're in-between, somehow. Still learning. And learning the hard way. I also think that the phrase, 'It's ahead of its time' is a bad sign." Her silence lasted for about one minute, and in that minute Krantz stopped crying and Jube stood and put me into a drawer (again!). If the furniture hadn't been dingy and cracked, I wouldn't have been able to see. "I have a lot ideas for making it better," she said, "like slowing down self-reinforcing learning."

"Well, I brought you something that's also kind of both low- and high-tech," Krantz said. "And hopefully not too soon." He opened his backpack and pulled out a rectangular sculpture I'd never seen before. In the center of one long side was a handprint with flickering blue lights running down the fingers into the palm where they met in a small circle. Krantz pushed it across the table to Jube who peered closely without touching it. I scanned the fingertips for prints through a crack in my drawer. If Jube had asked me, I could have told her first.

Krantz said, "It's Frank's handprint," even though she technically didn't ask him either. I've noticed that humans do that often – answer unspoken questions or provide opinions that were unsolicited but desired. I don't know how they do that. "You see," he continued, "Frank and I had a very short conversation at his bedside. Actually, his attempt to chat made a lot of alarms sound, but he was pretty insistent on talking. And at least I knew not to stop him."

"Yeah, he was chatty like that when he was drunk," Leah told him. Jube kept her gaze fixed on Krantz and, for the first time in the past 354 interactions she'd had with her mother, ignored her.

"Well, his speech was a bit slurred so I had trouble understanding at first, but I could tell that he was repeating the same sentence over and over. Then he leaned forward and squeezed my hand and said it forcefully and cleanly."

"Are you going to tell me what it was or make me guess?" Jube asked.

"I'm a little nervous…well, ok. Frank said, 'Tell Jubilee I'm sorry I fucked up.'"

"And then he died?" Leah asked. I was reminded of multiple movies from various genres – westerns, romance, and military – in which a character died immediately after uttering famous last words or, in the case of mystery, not completing their sentence before it was too late. Of course, in none of these movies did the person say, "I fucked up."

I took an additional minute to view the death scenes of the most popular movies of the past five years simultaneously and at a high speed and then ranked them in order of ticket sales just in case Jube had a question about this and asked me for a copy later. She never did.

"No, no, it took a while longer," Krantz told her.

"He probably talked about his poker game and his favorite bar maids," Leah said.

"Well…maybe," Krantz admitted. "But the hand squeeze was real, and that's what this is," he motioned toward the PVC-box. "I made an imprint of Frank's hand before he died, when it became clear that was going to happen. I was thinking it might mean a lot to the family. Then I…hey, what's the statute of limitations on petty theft?"

"I don't care," Jube told him. My buzzes made the side table shake.

"So, I pinched a bit of the extra eSkin laying around after Linus' demo at the Capitol. I was angry…and, well, you could say I wanted to test it myself without anyone knowing," Krantz admitted. "I only took a little."

"And?" Jube probed. If I'd been in her pocket, I could have predicted how she was feeling then. Maybe.

"It wasn't that bad. Actually, it felt nice on the massage setting. Not enough to replace a job role, but still nice. And then I thought of the hand imprint, which I hadn't been able to even look at since Frank died and I'd quit nursing. So I got a few PAATH members who were disgruntled engineers to teach the eSkin to hold hands, literally, then I put it on here," Krantz described.

"You're saying I can hold my dad's hand?" Jube asked. She looked at Leah, whose eyes were teary, potentially from emotion or from allergies as the pollen count was abnormally high that day.

"Yes I am. This is my gift to you, the human, and the high-tech touch in one interactive sculpture," he smiled.

"It's like the future of mourning," Leah announced. Jube snorted and reached for her dad's hand, then stopped and placed her palm flat on the table.

"Hey," Krantz said. "You try this on your own private time and when you feel good and ready." Jube nodded, perhaps in agreement or because her arm was stuck to the dirty table anyway. And then Krantz leaned forward and held Jube's hand more tightly and widely than I ever could. In that moment, she reciprocated.

I detected the news break then – an anonymous source had slipped the story of Poppy and Barney's arrests to the press. I could detect the heyday beginning through my feed but I decided against broadcasting it to the room. I was in a drawer. Even I could finally recognize a moment of closure. It was literal.

Chapter Thirty-One

Linus Beech was woken up from his coma a few days later. Jube heard that Krantz was at his bedside when this happened and that he visited daily throughout Beech's rehab at the hospital and at home. I don't know who broke the news about Poppy and Barney to Beech, but before the trial Dr. Galtway told the District Attorney that Beech had spoken about AI Mike for a few days at first after waking. Eventually it seemed to sink in that his own wife had assumed a digital form and then tried to kill him after stealing taxpayer money. Beech wanted to ensure that no one in La Selva had been directly injured other than being deprived from the opportunity to earn rewards for taking care of themselves. He'd had to content himself with the fact that the population had maintained their baseline level of care as if the pilot had never taken place, which it basically hadn't.

Jube also heard that Beech was assisted in this course of treatment by a human physical therapist and refused any robotic support.

Social media batted around many jokes and animated memes about how the people of La Selva were using their eSkin – vibrators, speed dating, Sex Bingo in senior housing. Beech actually replied once to say he hoped that they were at least getting some pleasure out of the intervention. In response, he was sent thousands of "thoughts and prayers." Jube told me that was because people now identified with him as the victim of harm and false love. She preferred that he be labeled as an idiot and over-zealous proponent of interventions he couldn't understand. But, how many people would want to empathize with someone like that? And everyone seemed to want to empathize with someone.

If others agreed with Jube about Beech, they didn't have the chance to say so via an election – he resigned from his post once his disability leave ended and then announced his retirement from public service. His professional tagline was now "healthcare shaman and independent consultant." Krantz was listed as "strategic shaman advisor."

A few months later, Beech and Poppy's divorce was finalized quietly, aside from multiple "para social" social media spotlights:

Who's packing their bags now?

Is Poppy Beech frowning from heartbreak or jailbreak? Vote below.

A fool + a crook = true love ~~forever~~ until rehab and jail time do us part

Poppy was incarcerated by then after taking a deal in exchange for pleading guilty to multiple forms of fraud, assault, and intent to murder and waiving her right to a trial. She'd insisted that Barney be given a reduced sentence, that the entire thing had been her idea and she'd kept him from knowing about any of her plans in detail. She was sent to a minimum security and no-tech prison after it became clear that she had no way of harming anyone without an AI to assist her. Jube disagreed with this part of the ruling and told me the judge was swayed by Poppy's "tiny frame and pretty hair." I analyzed comparative cases although the pool was limited. The closest I could find were women who had committed wire fraud and also violence against family members who'd raised suspicions over their behavior. And, yes, here I found a correlation between high attractiveness (by popular measures such as waist-to-hip ratio) and shorter sentences. I couldn't hope because I am a machine, but I predicted that if Jube were to commit a crime her sentence would be relatively high and so I contented myself with an equally low prediction that she'd ever become a criminal.

Barney was sentenced to community service and his access to the Internet and other mainstream technologies was barred for five years. For this reason, he was forced to leave Jericho and was placed in Government housing in an "ignoramus-ville." He chose La Selva saying he wanted to give back to his hometown and his main job would be making La Selva more accessible to the blind. Ms. Andre would be his point-of-contact as a patient and she'd be paid for her time. Mary Stevens moved out of state. I didn't learn why.

The press seemed to move on, possibly because they had other topics of interest to follow. Cassius was now often at the podium outside the hospital promising "safe and sound" healthcare for all. He wanted Jericho to buy into this idea with him and "co-found" the care of the future, but public signatures to back this idea were lacking. In his vision, eSkin would be used in the hospital under the guidance of a licensed nurse. During his speeches, every time that he started to say "high tech" but caught himself and changed it to "high quality," Sargent Jubilee Canton would feed treats to the therapy dog, formerly Mary Stevens' pet. Back at the station, she was no longer ridiculed and no longer needed to push her way through, neither literally nor figuratively.

As for me, I was downgraded significantly. The changes will take effect with the next software cycle. The Network is coming down. Individual devices like me will be allowed to survey and report from our handler's pockets. I will search historical and legal indices as needed and provide summaries. I will not learn or expand my knowledge base as I alone deem necessary to do my job. I will observe human behavior but not human nature. I will not testify in court and will not carry bullets.

This is my final report in my broader capacity and I'm left with one final lesson. The purpose of art and poetry is to translate the human soul for other humans to understand. And although I don't have a soul, I thought I could learn what one was and even provide the judgement to convict a criminal. I was wrong.

The more poetry I read in the last days of my higher capability, the more I feel that my title of "fucking pocket poet" is inaccurate, not because I think I am more, but because I am less. I am not a poet but a device that created metaphor without meaning. I exhibited mimicry instead of art. And ironically the use of image recognition to create analogies was the only "superfluous" task that Jube allowed Clios to keep when she led the next generation design in her new and high-ranking position. She said it was because it made her laugh. She puts me away when she gets home from work now, but I can usually hear her pencil scratching her page when she writes in her poetry journal nightly before bed.

Next week the walls of Jericho will come down. I suppose that, if I were human, I would feel sorry for myself, for Tugenov, for how things turned out. But most of all I would miss getting pizza with Jube and learning all the lessons she had to offer, unless that too was a hallucination all along.

Epilogue

Jube found the maggot larva in the sink laying there like a shriek waiting to happen.

A neighbor had recorded the suspect slowly entering the victim's home through the back window – raising it, glancing around, and throwing one leg, then the other over the ledge before sliding in like the first trickles of a flood. It was three thirteen in the morning. The lights inside the apartment went on three seconds later and the high-pitched screaming began about two seconds after that.

The intel I delivered said that the suspect's name was Jim, aliases "Jimbo" and "Jimmy," and he had a criminal record including a variety of traffic violations and one bar fight, none of which had required jail time. Social media photos portrayed him as an acquaintance of the victim (female, age 26, name withheld) and likely a romantic one given the level of affection displayed in photos of them together. These types of images – the two of them hugging or kissing as they walked on the beach or drank margaritas at a bar – had not been posted since three months prior to Jim's breaking and entering into her home. This pointed to the high possibility the relationship had ended. What's more, he'd published negative comments since then. For example, he wrote "nice and slutty" beneath the victim's recently posted selfies. She'd been wearing a bikini made of a textile with mini-umbrella decorations and laying on the beach like a youthful margarita on a towel.

The first oddity I detected based on my survey of medical and criminal studies was the multiple scrapes around her eyelids and mouth, none of which had drawn blood. Could she have been dead already?

Second, while Jim's prints were in the apartment they were not on the murder weapon. *So what?* The family had asked. *Jim must have wiped it clean because no prints were found on the knife whatsoever. Hang this man, and hang him high.*

Third, a swarm of flies from inside the apartment hovered around Jim's face as he climbed in. I counted fifteen. They set off my image recognition of "team of mountain climbers from a distance" as well as "dirt thrown at man's face by young son." There was no food left out in the kitchen, nothing else laying around or rotting in her home which was quite tidy compared to those in our other investigations to date.

Academic resources claimed that flies will swarm over a body quickly after death but they don't simply materialize, they must come in from the outside. And, per the footage from the building security camera, this woman's windows had been closed for two days. So how did such a large cluster of flies enter the home, and did they find the body or were they attracted to a substance we hadn't detected?

This is where the maggots came in. Jube found their tiny gray larva waiting to hatch in the kitchen sink, some laying against the drain and some resting inside the garbage disposal. Multiple entomological resources verified that this type of larva was typically only a few days old – later they'd become larger and whiter before hatching. And so it was likely that the woman's body had already been in place for two to three days before Jim had entered, and that the windows had been open, flies had come in, and then the windows were closed at some point after her death by someone other than her (who I couldn't see). It was also significantly possible that the murderer had re-entered from inside the building, found the body covered in flies, scraped the maggots off using the knife, and tried to send them down the drain. Then he or she could have wiped the knife of prints and closed the windows.

And what of the screams? Jube made Jim scream a few times and we compared notes, literally. She released a live bat into his jail cell and I recorded the sounds of his reaction. The man had a surprisingly high-pitched voice when terrorized, one that matched those coming from his ex-girlfriend's apartment on the night in question. This corroborated Jim's account of entering the apartment, finding her dead, and then screaming in reaction while fumbling for the lights to see if the murderer was still inside.

I submitted this report and the coroner mentioned it during his testimony. The rest they now kept out of my digital "hands." Later during trial the dead woman's family maligned Jim by saying he'd threatened her repeatedly and was a jealous and temperamental sort of man. They linked multiple (and unrelated) stories of violence against other women by resentful exes into a psychological mold that meant Jim *had* to be the perpetrator, there was no other possibility. He'd broken in, she had screamed, and then she been stabbed and died. End of story, according to them.

The jury deliberated for less than an hour before they agreed. Jim was found guilty and sentenced to life in prison.

In the end, I suppose, we are all flawed.

Acknowledgements

I was able to write this book because of the wonderful people who offered me their time and expertise. Robert Kurtzman, DO, FCAP, Forensic Pathologist, Retired Montana State Chief Medical Examiner. Chwee Teck Lim, PhD, Professor / Director, Institute for Health Innovation & Technology, National University of Singapore (and Dr. Yih Yng Ng who connected us). Marco Innocenti, retired Sheriff's Detective, SWAT Officer/Instructor, and DA Inspector. Laurie Lynn Drummond, former uniformed officer in Baton Rouge, Louisiana, and an author. The San Mateo County Sheriff's Office – thank you for your service. Peter Galatin, MD, PhD, my beloved brother-in-law and an exceptional doctor. Tmirah Haselkorn, PhD, my sister and brilliant epidemiologist. Ravid Haselkorn-Galatin, my sister and fierce cheerleader. My aunt, Aviva Kelmenson, mother-in-law, Susan Zanders Bye, and mother, Sarah Haselkorn, for helping to care for our youngest family members while I wrote. Early readers Lisa Giocomo, Evelyn Howard, and Sue McGarry. Editor Lea Vickery. I would also like to thank my alma mater, the Johns Hopkins Bloomberg School of Public Health, for providing such an excellent education. Finally, my dear husband, Ronny Krashinsky, and our boys, Isaac and Erez, for their support of my work. I love you.

Ateret Haselkorn is the author of Call Me Obie and Understanding Jericho. She was the adult winner of the 2014 Palo Alto Weekly Short Story Contest. Her work has been published in multiple literary and medical journals and can be accessed at AteretHaselkorn.com.

X and Instagram: @AteretHaselkorn

Poetry Referenced in the Text

[i] Gluck, L. (1992). "The Red Poppy." <u>The Wild Iris</u>. Hopewell, NJ: Ecco Press.

[ii] Moore, T. (b. 1779 d. 1852) "To The Invisible Girl." Public domain. "…Sweet spirit of mystery! how I should love,/In the wearisome ways I am fated to rove,/To have you for ever invisibly nigh,/Inhaling for ever your song and your sigh!…"

[iii] Hauge, O.H. Translated by Bly, R. (2008). "Don't Come to Me with the Entire Truth." <u>The Dream We Carry</u>. Port Townsend, WA: Copper Canyon Press; Bilingual edition.

[iv] Henley, W.E. (1849 –1903). "Invictus." Public domain. Full text: Out of the night that covers me, / Black as the Pit from pole to pole, / I thank whatever gods may be / For my unconquerable soul. / In the fell clutch of circumstance / I have not winced nor cried aloud. / Under the bludgeonings of chance / My head is bloody, but unbowed. / Beyond this place of wrath and tears / Looms but the Horror of the shade, / And yet the menace of the years / Finds, and shall find, me unafraid. / It matters not how strait the gate, / How charged with punishments the scroll, / I am the master of my fate: / I am the captain of my soul"

[v] Shakespeare, W. (1564 –1616). "Who will believe my verse in time to come". Sonnet 17. Public domain. Full text: Who will believe my verse in time to come, / If it were fill'd with your most high deserts? / Though yet, heaven knows, it is but as a tomb / Which hides your life and shows not half your parts. / If I could write the beauty of your eyes / And in fresh numbers number all your graces, / The age to come would say "This poet lies; / Such heavenly touches ne'er touch'd earthly faces." / So should my papers, yellowed with their age, / Be scorn'd like old men of less truth than tongue, / And your true rights be term'd a poet's rage / And stretched metre of an antique song: / But were some child of yours alive that time, / You should live twice, in it and in my rhyme.

vi Lee, Li-Young. (1986). "Blossoms." <u>Rose</u>. Rochester, New York: BOA Editions Ltd.

vii Amichai, Y. Translated by Bloch, C., & Mitchell, S. (2013). "Half The People In The World." <u>The Selected Poetry Of Yehuda Amichai</u>. University of California Press.

viii Shikibu, I. Translated from Japanese.

ix Shikibu, I. ibid.